Books by Yukio Mishima

THE SEA OF FERTILITY,
  A Cycle of Novels:

  Spring Snow
  Runaway Horses
  The Temple of Dawn
  The Decay of the Angel

Published by POCKET BOOKS

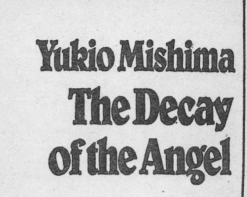

Yukio Mishima
The Decay of the Angel

Translated from the Japanese by
EDWARD G. SEIDENSTICKER

WASHINGTON SQUARE PRESS
PUBLISHED BY POCKET BOOKS NEW YORK

A Washington Square Press Publication of
POCKET BOOKS, a Simon & Schuster division of
GULF & WESTERN CORPORATION
1230 Avenue of the Americas, New York, N.Y. 10020

Japanese edition, *Tennin Gosui*, copyright
© 1971 by Yoko Hiraoka. English translation,
The Decay of the Angel, copyright © 1974 by
Alfred A. Knopf, Inc.

Published by arrangement with Alfred A. Knopf, Inc.
Library of Congress Catalog Card Number: 73-21525

ISBN: 0-671-44533-2

First Pocket Books printing September, 1975

10   9   8   7   6   5   4   3

WASHINGTON SQUARE PRESS, WSP and colophon are
trademarks of Simon & Schuster.

Printed in the U.S.A.

The Decay of the Angel

1

THE MISTS in the offing turned the distant ships black. Even so it was clearer than yesterday. He could pick out the ridges of the Izu Peninsula. The May sea was calm. The sunlight was strong, there were only wisps of cloud, the sea was blue.

Very small ripples broke on the shore. There was a certain distasteful quality, before they broke, about the nightingale colors at the bellies of the ripples, as if they had in them all the unpleasant varieties of seaweed.

The churning of the sea, day after day, a daily repetition of the churning sea of milk in the Indian legend. Perhaps the world would not let it rest. Something about it called up all the evil in nature.

The swelling of the May sea, endlessly and restlessly moving its points of light, a myriad of tiny spikes.

Three birds seemed to become one at the top of the sky. Then, in disorder, they separated. There was something wondrous about the meeting and separating. It must mean something, this coming so close that they felt the wind from each other's wings, and then blue distance once more. Three ideas will sometimes join in our hearts.

The black hull of a small cargo ship, its funnel mark a mountain over three horizontal lines, gave, in the heaping up of its mass, a sense of grandeur and sudden growth.

At two in the afternoon the sun withdrew into a thin cocoon of clouds, a whitely shining worm.

THE DECAY OF THE ANGEL

The horizon was a blue-black hoop of steel perfectly fitting the sea.

For an instant, at a single spot in the offing, a white wave sprang up like a white wing and fell back again. And what would that mean? It had to be some grand signal, or perhaps a grand whim.

The tide came slowly in, the waves were rising, the land lay before the most powerful of assaults. The sun was behind clouds and the green of the sea took on a somehow angry darkness. A long white line stretched across it from east to west in a sort of gigantic inverted triangle. It seemed to twist itself loose from the flat surface and, near at hand, toward the apex, fan-like lines lost themselves blackly in a black-green sea.

The sun came out again. Again the sea gave smooth lodging to the white light, and, at the ordering of a southwest wind, numberless shadows like the backs of sea lions moved northeast and northwest, limitless schools of waves aloof from the shore. The flood was held under strict control by the distant moon.

Mackerel clouds half-covered the sky, their upper line quietly severing the sun.

Two fishing boats were putting out to sea. There was a cargo boat farther out. The wind was stronger. A fishing boat came in from the west, as if to signal the opening of a ceremony. It was a poor little boat, and yet, wheelless and legless, it advanced with a proud grace as if sweeping in full-skirted.

By three the mackerel clouds were thinner. On the southern sky clouds fanned out like the tail of a white turtledove to throw a deep shadow over the sea.

The sea: a nameless sea, the Mediterranean, the Japan Sea, the Bay of Suruga here before him; a rich, nameless, absolute anarchy, caught after a great struggle as something called "sea," in fact rejecting a name.

As the sky clouded over, the sea fell into sulky contemplation, studded with fine nightingale-colored points.

8

It bristled with wave-thorns, like a rose branch. In the thorns themselves was evidence of a smooth becoming. The thorns of the sea were smooth.

Three ten. There were no ships in sight.

Very strange. The whole vast space was abandoned. There were not even wings of gulls.

Then a phantom ship arose and disappeared toward the west.

The Izu Peninsula was shrouded in mist. For a time it ceased to be the Izu Peninsula. It was the ghost of a lost peninsula. Then it disappeared entirely. It had become a fiction on a map. Ships and peninsula alike belonged to "the absurdity of existence."

They appeared and disappeared. How did they differ?

If the visible was the sum of being, then the sea, as long as it was not lost in mist, existed there. It was heartily ready to be.

A single ship changed it all.

The whole composition changed. With a rending of the whole pattern of being, a ship was received by the horizon. An abdication was signed. A whole universe was thrown away. A ship came in sight, to throw out the universe that had guarded its absence.

Multiple changes in the color of the sea, moment by moment. Changes in the clouds. And the appearance of a ship. What was happening? What were happenings?

Each instant brought them, more momentous than the explosion of Krakatoa. It was only that no one noticed. We are too accustomed to the absurdity of existence. The loss of a universe is not worth taking seriously.

Happenings are the signals for endless reconstruction, reorganization. Signals from a distant bell. A ship appears and sets the bell to ringing. In an instant the sound makes everything its own. On the sea they are incessant, the bell is forever ringing.

A being.

It need not be a ship. A single bitter orange, appearing no one knows when. It is enough to set the bell to ringing.

Three thirty in the afternoon. A single bitter orange represented being on the Bay of Suruga.

Hidden by a wave and appearing again, floating and sinking, like a ceaselessly blinking eye, the bright dot of orange floated slowly off toward the east through the ripples in near the shore.

Three thirty-five. Somberly, a black hull appeared from the west, from the direction of Nagoya.

The sun was behind clouds, like a smoked salmon.

Tōru Yasunaga looked away from the thirty-power telescope.

There was no sign yet of the cargo ship *Tenrō-maru*, due to make port at four.

He went back to his desk and absently scanned the Shimizu shipping notices.

Expected arrivals of nonscheduled ships, Saturday, May 2, 1970.
Tenro-maru, Japanese, 16:00. Taishō Shipping Company. Agent, Suzuichi. From Yokohama. Berth 4–5, Hinodé Pier.

2

SHIGEKUNI HONDA was seventy-six. He often traveled alone now that his wife Rié was dead. He chose easily accessible places that would not overtax him.

He had visited Nihondaira Heights below Fuji, and on his return had stopped by the Mio Grove and seen such treasures as the cloth, probably from Inner Asia, said to be a fragment of the angel's robe; and as he started back toward Shizuoka he found himself wanting to be alone for a time on the shore. There were three runs every hour of the Kodama Express. It would be no great matter if he were to miss his train. The return trip to Tokyo took only a little over an hour.

Stopping the cab, he walked with the help of a cane the fifty yards or so to the Komagoé shore. He asked himself, as he gazed out to sea, whether this would be the Udo Beach identified in the fourteenth century by Ichijō Kanera as the precise spot of the angel's descent. He thought too of the Kamakura coast of his youth. He turned back. The beach was quiet. Children were playing, and there were two or three anglers.

His attention on the sea, he had not noticed earlier, but now his eye caught, the rustic pink of a convolvulus below the breakwater. In the sand along the breakwater a great litter of garbage lay scoured by the sea winds. Empty Coca-Cola bottles, food cans, paint cans, nonperishable plastic bags, detergent boxes, bricks, bones.

The dregs of life on land cascaded down and came against infinity. The sea, infinity not met before. The

11

dregs, like man, unable to meet their end save in the ugliest and filthiest of fashions.

Straggling pines along the embankment sent out blossoms like starfish. To the left a radish patch put out forlorn little four-petaled white blossoms. Small pines lined the road. For the rest there was a solid expanse of plastic strawberry shelters. In vast numbers, under quonset huts of plastic, strawberries trailed their fruit over stone terraces among a profusion of leaves. Flies crawled along the saw-blade edges of the leaves. Quonset huts, as far as he could see, unpleasantly white, jammed in, one against another. Honda noticed —he had not before—a small tower-like structure among them.

Just in from the prefectural highway on which the cab had stopped, it was a two-story hut on a disproportionately high concrete platform. It was too tall for a watch shelter, too poor for an office building. Three sides were almost unbroken expanses of window.

Curious, he stepped into what appeared to be the yard. White window frames were heaped in great disorder on the sand. Fragments of glass faithfully caught the clouds. Looking up, he saw in a second-floor window what seemed to be shades for telescope lenses. Two huge iron pipes, rust red, protruded from the concrete platform and buried themselves in the earth. Uncertain of his footing, Honda made his way across the pipes and started up a flight of decaying stone steps.

At the foot of the iron stairs leading to the shelter was a shaded signboard.

In English:

TEIKOKU SIGNAL STATION

And in Japanese:

SHIMIZU OFFICE OF THE TEIKOKU SIGNAL
AND COMMUNICATIONS COMPANY

Notice of arrivals, departures, and moorings

Detection and prevention of accidents at sea
Land-to-sea communications
Marine weather information
Receiving and dispatching of ships
Various other matters related to shipping

The peeling white paint of the characters, here and there worn thin, with the name of the company in an antique hand, pleased Honda. The smell of the sea poured forth, quite without restraint, from the list of duties and functions.

He looked up the stairs. All was quiet.

Below and behind him, to the northwest, beyond the prefectural highway and the town, where pinwheels caught the light over carp streamers on new blue-tiled roofs, lay the complex of Shimizu Harbor, a crisscrossing of cranes on land and derricks on ships, white silos of factories and black hulls, iron bleached by the sea winds and thickly painted chimneys, one mass stopping at the shore, the other coming in from the several seas; there in the distance was the mechanism of the harbor laid bare, meeting at the appointed spot, glaring across the line. And the shining dismembered snake of the sea.

Fuji rose far above the hills. Only the summit was visible, as if a great sharp white boulder had been flung up through the uncertainty of the clouds.

Honda stopped to look.

3

THE CONCRETE PLATFORM was a water tank.

Water was pumped into it from a well and stored for irrigating strawberries. Teikoku Signal had seen the possibilities of the high platform and put up a wooden shelter. It was ideal for sighting ships from Nagoya to the west or Yokohama to the east.

Normally four signalmen worked eight-hour shifts. One of them had long been ill, however, and the other three took turns at twenty-four-hour duty. The first floor was the office of the superintendent, who from time to time came from the downtown office. The three signalmen had only a bare-floored room, some four yards square and surrounded on three sides by windows, on the second floor.

Attached to one window was a desk with a view on the three sides. Facing south was a thirty-power telescope, facing the harbor facilities to the east were fifteen-power binoculars, and at the southeast corner, for night signals, was a one-kilowatt beam. Two telephones on the desk at the southwest corner, a book shelf, maps, signal flags arranged on high shelves, and to the northwest a kitchen with a closet and a cot completed the furnishings. In front of the eastern window was a steel electric pylon, its porcelain insulators repeating the color of the clouds. The power line ran down to the beach, where it was caught by a second pylon. A turn to the northeast took it to a third, and so around the coast, a diminishing curve of

14

silver towers, to Shimizu Harbor. The third pylon was, from this vantage point, a good marker. A ship came into the harbor, and one knew as it passed the third pylon that it was approaching Basin 3-G, which included the piers.

Even now identification was by naked eye. So long as vagaries in cargoes and currents ruled the movements of ships, they would continue to come in too soon or too late, and a certain nineteenth-century romanticism would not disappear from welcoming parties. There was a need for more precise observations to tell the customs and quarantine officials and the stevedores and pilots and laundries and provisioners when to put out their welcoming flags. There was a still greater need for a just arbiter to decide which was to take precedence when two ships came in together and competed for the last berth.

That was Tōru's work.

A fairly large ship had appeared. The horizon was already obscure, and it took a quick and well-trained eye to determine a ship's origins. Tōru went to the telescope.

In the clear atmosphere of midsummer or midwinter, there would be an instant when a ship would move rudely in over the high threshold of the horizon; but in the mists of early summer such an appearance was a gradual separation from the inchoate. The horizon was like a long, white, soggy pillow.

The size of the black cargo ship seemed right for the 4,780-ton *Tenrō-maru*, and the stern bridge also corresponded to what the registry had told Tōru. The wake was white and clean, as was the bridge. There were three yellow derricks. What was the round red mark on the black funnels? Tōru strained his eyes. He made out the character for *tai*, "large," in a red circle. Taishō Shipping, no mistake about it. All the while

15

the ship kept up a speed of twelve and a half knots, and threatened to outrun the telescope. It was like a fly crossing a round window screen.

He could still not make out the name. He was sure that there were three characters, and foreknowledge told him that the first was *ten*, "heaven."

He returned to the desk and telephoned the agent. "Hello. This is Teikoku Signal. You should be ready for the *Tenrō-maru*. It's just coming past the pylon. The cargo?" Tōru conjured up an image of the waterline dividing the ship into red and black. "I'd think about half full. When will the stevedores be out? At five?"

That would give them an hour. The number of places that must be informed had grown.

Tōru moved busily back and forth between the desk and the telescope, and made some fifteen calls.

The pilot station. The tugboat *Shunyō-maru*. The pilot's house. Various provisioners. The Port Service Patrol. Customs. The agency once more. The Harbor Management Section of the Harbor Control Office. The Office of Statistics for weighing the cargo. Shipping offices.

"The *Tenrō-maru* is coming in. Hinodé four-five. If you will, please."

The *Tenrō-maru* was already at the third pylon. As the image moved past land it was distorted by heat shimmerings.

"Hello. The *Tenrō-maru* is coming into three-G."

"Hello. This is Teikoku Signal. The *Tenrō-maru* is in three-G."

"Hello. Customs? The police, please. The *Tenrō-maru* has come into three-G."

"Hello. The *Tenrō-maru* is in three-G. Sixteen fifteen."

"Hello. The *Tenrō-maru* came in five minutes ago."

• • •

Ships not from abroad but from Nagoya or Yokohama were more frequent at the end of the month than at the beginning. Yokohama was one hundred fifteen nautical miles away, nine and a half hours at twelve knots. Tōru had no duties except to be on watch for an hour or so before a projected arrival. There were no other arrivals today save the *Nitchōmaru* at nine in the evening, from Keelung.

Tōru always felt a little dejected when he had finished a round of calls. The harbor would be suddenly alive. He would light a cigarette as he watched the stir from remote isolation.

Actually he should not be smoking. The superintendent had had a sharp word or two when he had first noticed a boy of sixteen with a cigarette in his mouth. Afterward he had said nothing. No doubt he had concluded that inattention was the more profitable policy.

Tōru's pale, finely carved face was like ice. It conveyed no emotion, no affection or tears.

But he knew the happiness of watching. Nature had told him of it. No eye could be clearer or brighter than the eye that had nothing to create, nothing to do but gaze. The invisible horizon beyond which the conscious eye could not penetrate was far more remote than the visible horizon. And all manner of entities appeared in regions visible and accessible to consciousness. Sea, ships, clouds, peninsulas, lightning, the sun, the moon, the myriads of stars. If seeing is a meeting between eye and being, which is to say between being and being, then it must be the facing mirrors of two beings. No, it was more. Seeing went beyond being, to take wings like a bird. It transported Tōru to a realm visible to no one. Even beauty there was a rotted, tattered skirt. That had to be a sea never defiled by being, a sea upon which ships never appeared. There had to be a realm where at the limit of all the layers of clarity it was definite that nothing at all made an appearance, a realm of solid, definite indigo, where seeing cast off the shackles of consciousness and itself became transparent, where phenomena and consciousness dissolved like plumbic oxide in acetic acid.

Happiness for Tōru was sending his eyes into such distances. There was for him no more complete a throwing off of the self than in seeing. Only the eyes brought forgetfulness—save for the image in the mirror.

Tōru himself?

A sixteen-year-old who was quite certain that he did not belong to this world. Only half of him was in it. The other was in that realm of indigo. There were consequently no laws and no regulations that governed him. He but pretended that he was bound by the laws of this world. Where are there laws regulating an angel?

Life was strangely simple. Poverty and deprivation, the contradictions of society and politics, troubled him not in the least. Occasionally he would let a soft smile float to his lips, but it had in it nothing of sympathy. It was the final sign rejecting humanity, an invisible arrow released from the bow of his lips.

When he tired of looking at the sea, he would take a hand mirror from the desk and look at himself. In the pale, well-shaped face there were beautiful eyes, always brimming with midnight. The eyebrows were thin but proud, the lips were smooth and firm. But the eyes were the most beautiful feature. There was irony in the fact that his eyes should be the most beautiful part of his physical being, the fact that the organ for establishing his own beauty should be the most beautiful.

The eyelashes were long, and the eyes, utterly cruel, seemed at first sight to be lost in a dream.

This orphan, one of the elect, different from other men, had complete confidence in his own immaculateness, whatever evil he might work. His father, captain of a cargo ship, had died at sea, and his mother had died soon afterward, and he had been taken in by an impoverished uncle. A year in a prefectural training center upon his graduation from middle school and he was licensed as a third-class signalman and hired by Teikoku Signal.

Tōru knew nothing of the hard calluses built by outrage at poverty, like lumps of amber hardening from sap that oozes through wounded bark. His bark had always been hard. A thick, hard bark of contempt.

The joy of seeing, where everything was self-evident and given, lay only at the invisible horizon, far beyond the sea. Why need there be surprise? Despite the fact that deceit was delivered at every door every morning without fail, like the milk.

He knew his own workings to their smallest parts. His inspection system was flawless. There was no unconscious.

"If I had ever spoken or moved from the smallest subconscious impulse, then the world would have been promptly destroyed. The world should be grateful for my awareness of myself. Awareness has nothing to be proud of but control."

Perhaps, he sometimes thought, he was a hydrogen bomb equipped with consciousness. It was clear in any case that he was not a human being.

Tōru was a fastidious boy. He washed his hands any number of times every day. Constantly scrubbed at, they were white and dry. To the world he seemed no more than a clean, tidy boy.

He was indifferent to disorder outside himself. It seemed to him a symptom of illness to worry about wrinkles on another's trousers. The trousers of politics were a sodden, wrinkled mess, but what did that matter?

. . .

He heard a soft knock on the door downstairs. The superintendent always opened the badly fitting door as if crushing a matchbox and came stamping up the stairs. It would not be he.

Tōru slipped into sandals and went down the wooden stairs. He addressed the pinkish form at the undulant window, but did not open the door.

"It's still early. He might be as late as six. Come back after dinner."

"Oh?" Frozen for a moment in contemplation, the undulant form moved off. "I'll come back, then. I have lots of things to talk about."

"Yes, do."

Tōru shoved the stubby pencil he had for no reason brought with him behind his ear and ran back upstairs.

As if he had forgotten his caller, he gazed into the gathering dusk.

The sunset would be behind clouds, but it would come at six thirty-three, still more than an hour away. The sea was turning gray, and the Izu Peninsula, for a time out of sight, came dimly back, as if outlined in ink.

Two women made their way among the plastic houses, baskets of strawberries on their backs. Everything beyond was the sea, like unwrought metal. Just in line with the second pylon a five-hundred-ton cargo ship had been at anchor all afternoon. It had left early to save dockage, apparently, and then lowered anchor for a leisurely cleaning. The cleaning evidently finished, it was once more weighing anchor.

Tōru went into the kitchen, which contained a small washstand and a propane burner, and warmed his dinner. The telephone rang. Harbor Control. A message had come from the *Nitchō-maru*, confirming that it would arrive at nine.

After dinner he read the evening paper. He became aware that he was waiting for his caller.

Seven ten. The sea was enfolded in night. Only the white of the plastic houses, like a coat of frost, seemed to resist.

A pounding of light engines came through the window. The fishing fleet had put out from Yaizu to the right, making for the sardine banks off Okitsu. Green and red lights amidships, perhaps twenty of them, moved past, fighting for the lead. The quivering of the lights upon the sea gave visual manifestation to a primitive beating of hot-bulb engines.

The night sea was for a time like a village festival. It was like a roiling mass of festival-goers, each with a lantern in hand, pushing noisily for a dark shrine. Tōru knew that the boats would be talking to one another. Rushing, fighting for the threshold of the sea, dreaming of a huge take, vital and aggressive, fish-scented muscles shining, they would be talking to one another through speakers, out there on the sea.

In the quiet after the stir, the automobiles on the prefectural highway kept up a steady drone. Tōru heard a knocking on the door. It would be Kinué again.

He went down and opened the door.

Kinué, in a pink cardigan, stood in the light. She had a large white gardenia in her hair.

"Come in," said Tōru, with manly vigor.

Giving him a smile of delicate reluctance such as a great beauty might permit herself, Kinué came in. Upstairs she put a box of chocolates on Tōru's desk.

"For you."

"You're too good to me."

A crackling of cellophane filled the room. Tōru opened the oblong golden box and, taking a chocolate, smiled at Kinué.

He always treated her as if she were a great beauty. She took a seat beyond the signal light. Tōru seated himself at the desk. At a fixed and discreet distance, they took up their positions as if prepared to flee down the stairs.

When he was at the telescope he turned out all the lights; but otherwise it was bright from fluorescent ceiling lights. The gardenia in Kinué's hair took on a lustrous white glow. The ugliness beneath was rather splendid.

It was an ugliness that no one could miss. It cut off comparison with mediocre ugliness that could, given the right time and place, become beauty of a sort, or ugliness that revealed a beauty of spirit. It was ugliness, and could be described as nothing else. It was a bounty from heaven, a perfect ugliness denied to most girls.

But Kinué was constantly troubled by her beauty.

"The good thing about you," she said, worried about her knees and tugging at her short skirt, "the good thing about you is that you're the only one who never makes a pass at me. Of course you *are* a man, and I can never be too sure. I must warn you. If you ever do make a pass at me I won't come and see you any more. That will be the end. You promise that you at least never will?"

"I vow it most solemnly."

Tōru raised a hand in pledge. He had to be very earnest in such matters when he was with Kinué.

Every conversation was preceded by the pledge. Once it was made, her manner changed. She threw off uneasiness, her seated figure relaxed. She touched the gardenia in her hair as if it were breakable. She smiled from its shadow, and, with a sudden, deep sigh, began talking.

"I'm so unlucky I could die. I doubt if I can ever expect a man to understand what it means for a woman to be too beautiful. Men do not respect beauty. Every man who looks at me has the most contemptible urges. Men are beasts. I might have more respect for them if I hadn't been born so beautiful. The minute a man looks at me he turns into a beast. How can I respect a man? A woman's beauty is tied right away to the ugliest things, and for a woman there is no worse insult. I don't like to go downtown any more. Every man I pass, every last one of them, looks at me like a slobbering dog. There I am walking quietly down the street and every man that comes up to me has a look in his eyes that says I want her I want her I want her. Every one of them with a look in his eyes that can only be put into those words. Just walking through it all wears me out.

"On the bus just now someone made a pass at me. I hated it." She took a little flowered handkerchief from her cardigan and dabbed elegantly at her eyes.

"He was a good-looking boy, right beside me. From Tokyo, I'd imagine. He had a big Boston bag on his knee, and he was wearing a visor cap. From the side he looked a little like ———" and she mentioned the name of a popular singer. "He kept looking at me, and I said to myself, Here it comes again. The bag was all soft and white like a dead rabbit. He poked his hand in under it so no one else could see, and then stretched out a finger and touched my leg. Right here. On the thigh, and high up on it too. I was surprised, let me tell you. And it was worse because he was such a clean, nice-looking boy. I screamed and jumped up. The other passengers were all looking at me and my heart was beating so, I couldn't say anything. A nice lady asked me what was wrong. I was going to say to her this man made a pass at me. But he was all red and looking at the floor, and I'm too good-natured. I couldn't tell them what had happened. It wasn't any duty of mine to cover up for him, but I said I thought there must be a nail, people should be careful about this seat. Everyone said it was very dangerous and looked very bothered and stared at the cushion. It was a green one. Someone said I should turn in a complaint, but I said it didn't matter, I was getting off at the next stop. And I did get off. My seat was still empty when the bus pulled away again. Nobody wanted to risk it. All I saw was black hair shining under the visor cap. That's my story. I can congratulate myself on not having harmed anyone. I was the only injured party, and I'm glad. That's the fate of a beautiful person. Just accept all the ugliness in the world and hide the wound and die without letting out the secret. That's enough. Don't you suppose a beautiful, well-shaped girl has the best chance of getting to be an angel? I'm telling you, no one else. You can keep a secret.

"Yes, it's true. Only a beautiful woman can really know, and she sees it in the eyes of a man, the ugliness of the world, the way the real shape of a human being gets lost." Each time Kinué used the word "beautiful" it was as if she were mustering up all the saliva she had in her and spitting it out. "It's a beautiful woman that keeps hell at a distance. She gets these nasty things from the other sex and spite from her own, and she smiles and calls it fate. That's what a beautiful woman is. It's really a shame. Nobody knows what a shame. It's a misfortune only somebody as beautiful as she is can understand, and there's not a single person that can really sympathize. It makes my skin crawl when another woman says she wishes she were as beautiful as I am. Those people will never understand our misfortunes. Never. How can they be expected to understand the loneliness of a jewel? But then a diamond is always being washed clean by dirty greed and I am always being washed clean by dirty ideas. If people really knew what it is like to be beautiful, why all the beauty parlors and plastic surgeons would go broke. The ones who think it's good to be beautiful are the ones who aren't. Isn't it the truth?"

Tōru was rolling a hexagonal green pencil between his fingers.

Kinué was the daughter of a wealthy landowner. She had been somewhat strange since an unfortunate love affair, and she had been in a mental hospital for six months. She had a curious syndrome described as delirious depression or depressed intoxication or something of the sort. There had been no serious outburst since, and it had settled into a conviction that she was the most beautiful girl in the world.

Because of the delusion, she had been able to break the mirror that so tormented her and fly off into a mirrorless world. Reality became malleable, selective, a seeing of what was desirable and a rejection of everything else. The guiding principle would for most people have been a tightrope inviting almost certain disaster, but it brought her no complications and no sense of danger. Having thrown the old plaything of self-awareness into the garbage can, she had started to make a new plaything of wonderful ingenuity and intricacy, and now she had adapted it perfectly to her needs and set it to work like an artificial heart. When she had finished shaping it, Kinué had attained perfect happiness; or, as she would have put it, perfect unhappiness.

Probably the romantic misfortune had come about when a man made mention of her ugliness. In that instant Kinué saw the light down her only road, the defile open to her. If she could not change her own looks, then she must change the world. She set to work on her own secret plastic surgery and achieved a reversal, and a gleaming pearl emerged from the ugly, ashen shell.

Like a beleaguered soldier finding an escape, Kinué

came upon a basic but elusive link with the world. With that as her fulcrum, she stood the world upside down. A most extraordinary revolution. Exquisite craftiness in taking for misfortune what in her heart she desired above all.

His way of holding a cigarette somewhat old for his years, Tōru leaned back and stretched out long legs in blue jeans. He found nothing the least novel in her discourse, but he gave not a sign that he was bored. Kinué was very sensitive to her audience.

He never made fun of her as her neighbors did. That was why she visited him. He felt in this mad, ugly woman five years his senior a comrade in apartness. He liked people who refused to recognize the world.

If the hardness of the two hearts, the one protected by lunacy, the other by awareness—if the degree of hardness was about the same, then there need be no fear of wounds, however much they brushed against each other. Nor need there be a fear of carnal brushes. Kinué was now most off her guard. When Tōru got up with a creaking of his chair and moved toward her in great strides, she let out a shriek and ran for the door.

He was hurrying to the telescope. His eye glued to it, he waved a hand behind him.

"Work to do. Go on home."

"I'm sorry. I didn't mean it. I really believe you're not like other men, but you caught me by surprise. I've had such awful things happen to me, and when a man stands up all of a sudden I think it's happening again. You must understand that I live in constant fear."

"It's all right. Go on home. I'm busy."

"I'll go. But—"

"What is it?" His eye still on the telescope, he sensed that she was hesitating at the top of the stairs.

"I—I have a great deal of respect for you. Well, good-bye."

"Good-bye."

There were footsteps and the sound of a closing door. Tōru followed a light with the telescope.

He had glanced out the window as he listened to Kinué and caught a sign. Though it was cloudy there were lights scattered up and down the west Izu hills; and when the sign of an approaching ship came in among the lights of the fishing boats there came a faint, suspicious change like a spark in darkness.

The *Nitchō-maru* was not due for almost an hour. But one should not trust ships to keep their appointments.

Off in the obscurity, in the circle of the telescope, crawling along like a bug, were the lights of a ship. One cluster became two. The ship had changed direction, and the stern and prow lights separated. To judge from the distance and the lights at the bridge, it would not be a fishing boat of some hundreds of tons, but the *Nitchō-maru*, a good forty-two hundred tons. Tōru already had a practiced eye for reckoning the tonnage of a ship from its length.

As the telescope followed them, its lights moved away from the distant lights of Izu and the fishing boats. With grand confidence it pressed forward on its sea route.

It came like a shining death, casting bridge lights into the water. By the time he could clearly make out in the night, sketched in port and stern and deck lights, the form of a ship, that special form of a cargo ship, like a complex old ceramic piece, Tōru was at the signal light. He adjusted it by hand. If his signals were too fast, the ship would have trouble making them out, and if they were too full, the southeast pillar of the building might block out a part of them. And because recognition and quickness of response were moreover not easy to foresee, timing was not at all easy.

Tōru turned on the switch. Light leaked faintly from the old blinker. There were binoculars on top of it, like the eyes of a frog. The ship floated upon a round space in the dark night.

Tōru sent out three hallos. Dot-dot-dot-dash-dot.* Dot-dot-dot-dash-dot. Dot-dot-dot-dash-dot.

There was no response.

He again signaled three times.

A dash. It was like an oozing from beside the bridge.

He could feel the resistance of the distant shutter. "Your name?"

Dot-dash-dash-dot, dot-dash-dot-dash-dot, dash-dot-dot-dot-dash, dot-dash, dash-dot-dot-dot.

After that initial dash, the name of the ship, phantom-like.

Dash-dot-dash-dot, dot-dash-dash-dot, dot-dot-dot-dash-dot, dash-dash, dot-dot-dash, dash-dot-dot-dash, dash-dot-dash-dash-dot.

It was the *Nitchō-maru*, without question.

There was a wild restlessness in the long and short lights, as if in among the clusters of solid lights a single light were mad with joy. The voice calling out from afar over the dark sea was like the voice of the madwoman. A metal voice crying out sadly though not sad, pleading an agony of joy. It only reported the name of a ship, but the infinitely disturbed voice of light also conveyed in each fragment the irregularity of an overexcited pulse.

The signals would probably be from the hand of the second mate, on watch. Tōru could sense in the signals from a bridge the feelings of a second mate

---

* Translator's note: the code is that used by the Japanese for the Kana syllabary.

returning home. In that distant room, heavy with the smell of white paint, bright with the brass of compass and wheel, there would be the weariness of the long voyage and the lingering sun of the south. The return of a ship, battered by winds and its own cargo. A professionalism containing a masculine languor. A trained swiftness, and all the red-eyed intensity of a homecoming. Two bright lonely rooms faced each other across the dark sea. And as communication was struck up, the existence of another human spirit out in the darkness was like a ghost-light in the sea itself.

It would have to anchor offshore and come in to-morrow. Quarantine closed at five, and would not open until seven in the morning. Tōru waited until the ship had passed the third pylon. If there were later inquiries, he need only give the hour.

"The ones from foregn ports are always early," said Tōru to himself. He sometimes talked to himself.

It was approaching nine. The wind had stopped, the sea was quiet.

At about ten he stepped outside for a breath of fresh air to fend off sleep.

There was still traffic on the prefectural highway. The lights around Shimizu Harbor to the northeast blinked nervously. Mount Udo, which on clear days swallowed the setting sun, was a dark mass. There was drunken singing from the dormitory of H. Shipyards.

Back inside, he turned on the weather report. There would be rain and a high sea and bad visibility. Then came the news. American operations in Cambodia had incapacitated headquarters, supply points, and hospitals of the Liberation Front until October.

Ten thirty.

Visibility was already bad, and the lights of Izu had disappeared. It was better, thought Tōru sleepily, than a bright moonlight night. On moonlight nights it was difficult to make out ship lights in the glare of the water.

Setting the alarm clock for one thirty, he lay down on the cot.

4

AT ABOUT the same time Honda, at his house in Hongō, was having a dream.

He had gone to bed early and, exhausted from the journey, soon fallen asleep. Perhaps under the influence of the pine grove he had seen that day, the dream had to do with angels.

Flying over the pine grove of Mio was not an angel but a multitude of angels, male and female. The dream made good use of what Honda knew of Buddhist writ.

Dreaming, Honda told himself that the writ was true. He was filled with clean happiness.

There are the angels of the Six Worlds of Desire and the sentient beings of the several Worlds of Form. The first are the better known. Since the angels in Honda's dream were disporting themselves, the males with the females, it seemed likely that they were from the Worlds of Desire.

They carry lights of seven colors, fire, gold, blue, red, white, yellow, and black. It is as if giant hummingbirds with rainbow wings were weaving in and out.

The hair is blue, the teeth flash white as they smile. The bodies are softness itself, cleanness itself. The gazes are unblinking.

The male and female angels of the Worlds of Desire come constantly up to one another; but the angels the third world are content to hold hands, of the fourth to exchange thoughts, of the fifth to exchange glances, of the sixth and highest to exchange words.

It would be such a gathering, Honda told himself. There were scattered flowers, there were delicate perfumes and music. Honda was enrapt at this introduction to their several worlds. He knew that, though angels are sentient beings superior to humans, they still have not escaped the cycle of birth and rebirth.

It seemed to be night and yet it was bright afternoon, it seemed to be day and yet there were stars and there was a down-turned crescent moon. There were no human figures if one excepted Honda himself. He wondered if he might be the fisherman who at Mio tried to steal the angel's robe.

Buddhist writ has it thus: "Male angels are born at the knees of male archangels, and female angels at the shoulders of female archangels; and they know of their earlier places of birth, and they drink at the heavenly stream of sanctification."

Soaring up, dipping downward, the angels seemed to be making sport of Honda. With arched feet they came within brushing distance of his nose. He traced the white flower-fingers, and those that went behind the neck of the face smiling at him—it was the face of the Thai princess Ying Chan, crowned with flowers.

The angels were taking less notice of Honda. Coming near the dunes by the sea, they dipped under the lower branches of the pines. Honda was unable to take in everything. He was dazed by the whirling glitter. Heavenly flowers of white rained ceaselessly down. The sound of heavenly flageolet and lute. Blue hair and skirts and sleeves and scarves of raw silk, draped from shoulders down over arms, trailed in the breeze. An immaculate white bosom lingered for a moment before his eyes, the clean sole of a foot withdrew into the distance. A beautiful white arm, lighted by a rainbow, brushed past his eyes as if seizing at something. In that instant he saw the hollow of a gently opened finger, and, floating in it, the moon. Rich white arms permeated with a heavenly scent opened wide and soared skyward. The gentle lines of hips, outlined clearly against the blue sky, trailed like wisps of cloud. Then from afar a pair of unblinking black eyes came pressing down upon him, and, with a soft toss of a white forehead, reflecting the stars, the figure plummeted away, ankles raised.

Among the male angels he could clearly pick out Kiyoaki and a stern Isao. He tried to follow them, but, in the constantly shifting pattern of rainbow lights, he could not hold any one figure for more than an instant, however smooth its path.

Looking at the spot where he had seen Ying Chan, he wondered whether time might be more complex in the Worlds of Desire, and, changing form phantasmagorically, the past and the present might occupy the same space. The quiet little tragedy faded wistfully away even as new links seemed to be forming.

Only the pines were of this world. Their needles were etched in detail, the trunk of the red pine against which Honda leaned was rough and hard to the touch.

Honda presently came to find the constant motion irritating and even unbearable. He was still watching, as if from beneath a giant deodar in a park. A park of humiliation. Automobile horns in the night. He watched on and on, reducing everything to a common element, the most sacred and the most sordid of things. He made everything the same. Everything was the same. From start to finish. In deep depression

Honda opened his eyes and tore away the dream, as a man swimming in from the ocean might tear away clinging seaweed and fling it down on the shore.

He could hear his watch ticking softly in the hamper at his pillow. He turned on the night light. One thirty. He feared that he would be awake until daylight.

5

AROUSED by the alarm clock, Tōru went by habit to the washstand and scrubbed his hands. Then he went to the telescope.

The cushion at the viewer was warmly, repellingly damp.

He kept his eye a slight distance away. He could see nothing.

He had set the alarm for one thirty against the possibility that the *Zuiun-maru*, due at three, might come in early. He looked again, and saw nothing. From about three the sea came to life. Swarms of fishing boats approached from the left, their motors thumping and their lights fighting for the lead. For a time the sea below him was like a street fair. The boats were hurrying back for the morning market in Yaizu from the Okitsu sardine banks.

He took a chocolate and went to warm himself a bowl of noodles. A call came from the Yokohama signal station. The *Zuiun-maru* had been delayed and would not be in until four. He could have slept longer.

He yawned several times. The yawns seemed to force their way up from the farthest depths of his lungs.

Three thirty, and there was still no sign of the ship. To drive away the more and more insistent drowsiness, he went downstairs and outdoors and took long breaths of cold air. The moon should be rising, but it was cloudy and there were no stars. He could see only rows of red lights at the fire escapes of an apartment complex and, much farther off, a blaze of lights around Shimizu Harbor. A frog croaked softly and the first cock caught a hint of dawn in the cold air. The layers of clouds to the north were faintly white.

He came back indoors. It was five minutes till four. The first glimpse of the *Zuiun-maru* drove away sleepiness. The morning twilight was coming on, the plastic strawberry houses were like a snowy landscape. He had no trouble identifying the ship. He aimed the blinker at the red port light and the name promptly came back. In the dawn light the *Zuiun-maru* glided slowly into 3-G.

At four thirty there was a very faint flush over the clouds to the east. The line between sea and land was clear, the water and the reflections of the fishing boats took form and place.

At the desk, in light barely strong enough for writing, Tōru wrote over and over again, to no purpose: *Zuiun-maru, Zuiun-maru, Zuiun-maru.* The light was stronger by the moment. He glanced up, and could make out folds of waves.

The sun rose at four fifty-four. Tōru went to the east window and pulled back the glass to let in the beauty of the last moments before sunrise.

Just over the spot where the sun would rise, delicate clouds drew in deep relief pleats exactly like the folds of a skirt, as if there were a chain of mountains over the sea. Layers of rose-colored clouds trailed above, with here and there apertures of an ashen green.

Below the ridge of mountains clouds of light gray surged up like the sea. The mountain relief caught the rose glow down to its lower skirts. Tōru could almost see dots of houses on the far slopes. Above them was a vision of a rose coming into bloom.

It was from here, he said to himself, that he had come. From the mirage land, visible occasionally through openings in the dawn sky.

The morning breeze was chilly, the groves below the window had taken on a fresh green. The porcelain insulators on the pylons stood out white in the dawn. Eastward and eastward the line of pylons stretched, toward the distant point of the sunrise. But the sun did not come out. Just at the moment of sunrise the rose faded and was sucked up into blue clouds. In place of the vanished rose, clouds scattered like silk threads; but there was no sun.

It finally made its appearance at five past five. From an opening in the dark gray clouds at the horizon, just above the second pylon, came the first glimpse of the sun, carmine, melancholy, as if it were not rising but setting. The top and the bottom were cut off by a screen of clouds, like shining lips. An ironic smile of thin lips rouged in carmine floated briefly among the clouds. Thinner and thinner, fainter and fainter, they left a sardonic smile that was there and not there. The higher stretches of the sky carried a warmer, brighter light.

By six, when a ship with a cargo of sheet iron came in, the sun was astonishingly high, a ball of light dim enough for the naked eye. In its weak light, the sea to the east was a cloth of gold.

Tōru called the tugboat and the pilot's house.

"Good morning. The *Nitchō-maru* and the *Zuiun-maru* have came in. Yes, please."

"North Fuji? The *Nitchō-maru* and the *Zuiun-maru* are in. Yes. At four twenty, the *Zuiun-maru*, three-G."

6

THE CHANGE of shifts came at nine. Tōru left the chocolates for his successor. The weather forecasters had gone astray. It was a beautifully clear day. The sun as he waited for his bus was too bright for eyes that had not had enough sleep.

The road off toward the Sakurabashi station of the Shimizu Railroad had once gone through paddies, but they had all been filled in and subdivided. The bright flats were a tasteless jumble of new shops, like Main Street in an American country town. Getting off the bus, Tōru turned left across a brook. Beyond was the two-story apartment house where he lived.

He went up a stairway with a blue awning and opened the door at the end of the second floor.

It was as he had left it, neat and tidy, two rooms with kitchen, six mats and four-and-a-half mats, dim behind shutters. Before he opened the shutters he went to turn on the heater for the bath. He had a bath of his own, albeit a small one, heated by propane.

Worn out from looking, Tōru, who had no occupation but to look, leaned against the windowsill to the northwest and looked at the Sunday-morning bustle in the new houses beyond the orange grove. Dogs barked. Sparrows flitted among the orange branches. On south verandas men who finally had houses of their own were sprawled on rattan chairs reading newspapers. He caught glimpses of aproned women inside. The newly tiled roofs were a violent blue. The voices of children were like splinters of glass.

Tōru liked to look at people as at animals in a zoo. The bath was ready. Always after work he had a long bath and scrubbed every hollow of himself. He only had to shave once a week.

Naked, he creaked across the washing platform and got in without washing. No one would use the bath after him. He had set the thermostat, and it had missed by no more than a degree or two. Warmed, he got out and washed at his leisure. When he was tired and short of sleep, a cold sweat came out on his face and at his armpits. He stirred up a good suds and scrubbed industriously at his armpits.

The light from the window slipped down blue-white over his upraised arms and caught the left nipple, beside an armpit now hidden in suds. He smiled. He had been born with three inlaid moles, like the Pleiades. From he did not know when, they had seemed to him like proof in the flesh that limitless bounties were his.

·7

HONDA and Keiko Hisamatsu were perfect companions in old age. When he went walking with Keiko, everyone took them for an affluent, well-matched husband and wife. They could see each other every other day or so and not be bored. They worried about each other's cholesterol count and hemorrhoids and possible malignancies, and caused doctors much amusement.

They changed hospitals with great frequency, suspicious of all doctors. They even had an understanding on trivial economies. They were assiduous students of the psychology of the old, their own aside.

They had even struck a balance in irritability. The one would take on a discreet objectivity when the other was a victim of meaningless irritation, and each fed the other's pride. They nursed each other's lapses in memory. When either would forget what he had just said or say quite the opposite, the other (why it could as easily have happened to him) would politely refrain from laughing.

They were both a little vague on things that had happened these last ten or twenty years; but in ancient matters having to do with family and the like they competed in precision as if reading from a golden record. And often they would become aware of the fact that, neither of them listening to the other, they had been lost in concurrent soliloquies.

"Sugi's father—he was the founder of Sugi Chemical. It's since become Nihon Chemical. His first wife was from an old family in his home town, name of Honji. It didn't work and she took back her maiden name. Then she remarried, a second cousin. She was a nasty one, and she bought a house right beside his in Kagomachi. Then some diviner everyone was talking about—what was his name—anyway he told her the well was in a bad direction. So she did exactly what he told her and put up a shrine looking out from the garden. People came to pray at it in swarms and hordes. It only lasted until the air raids, but—" That was the sort of soliloquy in which Honda came to indulge himself.

And this is the sort of thing Keiko would say: "She was the daughter of a mistress, and that made her a half sister of Viscount Matsudaira. She fell in love with an Italian opera singer and got disinherited and chased him off to Naples and he ran out on her. She tried to commit suicide. It was in all the papers. A cousin of Baron Shishido's wife, Baron Shishido would have been her uncle, anyhow it was the Sawado family this cousin married into. She had twin boys, and no sooner had they turned twenty than they were killed in traffic accidents one right after the other. They were models for *Twin Buds of Sorrow*. It's very famous. You may have read it."

The audience was never attentive to this unraveling of genealogies, but that made no difference. Inattention was better than the look of boredom that came with attention.

They had in common an ailment which they wished no one else to know of: old age. Everyone wants to talk about his ailments, and it was clever of them to have found the right listeners. What made them a little different from most couples was that Keiko felt no need for dissimulation or youthful airs.

Fussiness, bias, hostility toward youth, excessive attention to detail, fear of death, indiscriminate irritability, these things Honda and Keiko found in each other, but not in themselves. And when it came to obstinacy, each was provided with a stock that quite balanced the other's.

They were very tolerant of young women and very intolerant of young men. They loved to complain about the young, and the Zengakuren and the hippies did not escape their lances. Smooth skins, rich black hair, a dreamy, bemused look, all of these were anathema, because attributes of the young. It is a sin for a man to be young, said Keiko, and Honda was pleased.

If old age was the reality most unpleasant to have to accept and most continuously to be lived with, then Honda and Keiko had each made the other a refuge from the reality. Their intimacy was not juxtaposition but a brushing past in the rush for a refuge. They exchanged empty houses and hurried to lock the doors behind them. Alone inside the other, each of them would breathe easily.

Keiko thought of her friendship with Honda as faithful adherence to Rié's last testament. As she lay dying, Rié had taken Keiko's hand and beseeched her to look after Honda. She thus saw to her husband's future in the most sagacious manner.

One fruit of the union had been a trip to Europe the year before. Keiko became a substitute for Rié, who had obstinately refused to go. Rié had loathed the thought of travel abroad and, each time he had suggested it, had asked Keiko to go in her place. She knew perfectly well that her husband did not like to travel with her.

In the winter Honda and Keiko went to Venice and Bologna. The cold was a bit trying, but they found the quiet and decay of hibernal Venice enormously to their liking. There were no tourists, the freezing gondoliers had no business, bridges would emerge one after another like ashes of ruined dreams. In Venice was the end at its most beautiful, beauty being gnawed to a skeleton by sea and factory. Honda caught cold and ran a high fever. The swiftness with which Keiko found a doctor who could speak English, the thoroughness of her ministrations, made Honda see that a companion in old age is a necessity.

On the morning his fever abated, his gratitude found expression in boyish embarrassment. "All this gentleness and maternal affection. I can see why the girls love you."

"The two are not the same at all." In fine spirits, Keiko feigned anger. "I am only kind to friends. To be liked by women I have to be cruel. If the girl I liked best were running a fever like this, I'd have to throw over all my worries and run out on her.

I'd rather die than have the sort of arrangement most of them do, living together as if they were husband and wife and taking care of each other in old age. There are plenty of haunted houses where mannish women are living with shrinking maidens of dreadful fidelity. Mushrooms grow in the dampness and that is what they feed on, and they spin soft cobwebs and sleep in them in each other's arms. The mannish woman is always a worker, and so there they are cheek to cheek, figuring out their taxes. No, it's not the sort of romance I want to be part of."

Thanks to the ugliness of masculine old age, Honda was an amply qualified sacrifice to this dauntless resolution. Such are the unexpected blessings of old age.

By way of recompense, perhaps, Keiko poked fun at Honda because he carried with him a small wooden cenotaph in Rié's memory. He had kept it secret; but when his fever went over a hundred he began leaving final instructions, sure that he was in the last throes of pneumonia. One was that she take the cenotaph back to Japan.

"That sort of love makes a person's flesh crawl," said Keiko, not at all gently. "She didn't want to come, and so you dragged her along against her will."

On the morning of his recovery Honda found the clear sky pleasant, and the tongue-lashing an added pleasure.

It was not clear to him, even after Keiko's ungentle remarks, what he was asking of Rié. She had been a chaste wife to the end, of that he had no doubt; but there were thorns in all the hollows and on all the corners of the chastity. The sterile Rié made always manifest the reservations Honda himself had about humanity. His unhappiness she made her happiness, and she immediately saw what was behind an occasional show of gentleness and affection. Even farmers were taking their wives abroad these days. Given

41

Honda's affluence, his proposal was a very modest one. Her refusal was extraordinarily stubborn. Sometimes she even shouted at him.

"What are London and Venice and Paris to me? I'm an old woman, and what do you expect me to get out of it, being dragged around to places like that?"

A young Honda would probably have been put off by such brusquenses; but the old Honda wondered whether his proposal to take his wife abroad had really had in it any sort of affectionate solicitude at all. Rié had become accustomed to look with suspicion upon evidences of affection, and Honda had fallen into a similar habit. Perhaps his travel plans had embodied an urge to play the role of the virtuous husband. Making everything its opposite, making his wife's resistance into womanly diffidence, her coldness into concealed ardor, he had sought evidence of his own benevolence. And perhaps he wanted to turn the whole voyage into a celebration marking the passage of some stage or other in life. Rié immediately picked out the vulgar motives behind his fabricated benevolence. She pleaded illness, and presently the averred illness became real. She drove herself into physical pain. Travel was out of the question.

Bringing the cenotaph with him was a post-mortem tribute to her honesty. If Rié had seen her husband tucking the cenotaph into his briefcase (the premise was of course a contradiction), how derisively she would have laughed! Today all manner of sentimental affection was permitted to Honda. And the one who permitted it was the new Rié.

On the night of their return to Rome, as if by way of compensation for her services in Venice, Keiko brought to their suite in the Hotel Excelsior a beautiful Sicilian girl she had picked up on the Via Veneto, near the hotel. The two enjoyed themselves the whole night through in Honda's presence.

Later Keiko said: "Your coughing was wonderful. You weren't entirely over your cold. You coughed all night, the strangest sort of coughing. I can't tell you how wonderful it was listening to that funny old cough while I had that marble body to enjoy in the next bed. It was background music better than the best I could have bought. I felt as if I were doing something or other, I don't quite know what, in a fine, luxurious tomb."

"You were listening to the skeleton."

"That's it. I was between life and death. Their intermediary. But you're not to say that you weren't having a good time yourself." Keiko was quite aware that Honda had come over and felt the girl's foot.

In the course of the trip Keiko taught Honda how to play cards. Upon their return she invited him to a canasta party. After lunch four tables were put up in the parlor.

With Honda were Keiko and two White Russian women. One was old and the other a portly person in her fifties. It was a gloomy, rainy afternoon. Honda could not understand why Keiko, who was so fond of young girls, should invite only old and aging women to these parties. There were only two men besides Honda, a retired businessman and an elderly teacher of flower-arranging.

The Russian women had been in Japan for several decades; and it was a source of surprise to Honda that their only Japanese consisted of vulgar pidgin uttered in very loud voices. They sat down to cards immediately after lunch. The Russians promptly retouched their faces with rouge and lipstick.

Since the death of their husbands, also White Russians, they had continued to operate a family enterprise manufacturing foreign cosmetics. They were very niggardly, but they did not mind spending money on themselves. Taken with persistent diarrhea on a trip to Osaka and wanting to avoid the embarrassment of countless trips to the lavatory on the way back, they had chartered a plane, and on their return to Tokyo been taken to a hospital where they were known.

The old woman, her hair dyed brown, was wearing a turquoise pullover and a spangled cardigan, and her pearl necklace was too heavy. She was bent, but the fingers that took up the compact and lipstick were still powerful, so powerful that the wrinkled lower lip was pulled to one side. She was a fierce battler at the canasta table.

Her favorite subject was death. Her last canasta party, she was sure. By the next one she would be dead. She would await protests when she had made her declaration.

The intricate design of the cards scattered over Italian parquetry quite dazzled the eye; and on her powerful finger an amber-colored cat's eye bobbed over the lacquer faces like a fisherman's float. Crimson fingertips on splotched hands like the belly of a shark that had been stranded for some days on a beach rapped nervously at the table.

With a graceful fanning of cards, Keiko expertly shuffled the two decks. The decks were left face down after each player had received eleven cards, and a single card was left face up beside them. It was the three of diamonds, a sort of lunatic freshness in its red. Honda caught his breath. He saw three moles, stained in blood.

The special sounds of a card game: laughter as of a table fountain, sighs, little cries of astonishment. It was a zone where there need be no inhibitions in such matters as chuckling, uncertainty and unease, the craftiness of old age. It was like night in a zoo of emotions. Cries and laughter came from all the pens and all the cages.

"It's your turn."

"No, it's yours."

"Doesn't anyone have a canasta yet?"

"But I'll be scolded if I play out of turn."

"She's a very good dancer. Go-go too."

"I've never been to a go-go hall."

"I have. Just once. Like an insane asylum. Have a look at an African dance some time. It's the same thing."

"I like to tango."

"I like the old dances."

"The waltz and the tango."

"The old dances are so graceful. These new ones are like spooks. The men and the women all dressed the same. And the colors. Like a nicky—you say?"

"A nicky?"

"You know. All sorts of colors in the sky."

"Oh, a *niji*. A rainbow."

"Yes. A *niji*, that's what it's like. Men and women, all sorts of colors."

"But a rainbow is beautiful."

"Rainbows will soon be animals too, at this rate. Rainbow animals."

"Rainbow animals."

"I haven't much longer. I want just one more canasta before I die. That's all I want, my very last wish. My last canasta, Mrs. Hisamatsu."

"Don't say it again, Galina."

This curious exchange made Honda, whose hand came to nothing at all, think of waking up in the morning.

What he had seen first each morning since turning seventy was the face of death. Sensing the arrival of dawn in the faint light at the paper doors, he would be awakened by a strangling accumulation of mucus. During the night mucus accumulated into a red-black mass and nurtured its own nightmarish stiffness. Some-day someone would perform for him the service of

45

taking it between chopsticks and cleanly lifting it away.

The lump of mucus, like bêche-de-mer, would inform Honda afresh each morning that he was still alive. And with the awareness of life it would bring a fear of death.

Honda was in the habit of giving himself over to a flow of dreams each morning. Like a cow, he would ruminate.

The dreams were bright and sparkling, much fuller of the happiness of life than life itself. Gradually dreams of boyhood and youth came to predominate. In a dream he would taste the hotcakes his mother had made one snowy morning.

Why should a meaningless little episode be so insistent? No doubt precisely because it was a meaningless little episode remembered hundreds of times over a half century. Honda could not himself understand the hold on his memory.

The last traces of the old breakfast room had probably disappeared, so often had the Hongō house been rebuilt. A fifth-year student in the secondary course at Peers, Honda had on his return from school —it would have been a Saturday—gone with a friend to call at a faculty house, and so proceeded homeward, hungry and without an umbrella.

He usually came in through the kitchen door, but today he went around to look at the snow in the garden. The matting to protect the pines from the winter cold was flecked with white. The stone lanterns were capped with white brocade. His shoes squeaking across the snow, he caught a distant glimpse of his mother's skirt at the knee-high window of the breakfast room. He was at home.

"You must be hungry. Come on in, but brush the snow off first."

His mother pulled her kimono tight together. Taking

off his coat, Honda slipped into the *kotatsu*. As if she were trying to remember something, his mother blew on the embers. She brushed a wisp of hair up away from the ashes.

"Wait just a minute," she said between breaths. "I have something good for you."

Placing a small pan on the embers, she rubbed it with greased paper. She poured neat circles of batter on the hot grease.

It was the taste of those hotcakes that Honda so often remembered in dreams: the taste of honey and melted butter that snowy afternoon. He could remember nothing more delicious.

But why should that one detail have become the germ of a memory he was to carry through life? There could be no doubt that this unwonted fit of gentleness on the part of his severe mother had added to the enjoyment. There was a strange sadness entangled with the memory: the profile of his mother as she blew on the embers; the glow on her cheeks as they lighted up, with each breath, embers that were not permitted to warm the parlor of this frugal house, dusky even in the light from the snow; the play of light and darkness, shadows coming over his mother's cheeks each time she took a breath. And perhaps concealed in the intensity of her motions and the rare display of gentleness was a pain that she had refused all her life to give voice to. Perhaps it had come transparently and immediately across to him, in the full round flavor of the hotcakes, through the untrained young palate, in the sense of affection. Only thus could the sadness find explanation.

Sixty years had gone by, as an instant. Something came over him to drive away his consciousness of old age, a sort of pleading, as if he had buried his face in her warm bosom.

Something, running through sixty years in a taste

of hotcakes on a snowy day, something that brought knowledge to him, dependent not on an awareness of life but rather on a distant, momentary happiness, destroying the darkness of life at least for that moment, as a light far out on a dark moor destroys an infinity of darkness.

A moment. Honda could feel that nothing at all had happened in the interval separating the Honda of sixteen from the Honda of seventy-six. An instant, time for a child in a game of hopscotch to hop over a ditch.

He had seen often enough how the Dream Diary kept so faithfully by Kiyoaki had come true. He had had evidence enough of the superiority of dreams to waking. But he had not thought that his own life would ever be so filled with dreams. There was happiness in the dreams that poured over him like floods over Thai paddy lands; but they had only nostalgia for a past that would not return to set against the delicious fragrance of Kiyoaki's dreams. A young man who had not dreamed had become an old man who dreamed occasionally, and that was all. His dreams had little to do with symbol or with imagination.

This chewing-over of dreams as he lay in bed each morning came in part from a fear of the arthritic pains that were certain to follow. With the memory of yesterday's scarcely endurable pain in the hips, the pain this morning would move to his shoulders and sides. He did not really know until he got out of bed where it would be. He did not know while he still lay in bed, flesh withered and bones creaking in the gelatinous remains of dreams, in thoughts of a day that was certain to bring nothing of interest.

It was a chore even to reach for the house phone he had had installed some five or six years before.

He would have to endure the housekeeper's shrill morning greetings.

He had kept a law student in the house after Rié's death, but he had soon come to find the youth irksome and sent him away; and since then there had been only Honda and two maids and a housekeeper in the big house. The women were constantly changing. At odds with the slovenliness of the maids and the dishonesty of the housekeeper, Honda became aware that his sensibilities were not up to the modish habits and words of today's women. However diligently they might work, all their mannerisms, up-to-date locutions like "fun game" and "well, sorta," a door opened without proper ceremony, a loud guffaw without a respectful hand over the mouth, a mistake in honorifics, gossip about television actors, all of them brought physical revulsion. When in his inability to control it he would let slip a word of complaint, he could be sure that the woman would be gone the next day. He would vouchsafe a complaint to the masseuse he called almost every night, and a domestic tempest would ensue. The masseuse had acquired the fashionable predilection for being called "Ma'am" and would refuse to answer if not so addressed; but Honda could not do without her.

However frequently he might complain, there was dust on the parlor shelves. The master of flower-arranging who came for a weekly lesson also spoke of it.

The maids would invite errand boys in for cups of tea, and the whiskey he valued so highly was being drunk up by he did not know whom. Occasionally he would catch a burst of insane laughter from far down a hallway.

His ear branded by the housekeeper's morning courtesies, he would have trouble bringing himself to order breakfast, and the sticky clinging of feet to the mats in the corridor as the two maids opened the shutters irritated him indescribably. The hot-water faucets were forever getting stopped up, and an empty toothpaste tube was never replaced until he ordered it to be. The housekeeper kept a good enough watch on his laundry and cleaning, but it took a laundry tag scratching at his neck to tell him that that was the case. His shoes were polished but the sand was carefully preserved within, the catch on his umbrella was left unrepaired. He had been unaware of such details while Rié lived.

The smallest tear or scratch and an article was discarded. There were unpleasant scenes.

"You tell me to have it repaired, but there isn't a place in town that would repair it."

"All right, go ahead and throw it away, then."

"It's not all that valuable."

"Whether it's valuable or not has nothing to do with the case."

There would be instant contempt for his penuriousness in the woman's eyes.

Such incidents made him more and more dependent on Keiko.

Keiko had become energetic in her pursuit of Japanese culture. It was her new exoticism. For the first time in her life she began to go to Kabuki, and she would compare inept actors with famous French actors. She began to learn Nō music and make the rounds of temples in pursuit of Buddhist art.

She was always asking him to go to likely temples with her, and once he had been on the point of suggesting the Gesshūji. But it was not a temple for a lighthearted outing with Keiko.

Not once in these six decades had Honda visited Satoko, Abbess of the Gesshūji. Though he had heard that she was still alive and well, he had not once exchanged letters with her. In the war years and after, he had any number of times been taken by an impulse to call on her and apologize for his neglect; but always misgivings had been stronger, and he had kept his silence.

He had not for a moment forgotten the Gesshūji. But as the years of silence went by, a self-imposed restraint grew stronger, a feeling that the Gesshūji was too precious, that he must not after all this time invade her sanctuary with memories, or look upon her in her old age. He had heard from Tadeshina in the bombed-out ruins of Shibuya that Satoko was only more beautiful, as a spring is more limpid. Nor was he himself beyond imagining the ageless beauty of the aging nun. He had heard an Osaka friend describe it in awed tones. But Honda was afraid. He was afraid to see a relic of past beauty, and he was more afraid of present beauty. Satoko would by now of course have reached a level of enlightenment far beyond Honda's reach, and were Honda in his old age to visit her he would cause not so much as a ripple upon the tranquillity. He knew that she was beyond being intimidated by memories. But the image of Satoko, safe in indigo armor from all the slings of memory, seemed when he looked through the eyes of the dead Kiyoaki another germ of despair.

And it weighed on him to think that he must visit Satoko as Kiyoaki's representative, bearing memories.

"The sin is ours, Kiyo's and mine, and nobody else's," she had said on the way back from Kamakura.

Sixty years had gone by and the words were still in his ears. Were he to visit Satoko she would probably after a quiet laugh talk easily about the chain of memories. But the journey was too much for him. Old and ugly and stained with sin as he was, the complications seemed only to increase.

The Gesshūji itself, gently enveloped in a spring

snow, was layer by layer more distant, with memories of Satoko, as the years passed. More distant, but not with a distance as of withdrawing into the heart. As he sought to remember it, the Gesshūji was on a snowy pinnacle, like a temple in the Himalayas, its beauty turned to harshness, its softness to a day of wrath. The ultimate in clarity, a moon temple quite at the ends of the earth, dotted a single dot with the purple cassock of an aging and ever more delicately beautiful abbess, seemed to send off an ice-light, as if it stood at the very limits of awareness and reason. Honda knew that he could be there in no time by airplane or express train. But the Gesshūji had become not a temple for a man to visit and look upon, but a ray of moonlight through a rent in the extremities of his consciousness.

It seemed to him that if Satoko was there then she must always be there. If he was chained to eternal life by consciousness then she must be up there an infinite distance from his hell. Doubtless she could see through it at a glance. And he felt that the deathless hell of a straitened and fear-ridden consciousness and her celestial immortality had struck up a balance. He could wait three hundred years, a thousand years, to see her.

He made all manner of excuses, and in the course of time all the excuses in the world came to seem like excuses for not visiting the Gesshūji. He was like a person denying beauty that was certain to bring destruction. His refusal to visit the Gesshūji became more than procrastination. He knew that to visit it had become an impossibility, perhaps the narrowest of the gates in his life. If he were to insist upon a visit, might the Gesshūji not withdraw from him, disappear in a mist of light?

All the same he came to think that, matters of an undying consciousness aside, senility had ripened the moment for a visit. Probably he would make his visit as he was about to die. Satoko had been a person whom Kiyoaki must meet at the risk of his life; and a young and beautiful Kiyoaki calling out still to Honda forbade a meeting unless Honda, witness to the cruel impossibility, gambled his own life. He could meet her if he met death too. Perhaps, in secrecy, Satoko too knew of a time and awaited its coming. An ineffably sweet well of memory flowed over the aging Honda.

That Keiko should be here with him was a little incongruous.

He had rather strong doubts about Keiko's understanding of Japanese culture. There was something admirable all the same in her expansive half-knowledge. She quite avoided pretense. She went her rounds of the Kyoto temples, and, like artistically inclined foreign ladies stuffed with misconceptions from a first visit to Japan, she would shrill forth her pleasure at objects that no longer interested most Japanese, and arrange them in false nosegays. She was fascinated with Japan as with the Antarctic. She would spread herself out with all the awkwardness of a stockinged foreign lady as she viewed a rock garden. All her life she had known only Occidental chairs.

She was in genuine intellectual heat. She fell into the habit of holding forth with her own peculiar notions about Japanese art and literature, albeit neglecting a detail here and there.

It had long been one of her indulgences to invite the foreign ambassadors in turn to dinner. Now they became the audiences for her proud lectures on Japanese culture. Older acquaintances had not dreamed that Keiko would one day honor them with discourses on gold-leafed screens.

"But they're passers in the night with no sense of gratitude at all." Honda warned her of the futility.

"They'll go on to their next posts with not a thought left in their heads for this one. What's the point in even seeing them?"

"The birds of passage are the ones you don't have to be on your guard with. You don't have to worry about ten years from now, and a new audience every night is rather fun."

But she was taking herself seriously, congratulating herself in a naïve way on furthering international cultural exchange. She would learn a dance and immediately unveil it before ambassadorial guests. It gave her strength to know that her audience was not likely to detect the flaws.

However assiduously Keiko might refine her knowledge, it was not up to plumbing the darkness where stretched the deepest roots of the Japanese. The dark blood springs that had agitated Isao Iinuma were far away. Honda called Keiko's store of Japanese culture a freezer full of vegetables.

Honda had become recognized at the embassies as Keiko's gentleman friend. He was always invited with her to dinner.

It angered him when at one embassy the footmen were in formal Japanese dress. "Displaying the natives, nothing more. It's an insult."

"I don't feel that way at all. Japanese men look better in Japanese clothes. Your dinner jacket does nothing for me at all."

When, at a diplomatic black-tie dinner, the guests would start for the dining room with a gentle stir, the ladies in the lead, and the flowers on the table would throw deep shadows from a forest of silver candlesticks, and outside there would be quiet summer rain, the shining sadness of it all was most becoming to Keiko. She allowed not a flicker of the ingratiating smile so common among Japanese women. There was grand tradition in the grand glowing back of the retreating figure. She even had the husky, melancholy voice of the old Japanese aristocrat. In the company of ambassadors whose weariness was showing through the gilt and of cold-blooded counselors each with his own special affectations, Keiko was alive.

Since they would be separated at the table, Keiko spoke to him quietly in the procession. "I brought up *Robe of Feathers*. But I've never been to Mio. Take me there some day soon. There are so many places I've never been."

"Any time. I've just been to Nihondaira Heights, but I wouldn't mind going again. I'll most happily be your escort."

His stiff shirt insisted on pressing at his chin.

8

AT THE OPENING of *Robe of Feathers*, two fishermen, one of them the deuteragonist, are engaged in conversation. "The boatmen call out as they make their way up the tempestuous Mio channel." There comes a description of the journey. "Suddenly, a thousand leagues off, the friendly hills are enshrouded in clouds." A fine long robe of silk hangs on the pine at center rear. Hakuryō starts off with it, thinking to make it his own. The protagonist, the angel, appears. He ignores her pleas that he return it. She is desolate, unable to fly back to the heavens.

"Hakuryō clutches the robe. She is helpless. Her tears like the dew in her jeweled hair, she weeps.

The flowers fade, the five signs of the decay of the angel come forth."

On the express from Tokyo Keiko was humming the prologue. "And what," she asked with sudden earnestness, "are the five signs of the decay of the angel?"

Honda was well informed. He had looked into the matter of angels after that dream. The five signs are the five marks that death has come to an angel. There are variations, depending on the source.

Here is the account in the twenty-fourth fascicle of the *Ekottara-āgama:* "There are thirty-three angels and one archangel, and the signs of death in them are fivefold. Their flowered crowns wither, their robes are soiled, the hollows under their arms are fetid, they lose their awareness of themselves, they are abandoned by the jeweled maidens."

And *The Life of the Buddha,* fifth fascicle: "There are five signs that the allotted time has run out. The flowers in the hair fade, a fetid sweat comes from under the arms, the robes are soiled, the body ceases to give off light, it loses awareness of itself."

And the last fascicle of the *Mahāmāyā-sūtra:* "And at that time Mahā gave forth in the heavens five signs of her decay. Her crown of flowers wilted, a sweat poured from under her arms, her halo faded, her eyes came to blink without pause, she lost all satisfaction with her rightful place."

So far the similarities are more striking than the variations. The *Abhidharma-mahāvibhāsā-sāstra* describes the five greater signs and the five lesser signs in considerable detail. The five lesser signs are first.

As an angel soars and pirouettes it usually gives forth music so beautiful that no musician, no orchestra or chorus can imitate it; but as death approaches the music fades and the voice becomes tense and thin.

In normal times, day and night, there floods from

within an angel a light that permits of no shadows; but as death approaches the light dwindles sharply and the body is wrapped in thin shadows.

The skin of an angel is smooth and well anointed, and even if it immerses itself in a lake of ambrosia it throws off the liquid as does the leaf of a lotus; but as death approaches, water clings and will not leave.

At most times an angel, like a spinning wheel of fire, neither stops nor is apprehensible in one place, it is there when it is here, it dodges and moves and throws itself free; but when death approaches, it lingers in one spot and cannot break free.

An angel exudes unblinking strength, but as death approaches the strength departs and blinking becomes incessant.

Here are the five greater signs: the once-immaculate robes are soiled, the flowers in the flowery crown fade and fall, sweat pours from the armpits, a fetid stench envelops the body, the angel is no longer happy in its proper place.

It will be seen that the other sources enumerate the greater signs. So long as only the lesser ones are present, death can still be put off, but once the greater signs appear the issue is not in doubt.

In *Robe of Feathers,* one of the greater signs has already made its appearance, and yet the angel will recover if the robe is returned. It may be imagined that Zeami allowed himself a poetic hint of decay and decline and did not worry about the meticulous letter of the law.

Honda remembered with extraordinary freshness the five marks of decay in the Kitano Scroll, a national treasure he had seen long before in the Kitano Shrine. He had a photographic copy which called up something, a song of horrid foreboding, perhaps, to which he had earlier been deaf.

In a garden blocked off by the beautiful founda-

tions of a Chinese pavilion, crowds of angels are pluck-
ing on zithers, beating on drums. But there is no
suggestion of vitality, the music has fallen to the dull
buzz of a fly on a summer afternoon. Pluck though
they may, beat though they may, the strings and skins
are slack and tired and decayed. There are flowers in
the forward parts of the garden, and among them a
grieving cherub presses its sleeves to its eyes.

Death has come too suddenly. Incredulity is written
on beautiful, otherwise inexpressive white angel faces.

Within the pavilion are angels in postures of dis-
array. Some seek ineffectively to cut graceful arcs with
their sleeves, some are twisting and writhing. They
stretch their hands languorously over finite spaces but
cannot touch, their robes are senselessly dirty, filth
pours from their bodies.

What is happening? The five signs have come. The
angels are as princesses with no escape, caught by the
plague in a close, tropical garden.

The flowers in their hair are limp, their inner spaces
are suddenly bloated with water up to the throat. The
gathering of soft, graceful figures has at some point
been pervaded by a transparent decay, and in the very
air they breathe there is already the smell of death.

These sentient beings who by the mere fact of their
existence lured men into realms of beauty and fantasy
must now look on helpless as, in an instant, their
spell is stripped away like flaking gold leaf and swept
up in the evening breeze. The classically elegant garden
is an incline. The gold dust of all-powerful beauty and
pleasure drifts down. Absolute freedom soaring in
emptiness is torn away like a rending of flesh. The
shadows gather. The light dies. Soft power drips and
drips from the beautiful fingers. The fire flickers in the
depths of flesh, the spirit is departing.

The brightly checkered floor of the pavilion, the vermilion balustrades, have faded not at all. Relics of

grandeur, they will be there when the angels are gone.

Beneath shining hair beautiful nostrils are turned upward. The angels seem to be catching the first forescent of decay. Petals twisting beyond clouds, azure decay coloring the sky, all pleasures of sight and of spirit, all the joyous vastness of the universe, gone.

"Good, good." Keiko sounded a full stop. "You are so well informed."

Nodding vigorously, Keiko touched a fashionable bottle of Estée Lauder to her ears. She had on pantaloons with a serpentine pattern and a blouse of the same material, a chamois belt reversed at the hips, and a black cordovan sombrero of Spanish make.

Honda had been somewhat startled by the ensemble when he had first caught sight of her at Tokyo Station, but he refrained from commenting upon her chic.

Five or six minutes more and they would be in Shizuoka. He thought of that last sign, a loss of awareness of place. He who had had no such awareness to begin with lived on. For he was no angel.

Vacantly, Honda remembered a thought he had had in the cab that had brought him to the station. He had asked the driver to hurry, and they had taken the expressway from West Kanda. An early-summer drizzle had been falling, he could not have said for how long. They made their way through the rows of banks and brokerages at fifty miles an hour. Huge, solid, the buildings spread great wings of steel and glass. Honda said to himself: "The moment I die they will all go." The thought came to him as a happy one, a sort of revenge. It would be no trouble at all, tearing this world up by the roots and returning it to the void. All he had to do was die. He took a certain minor pride in the thought that an old man who would be forgotten still had in death this incomparably destructive weapon. For him the five signs of decay held no fear.

9

THERE WAS one matter weighing on Honda's mind as he escorted Keiko to the pine grove at Mio. He feared ruining her good spirits by showing her the utter vulgarity to which this most beautiful of Japanese scenic spots had been reduced.

It was a rainy weekday, but the huge parking lot was jammed with automobiles, and the dirty cellophane in the souvenir shops caught an ashen sky. They did not seem to bother Keiko in the slightest.

"Beautiful. Perfectly lovely. Smell the fresh air and the salt. The sea is so near."

As a matter of fact the air was strangled with gasoline fumes and the pines were on the point of asphyxiation. Honda felt better. He had visited the place some days before, and he had known what Keiko would see.

Benares was sacred filth. Filth itself was sacred. That was India.

But in Japan, beauty, tradition, poetry, had none of them been touched by the soiled hand of sanctity. Those who touched them and in the end strangled them were quite devoid of sanctity. They all had the same hands, vigorously scoured with soap.

Even at the pine grove of Mio, angels in the empty skull of poetry answered to the unspeakable demands of men, and were forced into myriads and myriads of twists and turns, like circus performers. The cloudy skies were traced as if with a mesh of silver high-tension wires by their dances. In dreams men would meet with only the marks of the decay of angels.

THE DECAY OF THE ANGEL

It was past three. "The Pine Grove of Mio. Nihon-daira Prefectural Park." The rough-scaled bark of the tree was enshrouded in the green of moss. Above a gentle flight of stone stairs, the pines sent rude bolts of lightning across the sky. The blossoms, veils of green smoke that even the branches of strangling pines will send forth, shut off a lifeless sea.

"The sea!" said Keiko joyously.

Honda did not trust the joy. There was a little of her party manner in it, of flattery for the villa at which she was a guest. Yet exaggeration can spawn pleasure in something that is nothing at all. At least the two of them were not lonely.

Outside a pair of shops, their cantilever shelves bulging with red Coca-Cola cartons and souvenirs, stood a pair of photographer's dummies with apertures for two faces: Jirōchō, the boss of Shimizu Harbor, in a pale grove of pines, and Ochō, his lady friend. Jirōchō's name was on the triangle of the umbrella he cradled in his arm. He was in travel dress, with a walking stick, light-blue mittens and leggings, and a hitched-up kimono in narrow blue and white stripes. Ochō had a high chignon, and wore a black satin kimono and an obi of yellow Hachijō plaid.

Honda urged Keiko on toward the grove, but she was entranced by the dummies. She repeated Jirōchō's name over and over to herself. She knew nothing about him except his name, not even the elementary fact that he was a famous gambler; and Honda's lecture on the subject left her yet more entranced.

The nostalgic hues, the fresh, wild vulgarity, quite enthralled her. Wherever she might search in her own life with its distant harvest of the carnal, she could catch no sound so wild and sad in its vulgarity. Her great virtue was that she was without preconceptions. What she had never seen and never heard of was, the last bit of it, "Japanese."

Almost angrily, Honda sought to break up her love affair with the dummy.

"Oh, stop it .You're making a fool of yourself."

"You think the two of us still have the luxury of being fools?"

Serpent-twined legs spread wide, hands on hips, Keiko struck a pose as of an Occidental mother scolding a child. There was anger in her eyes. He had besmirched the poetry.

Honda surrendered. They were beginning to attract a crowd. The cameraman came running up with a tripod and a red velvet cloth. As Honda dodged behind the dummy to avoid curious eyes his face appeared at the aperture. The crowd laughed, the diminutive cameraman laughed, and, though it seemed not entirely appropriate that Jirōchō should be laughing, Honda laughed too. Keiko tugged at his sleeve and took his place. Jirōchō had changed sex, and so had Ochō. The merriment was louder. Honda was drunk. He had known much of peep holes, but he had not had the experience of mounting a guillotine for the pleasure of boisterous masses.

The cameraman took rather a long time with his lens, perhaps because he had become a cynosure.

"Quiet, please." The crowd was quiet.

Honda's austere face protruded from the low-slung hole over the yellow plaid. Stooped, hips thrust out, he had taken up his pose at the peep hole in Ninooka. Behind the scene of these humiliating antics a subtle quick change took place as, indifferent to the crowd's laughter, Honda confirmed that his whole world hung on the act of observing. He resumed this role, and the viewers became the viewed.

There was a sea, there was a great pine, its trunk roped off: the pine of the heavenly robe. The gentle, sandy slopes leading up to it thronged with spectators. Under the cloudy sky the several colors of their dress were uniformly somber, the wind in their hair made them look like a rotting upturned pine. There were clusters of people, there were couples off by themselves; and the great white eye of the sky crushed down upon them. And in the wall that was their foremost rank laughter was forbidden. They gazed at Honda with a stony blankness.

Women in kimono, shopping bags in their hands, middle-aged men in badly cut suits, boys in green-checkered shirts and plump-legged girls in blue miniskirts, children, old men, Honda saw them gazing at their own death. They were waiting for something, some occurrence so amusing that it must have its own grandeur. Lips were relaxed in good-natured smiles. Eyes were aglow with a naked bestiality.

"Quiet!" The cameraman raised his hand.

Keiko promptly withdrew her head from the hole. She stood before the multitude stately as a knight commander. Jirōchō, shaking her head, had become a person in serpentine pantaloons and a black sombrero. The crowd clapped. Keiko calmly wrote down her address for the cameraman. Several young persons, having decided that she was a famous actress from an earlier day, came up for her autograph.

Honda was exhausted by the time they reached the pine.

It was a giant pine on the point of death, spreading its arms in several directions like an octopus. Rents in the trunk had been filled with cement. People disported themselves around a tree that lacked even a proper supply of needles.

"Do you suppose the angel was in a swimming suit?"

"Is it a he-pine? Is that why the woman picked it?"

"She couldn't reach the top."

"Not much of a pine, when you get a good look at it."

"But isn't it nice they've managed to keep it alive. Just feel the sea wind."

And indeed the pine leaned more aggressively to sea than a sea-trained pine should have, and the sea scars on its trunk were numberless as on a beached hulk. Toward the sea from the marble enclosure a pair of binoculars stood perched on a fresh vermilion bipod like a tropical bird. The Izu Peninsula loomed whitely beyond. A large cargo ship was passing. As if the sea had set out its wares for sale, a circle of driftwood and empty bottles and seaweed marked the high tide.

"Well, there you have it, the spot where the angel danced the heavenly dance to get back her feathered robe. There they all are getting their pictures taken again. That's the way to do it. Don't even look at the pine, just get your picture taken. Do you suppose they think it makes so much difference that they should be at a spot where something remarkable happened and stay long enough to get a shutter clicked in their faces?"

"You take it too seriously." Keiko sat down on a stone bench and lighted a cigarette. "It's beautiful. I'm not in the least disappointed. It may be dirty and the tree may be about to die, but it has a spell. If it were all pretty and dreamy the way it is in the play, then it would be a lie. The naturalness is very Japanese. I'm glad we came." So Keiko seized the lead.

She enjoyed everything. That was her queenly prerogative.

In the vulgarity, as heavy and all-pervasive as a sultry sand-laden wind during the summer rains, she happily, gaily saw her sights, and she took Honda with her. On their return they looked in on the Mio Shrine. At the eaves of the sanctuary, on a rough framed board, was a votive painting in low relief of a newly built passenger ship. Sending out its wake over a blue sea, it seemed exactly right for a harbor shrine.

Against the rear wall of the sanctuary was a large fan-shaped board on which was carved the cast for a Nō performance. It had been given six years before in the Dance Pavilion.

"A ladies' day. *Kamiuta, Takasago, Yashima,* and then *Robe of Feathers.*" Keiko was impressed.

In the aftermath of the excitement she picked up and ate a cherry from under one of the trees that lined the path.

"See what I'm doing. I'm inviting death."

His steps somewhat uncertain, Honda began to regret that vanity had kept him from bringing his stick. Panting and gasping, he had fallen behind when Keiko called out the warning.

Low on the rope that joined the trunks of the trees, numbers of identical signs waved in the breeze.

"Danger. Poisonous insecticides. Do not pick or eat."

The branches, heavy with fruit from faint pink to blood red, were clustered with little knots of paper that carried prayers and petitions. Some of the cherries had been picked to bare seeds by the birds. Honda suspected that the signs were empty threats. And he knew that a small dose of poison was not enough to carry off Keiko.

10

WAS THERE nothing more to see, was there nothing more to see, asked Keiko. Though exhausted, Honda ordered the driver to go back to Shizuoka by the way of Mount Kuno. They stopped before the signal station Honda had seen some days earlier.

"Doesn't it strike you as a rather interesting building?" Honda looked up from the profusion of portulaca at the stone base.

"I think I see a pair of binoculars. What's it for?"

"It keeps watch on ship movements. Shall we look inside?"

Though curious, neither had quite the courage to knock.

They had climbed the stone steps that encircled the base and were at the foot of the iron stairway when a girl brushed past them with a clanging of iron, so near a miss that one of them called out a warning. Kicking up her skirts like a yellow tornado, she passed so quickly that they did not see her face; but she left all the same an impression as of a fleeting distillation of ugliness.

It was not that she had a bad eye or an objectionable scar. It was just that a hangnail of ugliness for an instant obstructed the view and went against all the careful, delicate ordering known as beauty. It was like the darkest of dark, fleshly memories rasping against the heart. But if one wished to view her in a more quotidian manner, she need be no more than a shy maiden returning from a tryst.

They climbed the stairs and paused at the door to catch their breath. It was half open. Honda pushed his way inside. The room seemed empty. He called up the narrow stairway to the second floor. Each time he called he was seized by a violent fit of coughing.

There was a creaking at the top of the stairs. "Yes?" A boy in an undershirt looked down.

In surprise, Honda note the blue flower hanging over his forehead. It seemed to be a hydrangea. As he looked down, the flower fell and rolled to Honda's feet. The boy was startled. He had forgotten the flower. It was brownish and worm-eaten and badly wilted.

Keiko, still in her sombrero, surveyed the scene over Honda's shoulder.

Though the stairway was dusky, it was apparent that the boy had a fair, handsome face. An almost disquietingly fair face, it seemed, despite the fact that the light was behind it to send down its own light. The need to return the flower his excuse, Honda carefully but briskly made his way up the steep stairs, his hand against the wall. The boy came halfway down to take it.

Their eyes met. Honda knew that the cogs of the same machine were moving both of them, in the same delicate motions at precisely the same speed. Honda's duplicate down to the finest detail, even down to an utter want of purpose, was there as if bared to a cloudless void. Identical to his own in hardness and transparency despite the difference in their years, the delicate mechanism within this boy corresponded precisely to a mechanism within Honda, in terror lest someone destroy it, the terror hidden in its deepest recesses. In that instant Honda saw a workerless factory polished to a perfection of utter bleakness, Honda's mature self-awareness in juvenile form. Producing interminably without consumers, endlessly throwing away, horribly clean and perfectly regulated for heat and humidity, rustling forever like a flow of satin. Yet there was a possibility that the boy, though he was Honda himself, misunderstood the machine. His youth would be the reason. Honda's factory was human from an utter want of humanity. If the boy refused to think of his own as human—that was all right. Honda rested in the confidence that though he had seen all of the boy, the boy could not have seen all of him. In the lyrical moods of his youth, he had been wont to think the machine the culmination of ugliness; but that was only because a youthful miscalculation had confused fleshly ugliness with the ugliness of the machine within him.

The ugliest of machines, very youthful, very exaggerated, romantic, self-advertising. But that was all right. Honda could so name it today with the coolest of smiles. Exactly as he could name a headache or a pain in the diaphragm. It was nice that the ugliest of machines should have so beautiful a face.

The boy was of course unaware of what had happened in that instant.

Halfway down the stairs, he took the flower. He crushed the source of his embarrassment in his hand.

"Damn her." He spoke to himself. "I'd forgotten all about it."

Most boys would have flushed. It interested Honda that no transformation at all came over the white composure.

The boy changed the subject. "Is there something I can do for you?"

"Not really. We're tourists, and we wondered if we might have a look around for our edification."

"Please. Come on in."

The boy bowed quickly from the hips and laid our slippers for them.

It was cloudy, but the naked outdoors seemed to be sweeping them suddenly from a dark attic to an open moor. Some fifty yards to the south were Komagoé Beach and the dirty sea. Honda and Keiko knew well enough that old age and affluence dispel reticence. Soon they were seated as if at their own veranda on the chairs pushed toward them. Yet the words that followed the boy back to his desk were very ceremonious.

"Go ahead with your work, please, quite as if we weren't here. Would you mind, I wonder, if we were to take a look through the telescope?"

"Please. I don't need it at the moment." The boy threw the flower into the wastebasket. After a noisy washing of hands the fair profile was bowed over the notebook on the desk as if nothing had happened; but

Honda could see curiosity swelling the cheek like a plum.

He invited Keiko to have a look through the telescope and then had a look himself. There were no ships, only a heaping of waves, like a culture of black-green bacteria squirming purposefully under a microscope.

The two were a pair children soon tired of their toy. They had no particular interest in the sea. All they had really wanted was to intrude for a moment upon a stranger's life and work. They looked around them, at the several instruments echoing the stir of the harbor, distantly and sadly but faithfully, at "Shimizu Docks" and the name of each dock in large black letters, at the wide blackboard listing the ships in port, at the books ranged on the shelf, *Shipping Ledger, Registry of Japanese Shipping, International Codes, Lloyd's Register of Shipowners 1968–69,* at the telephone numbers on the wall, those of the agent and the pilot and the customs and quarantine stations and the provisioners and the rest.

All these details had about them, undeniably, the smell of the sea, the light of the harbor some two or three miles distant. From whatever distance, a harbor announces its languorous turbulence in its own sad metallic tones. It was a gigantic, lunatic zither, sprawled out by the sea and sending an undulant image over the sea, sounding and for a time echoing destruction on all the seven giant strings of its docks. Entering the boy's heart, Honda dreamed of the sea.

Sluggishly pulling in, sluggishly tying up, sluggishly unloading—what an endless compromise it was, this trancelike mating of the sea and the land. They were joined in mutual deceit, the ship wagging a seductive tail and pulling coyly away again with a threatening bleat on its whistle, moving away and then coming in again. What a naked, unstable mechanism!

From the east window he could see the confusion of the harbor frozen under a smoky mist, but an unshining harbor was not a harbor, for a harbor is a row of white teeth bared tensely at a shining sea. The teeth of piers eaten at by the sea. It had to shine like a dentist's office and smell of metal and water and antiseptic, with cruel derricks pushing down overhead and antiseptics sinking the ships into a motionless sleep, and perhaps, from time to time, a trace of blood.

The harbor and this little signal room. The image of the harbor taken and firmly impounded as toll, until he could almost fancy that it was a ship grounded high on the rocks. There were more than a few likenesses to a dental office: the simplicity and the efficient disposition of the instruments, the freshness of the whites and the primary colors, the readiness for a crisis that could come at any time, the warped window frames gnawed at by the sea winds. And the watch, solitary in the field of white plastic, carrying on an intercourse almost sexual with the sea, through the day and through the night, intimidated by harbor and ship, until gazing became pure madness. The whiteness, the abandonment of the self, the uncertainty and loneliness were themselves a ship. He felt that one could not stay at it long without getting drunk.

The boy pretended to be lost in his work. But Honda knew that in point of fact he had no work when there were no ships in sight.

"When is the next ship due?"

"About nine in the evening. This has been a slack day."

He answered with an air of bland efficiency; and his ennui and curiosity came through like strawberries through plastic walls.

It may have been a matter of pride for the boy not to make himself more formal—in any case he put on nothing over his undershirt. In the hot air, still even with the window open, there was nothing unnatural in his way of dress. The fair body, with no fullness of flesh but with rather a sort of botanical slenderness, sent the immaculate shirt down from the shoulders in two circles and thence over the roundness of the stooped chest. It was a body with a firm coolness about it, and no suggestion of softness. The profile, aristocratic eyebrows and nose and lips, was well formed, as on a somewhat worn silver coin; and the eyes with their long lashes were beautiful.

Honda could see what the boy was thinking.

He was still embarrassed about the flower in his hair. He had had no trouble covering the embarrassment as he received his guests, but he was spun up in it as in a swirl of red threads. And since they had of course had a glimpse of the girl's ugliness he had to put up as well with misunderstanding and concealed smiles of solicitude. The cause of it all was in his own magnanimity. It had inflicted an incurable wound upon his pride.

Of course. One could scarcely believe that the ugly girl was his paramour. They were altogether too ill-matched. One had only to look at the frangibility of the earlobes, like the most delicately wrought glass, and at the supple whiteness of the neck to know that the boy was one who did not love. Love was alien to him. He washed his hands industriously after crushing the flower, he had a white towel on the desk, he was constantly wiping at his neck and armpits. The freshly washed hands on the ledger were like sterilized vegetables. Like young branches trailing out over a lake. Aware of their own elegance, the fingers curved haughtily, intimate with the supernal. They clutched at nothing material, and their business seemed to be with the void. They seemed to stroke the invisible, but without humility or petition. If there are hands to be used only for addressing the infinite and the universe, they are a masturbator's hands. I have seen through him, thought Honda.

Beautiful hands for touching the moon and the stars and the sea, meant for no practical work. He wanted to see the faces of the persons who sought to hire them. When they hired a man, they learned nothing from such tiresome details as family and friends and ideology and transcripts of grades and state of health. It was this boy himself they had hired, knowing none of these things; and he was unmixed evil.

Look at it if you will. Unmixed evil. The reason was simple. The insides of the boy were wholly and utterly those of Honda himself.

An elbow against the table at the windowsill, pretending to gaze unblinkingly out to sea, under a natural covering of senile gloom, Hondo from time to time stole a glance at the boy's profile, and felt that he was seeing in that glance his own life.

The evil suffusing that life had been self-awareness. A self-awareness that knew nothing of love, that slaughtered without raising a hand, that relished death as it composed noble condolences, that invited the world to destruction while seeking the last possible moment for itself. But there was a ray of light in the empty window. India. India, with which he had had his encounter as he became aware of evil and wanted to flee it for even an instant. India, which taught that there had to exist in response to moral needs the world he had been so intent on denying, enfolding in itself a light and a fragrance which he had no devices for touching.

But his own inclinations all through his long life had been to make the world over into emptiness, to lead men to nothing—complete destruction and finality. He had not succeeded; and now at the end of it, as he approached his own separate finality, he had come upon a boy sending out identical shoots of evil.

Perhaps it had all been an illusion. Yet, after missteps and failures, he could congratulate himself on an ability to see through pretense. His vision, so long as it was not obstructed by desire, did not fail him. Most especially in what did not suit his deeper inclinations.

Sometimes evil took a quiet, botanical shape. Crystallized evil was as beautiful as a clean white powder. This boy was beautiful. Perhaps Honda had been awakened and bewitched by the beauty of his own self-awareness, which had sought to recognize neither self nor other.

Somewhat bored, Keiko was putting on lipstick. "Perhaps we should go?"

Faced with the old man's equivocation, she took on protective coloring from her dress and began slipping around the room like a great languid tropical serpent. Her discovery was that the shelf nearest the roof was divided into some forty compartments, and each of them contained a dusty little flag.

Drawn to the bright reds and yellows and greens of the loosely rolled flags, she stood gazing up at them for a time, arms folded. Then, suddenly, she laid a hand on the sharp, gleaming ivory of the boy's naked shoulder.

"What are these flags for?"

He pulled back in surprise. "We're not using them just at the moment. They're signal flags. We only use the blinker. At night."

He pointed at the signal light in the corner of the room. Hurriedly his gaze returned to the desk. Keiko looked over his shoulder at sketches of ship funnels. He paid no attention.

"May I see one?"

"Please."

He had been hunched as low as possible over the desk. Now he stood up and moved to the shelf, avoiding Keiko as he might avoid a hot jungle undergrowth. He passed in front of Honda. Standing on tiptoes, he took a flag from the shelf.

Honda had been lost in his own thoughts. He looked at the boy, arms outstretched beside him. A faint sweet smell flooded Honda's nostrils. There were three moles on the left side of the chest, yet whiter, until now covered by the undershirt.

"You're left-handed," said Keiko, not one for reticence.

The boy darted a glance of annoyance at her as he took down the flag.

Honda had to be quite sure. He came nearer the boy. The arm was folded once more, like a white wing; but at each motion two moles were darkly hidden behind the hem of the undershirt, and a third was exposed. Honda's heart raced.

"What a beautiful design. What is it?" Keiko spread out a flag of checkered yellow and black. "I'd like a dress made of it. What do you suppose the material is? Linen?"

"I wouldn't know about the material," said the boy roughly, "but it's an 'L.' "

" 'L.' for 'love.' "

The boy went back to his desk, now openly annoyed. "Take your time," he mumbled, as if to himself. "There's no hurry."

"So this is an 'L.' Not at all what I would expect an 'L' to be. Let's see, now. 'L' should be a murky green. Black and yellow checkers are entirely wrong. Heavier and stronger, like knights at a joust. A 'G' maybe?"

" 'G' is yellow and blue vertical stripes," said the boy, somewhat desperately.

"Yellow and blue vertical stripes? Entirely wrong. 'G' is as far from vertical stripes as it can be."

"I'm afraid we're keeping you from your work. Thank you very much indeed. I hope you won't mind if I send candy or something from Tokyo? Do you have a card?"

Surprised at this rather exaggerated politeness, Keiko put the flag on the desk and went to take her sombrero from the little binoculars at the east window.

Honda laid his card politely before the boy. The boy took out a card of his own with the address of the signal station. "Honda Law Offices" on the card before him seemed to dispel his suspicions.

"You seem to have heavy responsibilities," said Honda casually. "Can you manage all by yourself? How old might you be?"

"Sixteen." It was a brisk, businesslike answer that deliberately omitted Keiko.

"Very useful work. Keep at it." Each syllable formal and precise through his false teeth. Honda cheerfully motioned Keiko toward the door and started to put on his shoes. The boy saw them downstairs.

Back in the car, Honda felt too tired to look up. He directed the driver to a hotel on Nihondaira, where he had taken rooms for the night.

"I want a quick bath and a massage." Then, casually, he said something that left Keiko open-mouthed. "I'm going to adopt that boy."

11

Tōru was feeling irritable and restless.

He had idle visitors frequently enough. The building seemed to arouse curiosity. Most of them had children and came in at the children's urging. Tōru would lift them up to the telescope, and that would be that. This pair had been different. They had come as if trying to pry into something, and left as if they had stolen something. Something that Tōru himself had not been aware of.

It was five in the afternoon. Rain was threatening, and darkness came early.

The long line of indigo across the sea was like a great badge of mourning. It gave an air of repose. A single cargo ship was visible, far to the right.

There was a telephone call from Yokohama informing him of a sailing. There were no other calls.

It was time for dinner, but he was not hungry. He turned on the desk light and leafed through pages of ship funnels. They were good for driving away boredom.

He had his favorites among them, and reveries about them. He liked the mark of the Swedish East Asia Line, three yellow crowns on a white circle, and he liked the elephant of Osaka Dockyards.

On the average of once a month a ship bearing the elephant came into Shimizu. The white elephant over a yellow crescent on a black ground was visible from a considerable distance. He liked that white elephant riding in from the sea on its moon.

76

He liked the Prince Line of London, a coronet with three rakish feathers. When a Canadian transport came in, it seemed to him that the white ship was a gift and the mark was a brisk greeting card.

None of these marks was a continuing part of Tōru's consciousness. When they came within range of the telescope they were with him for the first time. Like bright cards scattered over the world, they had been part of a gigantic game in which he had not been a participant.

He loved only distant images that were no reflection of himself. If, that is to say, he loved anything.

Who and what might the old man have been?

Here in the room he had only been someone for that spoiled, overdressed old woman to bother; but now a separate presence remained behind, that of a quiet old man.

Tired, erudite, intelligent old eyes, a voice so low that Tōru had had difficulty in catching it, a politeness that almost seemed to verge on ridicule. What was he enduring?

Tōru had never before met anyone quite like him. He had never before seen the will to dominate take such quiet form.

Everything should have been old knowledge; and yet there was something in the old man that caught on a corner of Tōru's awareness like a rock snag and would not give way. What might it be?

But presently cool arrogance returned, and he ceased to speculate. The old man was a lawyer in retirement. That was enough. The politeness was a professional manner, nothing more. Tōru detected and was ashamed of a tendency in himself toward rustic wariness.

Getting up to warm his dinner, he threw a wad of paper into the wastebasket, and caught a glimpse of the withered hydrangea.

"Today it was a hydrangea. She poked it in my hair

77

as she left. Yesterday a cornflower. The time before a gardenia. The wanderings of a demented mind? Or have they some meaning? Maybe it's not just her idea. Maybe someone puts a flower in her hair every day and she carries some sort of signal without knowing it? She always does all the talking, but next time I have to ask her."

Perhaps there was nothing of the accidental or the random in events that took place around Tōru. Suddenly it seemed that a fine pattern of evil was taking shape around him.

12

HONDA WAS SILENT through dinner, and Keiko was too startled to talk.

"Are you coming to my room?" she asked as they left the table. "Or shall I go to yours?"

Always when they traveled together they went after dinner to the room of one or the other and talked over whiskey. If either pleaded fatigue the other understood.

"I'm not feeling as tired as I did. I'll be with you in maybe a half hour." He took her wrist and looked at the number on her key. She found endlessly amusing the pride he took in this little public display of intimacy. He could be amusingly intimate one instant and somberly, threateningly judicial the next.

She changed clothes. She would make fun of him. But she reconsidered. She saw that she could make fun of him without restraint when the matter was a serious one; but it was a law between them that the frivolous must always be serious.

They sat at the small table by the window. Honda ordered the usual bottle of Cutty Sark. Keiko was looking at the swirls of mist outside. She took out a cigarette. Cigarette in hand, she wore a sterner, tenser expression than usual. She had long ago given up the foreign affectation of waiting for him to light a match. He had always disliked it.

Abruptly she spoke. "I'm shocked, utterly shocked. The idea of taking in a child you know nothing about. I can think of only one explanation. You've kept your proclivities hidden from me. How blind I've been. We've known each other for eighteen years and I never suspected. I see now. There can be no doubt about it. We've had the same urges all along, and all along they've brought us together and made us feel secure, comrades and allies. Ying Chan was just a stage property. You knew about her and me, and were playing your part. A person can't be too careful."

"That isn't it at all. She and the boy are identical." He spoke with great firmness.

Why, she asked over and over again. How were they identical?

"I'll tell you when the whiskey comes."

It came. She had no choice but to await his words. She had lost the initiative.

Honda told her everything.

It pleased him that she should listen so carefully. She refrained from the usual overgeneralized response.

"You have been wise to say and to write nothing about it." Whiskey had produced a voice of smooth charity and benevolence. "People would have thought you mad. The trust you have built up would have collapsed."

"Trust no longer means anything to me."

"That's not the point. Something else you've kept hidden from me is your wisdom. No, a secret as violent as the most violent poison, capable of everything horrible, a secret that makes any sort of social secret seem like nothing at all. You could tell me that there are three lunatics in your immediate family, you could tell me you have sexual inclinations of a most curious sort, you could tell me the things most people would be most ashamed to tell me. It would be a social secret, nothing at all. Once you know the truth then murder and suicide and rape and forgery are easy, sloppy things. And what an irony that a judge should be the one. You find yourself caught up in a ring bigger than the skies, and everything else is ordinary. You have discovered that we've only been turned out to graze. Ignorant animals, out on loose tether." Keiko sighed. "Your story has cured me. I think I have fought rather well, but there was no need to fight. We are all fish in the same net."

"But it is the final blow for a woman. A person who knows what you know can never be beautiful again. If at your age you still wanted to be beautiful, then you should have put your hands over your ears.

"There are invisible signs of leprosy on the face of the one who knows. If leprosy of the nerves and leprosy of the joints are visible leprosy—then call it transparent leprosy. Immediately at the end of knowledge comes leprosy. The minute I set foot in India I was a spiritual leper. I had been for decades, of course, without knowing it.

"Now you know too. You can put on all your layers of makeup, but someone else who knows will see through to the skin. I will tell you what he will see. A skin that is too transparent; a spirit standing dead still; flesh that disgusts by its fleshiness, deprived of all fleshly beauty; a voice that is hoarse; a body stripped of hair, all the hair fallen like leaves. We will soon be seeing all the symptoms in you. The five signs of the decay of the one who sees.

"Even if you don't avoid people, you'll find, slowly,

that you are being avoided. Unknown to themselves, those who know give off an unpleasant warning odor.

"Fleshly beauty, spiritual beauty, everything that pertains to beauty, is born from ignorance and darkness and from them alone. *It is not allowed to know and still to be beautiful.* If the ignorance and darkness are the same, then a contest between spirit that has nothing at all to hide them and flesh that hides them behind its own dazzling light is no contest at all. Beauty is only beauty of the flesh."

"Yes, it is true. It was true of Ying Chan," said Keiko, light reminiscence in her eyes as she looked out at the mists. "And that I suppose is why you told neither Isao the Second nor Ying Chan the Third."

"A cruel sort of solicitude, I suppose, from a fear of obstructing fate. It kept me from speaking. But it was different with Kiyoaki. I did not then know the truth myself."

"You want to say that you were beautiful yourself." She cast a sarcastic eye from his head to his feet.

"No. I was industriously polishing the instruments to let me know."

"I understand. I am to keep it absolutely secret from the boy until he is twenty and ready to die."

"That is correct. You only have to wait four years."

"You are quite sure you won't die first?"

"I hadn't thought of that."

"We must make another appointment with the Cancer Research Institute."

Glancing at her watch, Keiko took out a small box filled with multicolored pills. She quickly selected three with her nail tips and drank them down with Scotch.

Honda had kept one thing from Keiko: that the boy they had met today was clearly different from his predecessors. The mechanism of his self-awareness was as apparent as if it lay behind a window. He had seen nothing of the sort in the other three. It seemed to him that the internal workings of the boy and his own were as alike as two peas. It was impossible that such could be the case—and yet, might the boy be that rarity, someone who knows and is all the more beautiful for knowledge? But that was impossible. If it was impossible, then, carrying all the proper marks, the proper age and the three moles, might the boy be the first instance of a cleverly wrought counterfeit set down before Honda?

They were beginning to feel sleepy. The talk moved to dreams.

"I very seldom dream," said Keiko. "Even now I sometimes do dream of examinations, though."

"They say you go on having dreams of examinations all through your life. I haven't had one in ten years."

"That's because you were a good student."

But it seemed altogether inappropriate to be talking with Keiko of dreams. It was like talking to a banker about knitting.

Finally they went off to their rooms. Honda had the sort of dream he had denied ever having, a dream of an examination.

On the second floor of a wooden frame schoolhouse, rocking so violently that it might have been hanging from a branch of a tree, Honda, in his teens, took up the answer sheets being passed briskly down rows of desks. Kiyoaki, he knew, would be two or three seats behind him. Looking from the questions on the blackboard to the answer sheets, Honda felt very sure of himself. He sharpened his pencils to chisels. He had the answers immediately. There was no need to hurry. The poplars outside were swaying in the wind.

He awoke in the night and every detail of the dream came back to him.

It had without question been a dream of an examination, and yet Honda had had none of the harried feelings that should go with such dreams. What had made him dream?

Since only he and Keiko knew of their conversation and it was not Keiko, then it had to be Honda himself. But he had not had the slightest wish to dream. He would not have made himself dream without consulting his own wishes in the matter.

Honda had of course read many books on Viennese psychoanalysis; but he could not accept the principle that one's wish was to betray oneself. No: it was more natural to believe that someone outside was keeping a close watch, and importuning.

Awake he had volition and, whether he wished it or not, was living in history; but somewhere back in the darkness was someone, historical perhaps, nonhistorical perhaps, setting him against dreams.

The mists would seem to have cleared and the moon to have come out. The window, a little too tall for the curtain, was shining at the bottom a faint silver-blue, like a shadow of the giant reclining peninsula beyond the waters. So India would look, thought Honda, to a ship approaching from the Indian Ocean at night. He went back to sleep.

13

AUGUST 10.

Beginning his shift at nine in the morning, Tōru as always opened the newspaper once he was alone. No ships were due until afternoon.

The paper was filled with stories of the industrial wastes that had floated ashore at Tago. There were some fifty paper mills at Tago, but Shimizu had only one, and that a small one. The prevailing currents were moreover eastward, and industrial wastes rarely came into Shimizu Harbor.

It seemed that the Zengakuren had come in considerable numbers for antipollution demonstrations. They were much beyond the range of even the thirty-power telescope. Things beyond the range of the telescope were of no relevance to Tōru.

It was a cool summer.

The sort of summer day was rare when the Izu Peninsula comes clearly forward and thunderclouds boil in a clear sky. The peninsula was in mists, the sunlight was dim. He had seen pictures taken recently from a weather satellite. Suruga Bay seemed to be always half hidden in smog.

Kinué stopped by in the morning, an unusual time. She asked if it would be all right to come inside.

"I'm all alone. He's gone to the main office in Yokohama."

There was fright in her eyes.

During the early summer rains he had taxed her considerably with the practice of bringing flowers for his hair, and for a time she had stopped coming. Now her visits were frequent again. She had stopped bringing flowers, but the fright and insecurity that were the excuse for the visits were more and more exaggerated.

"The second time. It's the second time, and a different man each time."

The story began the moment she sat down. Her breathing was heavy.

"What happened?"

"Someone is after you. When I come to see you I always make sure that no one sees me. If I didn't I might cause complications. If they were to kill you it would be my fault. and I'd have no choice but to kill myself."

"What are you talking about?"

"The second time, I tell you. That's why I'm so worried. I told you about last time. Remember? It was the same this time, but a little different. I went for a walk on Komagoé Beach this morning. I picked some beach lilies and then I went down to the water, and was looking out to sea with nothing very much on my mind.

"There aren't many people on Komagoé Beach, and I do get tired of having people stare at me. I love looking out to sea. I feel so relaxed. I sometimes think that if I put my own beauty on one side of the scales and the sea on the other they'd balance perfectly. So it's as if I'd turned my beauty over to the sea, and had no worries left.

"There was no one there. Just two or three people fishing. Maybe because he wasn't catching anything, one of them kept staring at me. I pretended not to notice, but that stare was on my cheek like a fly.

"I doubt if you can understand how awful it makes me feel. Here it is happening again, I say to myself. My beauty taking off on its own, robbing me of my freedom. It seems like something apart from me, beyond my control. Here I am, bothering no one, just wanting to be left alone, and it's off making trouble. It's a sign of true beauty, I know. But beauty's the worst sort of nuisance when it's off on its own.

"It's excited a man again, I say to myself. I barely have time to think how I hate it, and there it is, all busy tying a man up again. He's been an innocent bystander and now all of a sudden he's an ugly beast.

"I've stopped bringing you flowers, but I like putting flowers in my own hair when I'm by myself. I was singing and had a pink lily in my hair.

"I don't remember what I was singing. Isn't it odd,

when it was just a little while ago. But I think it must have been a sad, faraway sort of song, right for my beautiful voice. It's such a bore. The stupidest song in the world is beautiful when I sing it.

"Finally the man came up to me. He was young, and so polite it made me want to laugh. But there was something dirty in his eyes. He couldn't hide it. His eyes were like glue on my skirt. He talked about all sorts of things. But I was able to protect myself. You needn't worry about me. I was able to protect myself. It's you I'm worried about.

"He tried to confuse me by talking about all sorts of other things, but he kept coming back to you. He asked what sort of person you are, and how hard you work, and whether you are nice to people. I told him, of course. I told him that you are the kindest, most industrious person in the world. One thing seemed to surprise him. When I said you're superhuman.

"I knew by instinct. It was the second time, remember? Almst the same thing happened a week or ten days ago. Somebody suspects something about the two of us. Some awful person who hasn't shown himself has heard about me or maybe seen me from a distance, and he's lost his senses over me, and he's hired someone to spy on me, and wipe out a man he thinks might be fond of me. Insane love is coming nearer and nearer. I'm terrified. What will I do if harm comes to you through no fault of your own, just because I'm so beautiful? There's a conspiracy of some sort, I know it. A conspiracy hatched up by hopeless love. Some man is so rich and powerful that it's terrifying, and as ugly as a toad, and he's stalking me from way off, and he's out to get you."

Not pausing for breath, she was trembling like a leaf.

One blue-denim leg across the other, Tōru was smoking a cigarette. He was wondering what the point to it all might be. Kinué's dramatic imaginings quite aside, he was certain that someone was investigating him. Who would it be? And why? The police? But he was guilty of no offense more serious than smoking while still a minor.

He would think the problem over by himself; and in the meantime he would help the imaginings by giving them a logical turn.

He spoke solemnly. "Probably it is as you say; but I would have no regrets at all if I were to be murdered for the sake of a beautiful woman. Somewhere a rich and powerful and ugly man is waiting like a tiger to pounce on someone pure and beautiful. And his eye has landed on the two of us.

"You have to know what you're doing when you fight a person like him. He has his nets out everywhere. The thing to do is pretend you're not resisting and take plenty of time and seek out his weak points. The thing is to muster your strength and strike when you know what his weak points are.

"You must never forget for a moment that pure beauty is the enemy of the human race. His great advantage is that he has the whole race on his side. He won't let up for a minute until we've knelt down and admitted that we're human beings too. And so when the time comes we have to give in and pray to his gods. Unless we pray like mad he'll murder us. And when we do he'll relax and let us see his weak points. We have to hold out till it happens, all the while hanging on to our own self-respect."

"I understand perfectly. I'll do exactly as you say. But you must help me. This poisonous beauty of mine has me always feeling that I might stumble and fall. If the two of us go together hand in hand, why, we might wash the whole human race clean. And then the world would be a paradise, and we'd have nothing more to be afraid of."

"Exactly. Everything is all right."

"I like you better than anyone else in the world." She blurted out the words as she backed through the door.

Tōru always enjoyed her absence. When such ugliness became absent, how did it differ from beauty? Since the beauty which had been the premise for the whole conversation was itself absent, Kinué continued to pour forth fragrance after she was gone.

• • •

It sometimes seemed to him that beauty was crying in the distance. Just beyond the horizon, perhaps. It called out in a high voice, like a crane's. The call echoed and disappeared. If it took human form, it did so for but an instant. Only Kinué, a snare of ugliness, had captured the crane. And had long been feeding it with self-awareness.

The *Kōyō-maru* came in at three eighteen in the afternoon. No other ship was due until seven. Including nine ships awaiting berths, there were twenty ships in Shimizu Harbor.

Offshore in Third Area were the *Nikkei-maru II*, the *Mikasa-maru*, the *Camellia*, the *Ryūwa-maru*, the *Lianga Bay*, the *Umiyama-maru*, the *Yōkai-maru*, the *Denmark-maru*, and the *Kōyō-maru*.

At the Hinode Pier, the *Kamishima-maru* and the *Karakasu-maru*.

At the Fujimi Pier, the *Taiei-maru*, the *Hōwa-maru*, the *Yamataka-maru*, and the *Aristonikos*.

On buoys at Orito, a lumber port, the *Santen-maru*, the *Donna Rossana*, and the *Eastern Mary*.

Because of the danger, a single tanker, the *Okitama-maru*, was at a pipe in the Dolphin Area, reserved for tankers. It was on the point of sailing.

Large tankers with crude oil from the Persian Gulf anchored in the Dolphin Area, smaller tankers with refined oil could come into the Sodeshi Dock, at which there was a single ship, the *Nisshō-maru*.

A rail spur led from Shimizu Station past a number of berths and lonely customs warehouses deflecting the intense summer light, and deeper into the summer grasses, where from between warehouses the light on the sea told in derision of the end of land, and yet on and on as if it were meant for casting old steam engines into the sea. Then, suddenly, the crooked, rusty track came out upon the shining sea, and at its terminus was what is called the Railroad Dock. It was host to no ships at all.

Tōru had just entered the *Kōyō-maru* on the register for the Third Area.

It was anchored offshore, and loading operations would have to wait until the next day. There was no great urgency in sending out word of its arrival. At about four there came a call asking if it had in fact arrived.

At four there was a call from a pilot. Eight pilots worked in shifts, and the call was to inform him of the next day's assignments.

Time heavy on his hands, Tōru gazed out to sea through the telescope.

But as he gazed the uncertainty and the phantom of evil brought by Kinué came back to him. It was as if a dark filter had been slipped over the lens.

Indeed it was as if a dark filter had lain over the whole of this summer. Subtly, evil had come over the light, to dim the radiance and to thin the strong shadows of summer. The clouds lost their sharp outlines, the sea was a blank, the Izu Peninsula invisible on the steely blue-black of the horizon. The sea was a dull, monotonous green. Slowly, the tide was coming in.

Tōru lowered the telescope to the waves on the beach.

As they broke, a spray like the dregs of the sea slipped from their backs, and the pyramids of deep green changed, rose and swelled into an uneasy white. The sea lost its serenity.

Even as it rose it broke at the skirts, and ragged spots of white from its high belly like a call of inexpressible sorrow became a sharply smooth yet infinitely cracked wall of glass, like a vast spray. As it rose and broke, the forelocks were combed a beautiful white, and as it fell it showed the neatly arrayed blue-white of its crown, and the lines of white became a solid field of white; and so it fell, like a severed head.

The spread and the falling away of foam. Little patches of foam trailing off to sea like lines of water bugs.

Foam trailing off over the sand like sweat from the back of an athlete at the end of his exertions.

What delicate changes passed over the white monolith of the sea as it came in upon the shore and broke. The myriad confusion of thin waves and the fine partings of the foam became in desperation an infinity of lines spewed out over the sea as from silkworms. What a subtle evil, overcoming by sheer force even as it took into itself this delicate white.

Four fifteen.

The sky in its upper reaches was blue. It was an affected, pompous sort of blue. He had seen a similar blue in the library, in a collection from the School of Fontainebleau. Composed all lyrically with just an apology for clouds, it was not a summer sky at all. It was laid over with a saccharine hypocrisy.

The lens had left the shore, and was turned on the sky, the horizon, the sea.

It caught a sheet of spray that seemed to hurl itself into the very heavens. What could it be up to, this single point of foam flinging itself above the rest? Why had it been elected?

Nature was a cycle, the whole to the fragment, the fragment back to the whole. Compared to the fleeting cleanness of the fragment, the whole was dark and sullen.

And was evil a matter of the whole?

Or of the fragment?

Four forty-five. Not a ship in sight.

The beach was lonely. There were no swimmers, and only two or three anglers. The sea without ships was worlds away from dedication and service. Suruga Bay lay utterly sober, without love and without joy. There had to be ships sliding in and out, cutting razor lines of white through this sluggish, flawless perfection. A ship was a weapon of cool contempt against the perfection, gliding over the thin taut skin of the sea and wounding it. Yet going no deeper than the surface.

Five o'clock.

The white of the waves become for an instant the color of a yellow rose, to tell that evening approached.

He saw two black tankers, large and small, making for sea to the left. The fifteen-hundred-ton *Okitama-maru*, which had left Shimizu at four twenty, and the three-hundred-ton *Nisshō-maru*, at four twenty-three.

They were like mirages in the mist. Not even their wakes were distinct.

He lowered the lens to the shore.

As they took on the color of evening, the waves were stern and hard. The light had more and more the color of evil, the bellies of the waves were uglier.

Yes. The waves as they broke were a manifest vision of death. It seemed to him that they had to be. They were mouths agape at the moment of death.

Gasping in agony, they trailed numberless threads

of saliva. Earth purple in the twilight became a livid mouth.

Into the gaping mouth of the sea plunged death. Showing death nakedly time and time again, the sea was like a constabulary. It swiftly disposed of the bodies, hiding them from the public gaze.

Tōru's telescope caught something it should not have.

He suddenly felt that a different world was being dragged forth from those gaping jaws. Since he was not one to see phantasms, there could be no doubt that it existed. But he did not know what it was. Perhaps it was a pattern drawn by micro-organisms in the sea. A different world was revealed in the light flashing from the dark depths, and he knew it was a place he had seen. Perhaps it had something to do with immeasurably distant memories. If there was such a thing as a previous life, then perhaps this was it. And what would its relation be to the world Tōru was constantly looking for, a step beyond the bright horizon? If it was a dance of seaweed caught in the belly of the breaking waves, then perhaps the world pictured in that instant was a miniature of the mucous pink and purple creases and cavities of the nauseous depths. But there had been rays and flashes—from a sea run through by lightning? Such a thing was not probable in this tranquil twilight sea. There was nothing demanding that *that* world and *this* world be contemporary. Was the world he had had a glimpse of in a different time? Was it of a time different from that measured by his watch?

He shook his head. As he fled the unpleasant sight, the telescope too became unpleasant. He moved to the fifteen-power binoculars in another corner of the room. He followed the great hull of the ship leaving the harbor.

It was the *Yamataka-maru* of the Y.S. Line, 9,183 tons, bound for Yokohama.

"A Yamashita ship has just left, bound in your direction. *Yamataka, Yamataka.* It's now seventeen twenty."

Having telephoned his message to the main office in Yokohama, he returned to the binoculars and once more followed the *Yamataka-maru,* its masts now disappearing into the mist.

The mark was a single black line near the top of a persimmon-colored ground. Y.S. LINE in large black letters on the hull. White bridge, red cranes. The ship was in desperate flight from the circle in the telescope. Sending white lines from its prow, it moved out to sea.

It was gone.

There were bonfires in what had been strawberry patches below the window.

The plastic shelters which had until about the end of the summer rains covered the whole expanse had all been taken away. The strawberry season was past. Cuttings for forced cultivation were off at the fifth station of Fuji welcoming a man-made winter. They would return late in October, to be ready for the Christmas market.

People were working among the foundations and on black paddies from which even the foundations had been removed.

Tōru went to get dinner.

He had a simple dinner at his desk. It was nightfall. Five forty.

A half moon came from the clouds, high in the southern sky. Another moment and the half moon, like an ivory comb dropped down into the sky, was indistinguishable from a cloud.

The pines along the sea were black. It was already dark enough to make out the red taillights of the anglers' cars parked on the beach.

Children were swarming over the road through the

strawberry patches. Strange children of the evening. Weird children, coming out into the dusk from nowhere, cavorting insanely through the fields.

The bonfires sent up tongues of flame beyond.

Five fifty.

Tōru glanced up. He caught a ship mark quite indistinguishable to the ordinary naked eye, and reached for the telephone. Such was his confidence that his hand went for the telephone even before he had verified the mark.

The ship's agent answered.

"Hello? This is Teikoku Signal. The *Daichū*. I've just sighted it."

It was like a smudge drawn by a dirty finger across faint pink on the southwest horizon. As if examining a fingerprint on the glass, he picked it out and identified it.

The register told him that the *Daichū-maru*, 3,850 tons, was a lauan transport, one hundred meters long, speed 12.4 knots. The only ships capable of more than twenty knots were international freighters. Lumber ships were slower.

He felt particularly close to the *Daichū-maru*. It had been launched the spring before from the Kanazashi Shipyards here in Shimizu.

Six.

In the pink offing, the dim form of the *Daichū-maru* was edging past the *Okitama-maru*, leaving the harbor. It was a strange moment when an image oozes from a dream into everyday life, an actuality from an abstraction—a poem becomes corporate, a fantasy an object. If something meaningless yet ominous is through some process taken into the heart, there is born in the heart an urgency to give it shape, and so a something comes to exist. Perhaps the *Daichū-maru* was born of Tōru's heart. An image indistinct as the sweep of a brush had become a gigantic hull of some four thousand tons. And the same thing was forever happening, somewhere in the world.

Six ten.

Foreshortened by the angle of its approach, it raised its two derricks like the horns of a great black beetle.

Six fifteen.

It was quite clear now to the naked eye, but it hesitated black on the horizon like an object forgotten on a shelf. The distance was accordioned, and it stayed on and on, a black beetle left on the shelf of the horizon.

Six thirty.

Through the lens, diagonally, he could see the funnel mark, a red "N" in a circle on a white ground. He could make out piles of lauan.

Six fifty.

Now broadside in the channel, the *Daichū-maru* was showing red mast lights against a cloudy twilight sky which no longer held a moon. It slipped past the *Okitama*, making its mirage-like way out to sea. There was a considerable distance between them, but the lights were caught in foreshortened perspective; and it was as if, out on the dark sea, the embers of two cigarettes were brushing and parting.

In from a foreign port, the *Daichū-maru* had two great iron rails on its deck to keep the lauan from falling overboard. In such quantities that the waterline was not showing, great trunks burned by the tropical sun lay piled one on another, like the bundled corpses of huge, powerful brown slaves.

Tōru thought of the new regulations for waterlines, jungle-like in their details. Waterlines for lumber vessels were of six varieties, summer, winter, winter North Atlantic, tropical, freshwater summer, and freshwater tropical. The tropical category was further divided into tropical by zone and tropical by season. The *Daichū-maru* fell into the former, and under the "special regulations for deck lumber transport." Tōru had memorized with fascination the lines that define the tropical zone.

From the east coast of North America along the thirteenth parallel east to sixty degrees west longitude; thence directly to ten degrees north by fifty-eight degrees west; thence along the tenth parallel to twenty degrees west; thence along the twentieth meridian to thirty degrees north; thence to the west coast of Africa . . . thence to the west coast of India . . . to the east coast of India . . . to the west coast of Malaya . . . thence along the southeast coast of Asia to the tenth parallel on the coast of Vietnam . . . from Santos . . . the east coast of Africa to the west coast of Madagascar . . . the Suez Canal . . . the Red Sea, Aden, the Persian Gulf.

An invisible line was drawn from continent to continent and ocean to ocean and what was within was named "tropical," and so, suddenly, a "tropical" made its appearance, with its coconuts, its reefs, its cobalt seas, its storm clouds, its squalls, the screams of its multicolored parrots.

Trunks of lauan, splashed with the scarlet and gold and green labels of the tropics. Heaped-up logs of lauan: they had been wet by tropical rains and they had reflected warm starlit skies, they had been attacked by waves and eaten by the shining bugs of the deep; and they could not dream that they were headed at the end of the journey for the boredom of everyday life.

Seven.

The *Daichū-maru* passed the second pylon. The lights of the harbor were aglow.

Since it had come in at an odd hour, quarantine and unloading would have to wait until the next morning. Even so, Tōru made the usual calls: the pilot, the police, the harbor superintendent, the agent, the provisioners, the laundry.

"The *Daichū* is coming into three-G."

"Hello? This is Teikoku Signal. The *Daichū* is coming into three-G. The cargo? The line is barely showing."

"Shimizu Provisioners? This is Teikoku Signal. Thank you for everything. The *Daichū* has just come into three-G. It's off the Mio lighthouse at the moment."

"Shizuoka Police? The *Daichū* is coming in. Tomorrow at seven, if you will, please."

"The *Daichū*. *D-a-i-c-h-ū*. Yes, if you will, please."

14

OFF DUTY on an evening in late August, Tōru had finished his dinner and bath. He went out to take the cool of the south wind under the blue awning of the veranda, still warm from the heat of the day. There were doors all along the shabby veranda, which he reached by iron stairs.

Immediately to the south was a lumber yard more than a hundred yards square, its huge cross-section dark under lights. The lumber sometimes seemed to Tōru like a great silent beast.

There was a crematory in the grove beyond. Tōru would like to have seen a flame that could show itself in the smoke from such an enormous chimney. He never had.

The summit of the dark mountain to the south was Nihondaira. He could see the streams of automobile lights on the road leading up to it. There were clusters of hotel lights, and the red lights of television towers.

Tōru had not been to the hotels. He knew nothing of the affluent life. He did know that wealth and virtue were incompatible, but he had no interest in making the world virtuous. Revolution could be left to others. There was no concept for which he had a greater dislike than equality.

He was about to go inside when a Corona pulled up at the stairs. He could not make out the details, but he was sure he had seen it before. He was startled when the superintendent got out.

A large envelope clutched in his hand, the superintendent lurched up the stairs, as he always did when he came to the signal station.

"Yasunaga is it? Good evening. I'm glad I caught you at home. I've brought something to drink. Let's have a drink and a talk." He did not mind being overheard.

Overwhelmed by this unique visit, Tōru reached for the door behind him.

"You're very neat." The superintendent seated himself on the cushion Tōru offered, and, wiping at his forehead, looked around him.

The building had been finished only the year before. It was as if the dust had not been allowed to gather. There was a maple-leaf pattern on the frosted glass of the aluminum-sashed windows, inside which were paper doors. The walls were lavender, the wood of the ceiling was of almost too good a grain, waist-high at the door was a frosted pane with a bamboo pattern, and the doors between the rooms too were decorated in unusual patterns. The tastes of the occupant demanded the newest wares.

The rent was twelve thousand five hundred yen a

month, and two hundred fifty yen besides went each month into a common maintenance fund. Tōru thanked the superintendent for the half of the rent paid by the company.

"But aren't you lonely, all by yourself?"

"I'm used to being alone. I'm alone at the station too."

"That's true, of course."

The superintendent took a bottle of Suntory Square from his bag, and side dishes as well, shredded cuttle-fish and prawn crackers. If Tōru had no glasses, he said, cups would do as well.

Something unusual was afoot. It was not the superintendent's practice to come calling upon subordinates thus provisioned. The visit could mean no good. Since Tōru had nothing to do with the accounts, it was not likely that he was about to be charged with fiscal venalities; but he must have made a grievous blunder without himself being aware of it. And here was the superintendent pressing liquor upon the boy he had scolded for his addiction to tobacco. Tōru was recon-ciled to dismissal; but he knew well enough that, even without a labor union, it was a world in which in-dustrious young men were not to be treated roughly, though they might be no more than signalmen third class. There were plenty of other jobs, if he took the trouble to look for them. In control of himself once more, he glanced at the superintendent with something like pity. He was confident that he could meet with dignity whatever came, even if it be notice of his dismissal. Whatever his adversary might think, Tōru knew that he was a jewel not easily come by.

Refusing the whiskey the superintendent pressed upon him, Tōru sat in an airless corner, his beautiful eyes alight.

He might be alone in the world, but he lived in a small castle of ice, quite free of the ambition and greed and lust upon which people lose their step. Because he disliked comparing himself with others, he was quite free from envy and jealousy. Because he had cut off the road to mundane harmony from the outset, he quarreled with no one. He let people think of him as a gentle, harmless, cuddly white bunny. The loss of a job was the smallest triviality.

"I had a call from the main office the other day." The superintendent was drinking to build up courage. "I wondered what it might mean, and it turned out to be a summons from the president himself. Let me tell you I was surprised. I went into his office wondering what would come next, and I have to admit that I was shaking in spite of myself. And there he was, all smiles. Have a seat, he said. I knew the news wasn't going to be bad, but it turned out not to be good and not to be bad either as far as I myself was concerned. What do you think it was? Well, it had to do with you."

Tōru's eyes were fixed on him. The news proved to be quite beyond his imagining. Dismissal had nothing to do with the case.

"Wasn't I surprised, though. It had come through an older man who had done a great deal for the president. There's someone who wants to adopt you. And it's up to me to make you agree, even if I have to force you. That's quite a responsibility, coming from the president himself. Someone's put a high price on you. Or it might be that someone knows a good article when he sees it."

An intimation came to Tōru. It had to be the elderly lawyer who had left his calling card.

"I should imagine his name is Honda."

"That's right. How did you know?" The superintendent was astonished.

"He came once to look at the station. But it seems

odd that he should want to adopt me after just the one time."

"It seems that he's made two or three very careful investigations."

Tōru frowned. He remembered the tidings from Kinué. "Not a very pleasant sort of thing to do to a person."

The superintendent hurried on in some confusion. "But it's all right. He found out that you're a model young man. Not a mark against you."

It was not so much the elderly lawyer Tōru was thinking of. It was that spoiled, Westernized old woman, from a world utterly alien to Tōru, spreading her scaly powder like a gaudy moth.

The superintendent kept Tōru awake until eleven thirty. Sometimes, his knees in his arms, Tōru would doze off; but the superintendent, now in his cups, would shake him and go on talking.

The man was a wealthy and famous old widower. He saw that it would far better serve the interests of the Honda family and of Japan to adopt a truly talented and willing young man than to take in a dolt from a high-placed family. He would hire tutors as soon as the adoption had been accomplished, to put Tōru into the best preparatory school and university. The prospective father rather hoped that Tōru would choose law or business, but the final choice must of course be his own, and the father would be quite unstinting with his help. He did not have long to live, but there were no family complications, and the whole of his estate would go to Tōru. Could any proposal be more attractive?

But why? The question tickled at Tōru's self-respect.

The other person had jumped over something. It corresponded, by wonderful coincidence, to something Tōru himself had jumped over. It seemed to the other and to Tōru himself that the irrationality of it all was natural; and the ones who had been taken in were the common-sense ones in between, the president and the others.

The news came to Tōru as nothing to be surprised by at all. He had been prepared for a curious denouement the moment he had met the quiet old man. He was confident that no one would find him out, but the faculty of not being caught by surprise had given him the confidence to pass generous judgment on wholly outrageous mistakes about himself and to swallow the results. If in the end they came to nonsense, they were the results of beautiful error. If a confusion in the world's awareness was taken to be a self-evident premise, then anything could follow. The view that all the benevolence and malevolence directed at him were based upon error brought a blinding of self-respect, and self-denial as the final conclusion to cynicism.

Tōru had only contempt for inevitability, and to him volition was nothing. If he imagined himself caught up in an antiquated comedy of errors, he had ample reason. There could be no doubt that nothing was more ridiculous than the anger of a volitionless person who thought his volition was being trampled on. If he behaved in a coolly rational manner, then to say that he had no particular wish to become an adopted son amounted to the same thing as saying that he was quite prepared to become an adopted son.

Most people would immediately have become suspicious of the inadequate reasons offered. But that was a matter of weighing the appraisal of another against one's self-esteem, a road which Tōru's thoughts did not choose to travel. He compared himself with no one. In the measure, indeed, that the proposal was child's play lacking inevitability and became something very like the whim of an old man, the element of the inescapable grew more tenuous, and the proposal easier for Tōru to accept. A person without fate or destiny is not bound by the inescapable.

The proposal came, in sum, to alms masking themselves as educational endeavor.

An ordinarily proud and high-spirited boy could have said: "I'm no beggar."

But that sort of protest had about it the smell of boys' magazines. Tōru had the more enigmatic weapon of a smile. He accepted by denying.

As a matter of fact, the play of light, when he investigated his enigmatic smile in a mirror, sometimes made it seem like that of a young girl. Perhaps a young girl in some distant land, speaking some incomprehensible language, had just such an enigmatic smile as her only route of communication. He did not wish to be understood as saying that the smile was girlish. Yet it was not a man's smile. It had in it a quality as of a bird waiting in its nest at the most delicate moment, free of either coquetry or timidity, between hesitation and resolution, preparing because of an adversary for a crisis as of walking a dark path. Between dark and dawn, neither road nor hill could be made out, and each step might mean drowning. It sometimes seemed to Tōru that it was a smile he had inherited from neither of his parents, but acquired rather from a young girl, a stranger he had met in his distant youth.

Nor was it conceit that made him think so. He could see himself from corner to corner and the confidence that the most perceptive of persons could not see him as he saw himself was the basis of his self-respect; and so long as it was to the Tōru seen by others, the offer of alms was an offer to a shadow of the real Tōru, quite incapable of wounding his self-respect. Tōru was secure.

But were the motives of the man so incomprehensible? There was nothing in the least incomprehensible

about them. Tōru understood perfectly. The victim
of boredom is quite capable of selling a world to a
rag-picker.

His knees in his arms, Tōru was nodding sleepily.
He had made up his mind. But good manners demanded that he defer his assent until the superintendent could be a little prouder of the sweat he had
expended.

He was happier than ever with his faculty for not
dreaming. He had lighted mosquito repellent for the
benefit of the superintendent, but the mosquitoes were
at his own feet and ankles. The itching shone through
his drowsiness like moonlight. He thought vaguely
that he must again wash the hands with which he was
scratching.

"Well, I'm afraid you're sleepy. You have every
right to be. The night's practically over. Dear me.
Eleven thirty already. I've stayed much too long. So
the story sounds good to you? You agree?" As he
stood up to leave, the superintendent laid a persuasive
hand on Tōru's shoulder.

Pretending to have awakened only now, Tōru said:
"Yes. I agree."

"You agree?"

"I agree."

"Thank you, thank you. I'll take care of everything
else. Think of me as your father. All right?"

"Yes. I'd be very grateful if you would."

"But it will be a loss for the station, letting a good
boy like you go."

He was far too drunk to drive. Tōru went for a
taxi and saw him home.

15

Tōru was off duty the next day. He spent the day at a movie and watching the ships in the harbor. He was on duty from nine the next morning.

After a number of typhoons, the late-summer sky for the first time displayed summery clouds. He was more attentive than usual to the clouds, thinking that this would be his last summer at the station.

The sky that evening was beautiful. Lines of cloud hovered over the ocean like the god of storms himself.

But the grand, orange-tinted forest of clouds was decapitated by yet another layer of clouds. Here and there the powerful muscles of the storm clouds were flushed over with shyness, and the blue sky behind poured over them in an avalanche of high azure. This layer was dark, that shone like a bright bow.

It was the nearest and highest layer of clouds. In exaggerated perspective, the layers that trailed off behind seemed to descend in steps beyond the clear sky. Perhaps, thought Tōru, it was a fraud perpetrated by the clouds. Perhaps the clouds, making a show of perspective, were deceiving him.

Among clouds like antique white clay images of warriors were some that suggested dragons twisting angrily and darkly upward. Some, as they lost their shape, were tinged rose. Presently, they separated themselves into bland reds and yellows and purples, and their stormy powers left them. The white shining face of the god had taken on the ashen hue of death.

16

SURPRISED TO learn that Tōru's birth, on March 20, 1954, came before the death of Ying Chan, Honda ordered further investigation. He went ahead with the adoption proceedings all the same.

He regretted that he had learned from her sister only that her death had come in the spring, and that he had not sought more specific information. Inquiring at the American Embassy about the residence of the sister, who had returned to America, he sent off two or three queries, but not the smallest fragment of information came in response. He had a friend in the Foreign Office make inquiry through the Japanese Embassy in Bangkok, but the only reply was that an investigation was in progress. There followed silence.

He could think of any number of devices if he did not mind the expense; but, with badly misplaced frugality and the impatience of old age, he neglected looking into the matter of the princess's death even as he pushed forward with arrangements for the adoption. It seemed too much trouble.

The nerves of the Honda of 1944, uneasy about classic monetary principles, were probably still young and resilient. Now, when the classic common sense was falling apart, Honda clung to it stubbornly, and the result was a quarrel with a financial consultant fifteen years younger than he.

This last quarter of a century he had all the same amassed a fortune of perhaps two million dollars. The million that had come to him in 1948 he had cleanly divided into three parts, which he had put into stocks, real estate, and savings. The portion in real estate had increased tenfold and the stocks threefold and the savings had diminished.

He had not lost his taste for the stocks preferred by old gentlemen who, in wing collars, played billiards at English-style clubs. He was not free from the tastes of an age when the mark of class was to be the holder of "elegant, reliable" stocks like Tokyo Fire and Marine, Tokyo Electric Power, Tokyo Gas, and Kansai Electric Power, and to have a contempt for speculation. Yet the uninteresting stocks that exclusively made up his portfolio had tripled in value. Because of the fifteen-percent tax deduction for dividends, he paid scarcely any taxes at all from his dividend income.

Tastes in stocks were like tastes in neckties. Wide, gaudy, modish prints were not for an old man. If he did not reap the benefits of bold tastes, neither did he take the risks.

In the decade since 1960 it had become possible, as in America, to guess a man's age from the stocks he owned. The bright celebrities among stocks were day by day becoming more vulgar, day by day taking on the look of the hoi polloi. The makers of small transistor parts, recording annual sales of ten billion yen, with stocks once fifty yen a share now touching fourteen hundred—they were altogether too ordinary.

While paying careful heed to his taste in stocks, Honda was quite insensitive to taste in real estate.

He had made a very good profit from the houses he had put up in 1953 for American soldiers near the Sagamihara Base. In those days it took more money to build houses than to buy land. Upon the advice of his financial consultant, Honda at first ignored houses and bought up some ten acres of unimproved land at a hundred yen or so per square yard. Each square yard was now worth perhaps twenty thousand yen. Land for which he had paid three million yen was now worth perhaps seven hundred and fifty million.

This was of course a windfall. He had had good luck with some of his land, rather poorer luck with other, but none of it had lost value. He regretted now that he had not left half that million dollars' worth of forest land as it was.

His experience in making money had been a strange one. He could, to be sure, have made tenfold more if he had been bolder; but he could not think that he had come the wrong way. His prudence had guaranteed against loss. Yet there were small regrets and feelings of dissatisfaction. Pushed to their conclusion, they amounted to a dissatisfaction with his own innate nature; and a certain morbid lyricism was an inevitable result.

Honda had achieved security by clinging to his old-fashioned principles even though he was quite aware of the sacrifices they required. He worshipped the trinity of classical capitalism. There was something sacred about it, the harmony of liberal economics. It was symbolic, it had in it the slow, studied intellectual arrogance and sense of balance the gentlemen of the home country had toward colonies still in the primitive insecurity of monoculture.

Such things survived in Japan, then? As long as the tax laws remained unchanged, and enterprises continued to depend on sources of money other than their own capital, and as long as banks continued to demand land as security for loans, the giant article in pawn known as the land of Japan would have no part of the classic principles, and land prices would continue to rise. Inflation would cease only with the end of economic growth or with a Communist government.

While perfectly aware of these facts, Honda remained faithful to the old illusion. He took life insurance, and became an almost foolish defender of a currency system that was day by day falling to pieces. Perhaps a distant mirage of the age of the gold standard, when Isao was living so passionately, remained with Honda.

It had been long ago that the beautiful dream of harmony so dear to the liberal economists had faded, and the dialectical inevitability of the Marxists too had come to look rather peculiar. What was supposed to die had increased and multiplied, what was supposed to grow (it did grow, of course) changed into something quite different. There was no room left for pure doctrine.

It was simple to believe in a world headed for destruction, and had he still been twenty Honda himself would perhaps have so believed; and the very refusal to collapse kept the person who had to slip over life like a skater and presently die constantly on the alert. Who would be so foolish as to skate if he knew the ice was cracking? And if the ice was quite certain not to crack, then a person was denied the pleasure of seeing others fall in. The only question was whether the ice would crack or not while one was skating, and Honda had not a great deal of time left to skate.

And while he was about it, his holdings gradually increased from interest and various sorts of profit.

People thought at any rate that their holdings increased. If they kept ahead of inflation they did increase. But something that increased by laws fundamentally in opposition to those of life could exist only by eating away at what stood on the side of life. Growing profits were the incursions of the white ants of time. A slight increase here and there brought the gentle, steady gnawing.

And then one became aware of the fact that time bearing profits and time for life were of a different nature.

These were thoughts that inevitably went through Honda's mind as he lay awaiting daylight, altogether too awake, and indulged in the sport of chasing thoughts.

Interest accrues like moss over a great plain of time. We are not up to pursuing it forever. That is because our own time leads us relentlessly downhill to a cliff.

It had been a still-young Honda who thought that self-awareness was entirely a matter of the self. It had been a still-young Honda who had named "self-awareness" the awareness of a reality like a dark, thorny sea cucumber floating in the transparent cask of the self. "Like unto a violent torrent, ever flowing, ever changing." He had apprehended the principle intellectually when he was in India, but it had taken him thirty years to make it a part of himself.

As he grew older, awareness of self became awareness of time. He gradually came to make out the sound of the white ants. Moment by moment, second by second, with what a shallow awareness men slipped through time that would not return! Only with age did one know that there was a richness, an intoxication even, in each drop. The drops of beautiful time, like the drops of a rich, rare wine. And time dripped away like blood. Old men dried up and died. In payment for having neglected to stop time at the glorious moment when the rich blood, unbeknownst to the owner himself, was bringing rich drunkenness.

Yes. The old knew that time held intoxications. And when the knowledge came there was no longer enough liquor left. Why had he not stopped time?

Even though he reproved himself, Honda did not think that it had been because of his own laziness and cowardice that he had not stopped time while he could.

Feeling the approach of daylight through his eyelids, Honda indulged in a soliloquy.

"No, there was never for me a moment when I had to do it, stop time. If I have something that might be called a destiny, then it has been in this inability to stop time.

"There was for me nothing that might have been called the pinnacle of my youth, and so no moment for stopping it. One should stop at the pinnacle. I could discern none. Strangely, I feel no regrets.

"No, there is still time after youth has gone by a little. A pinnacle comes, and then the moment. But if the eye that discerns the pinnacle is called an eye of awareness, then I must offer a small objection. I doubt that anyone has been more diligent than myself in putting the eye of awareness to work, more relentless in keeping it open. It is not enough for detecting the pinnacle. The help of destiny is needed. I am quite aware that few have been given that in shorter supply than myself.

"It is easy to say that strength of will kept me back. Was that really the case? Is not the will the leavings of destiny? Between will and determination, are there not inborn differences, as between castes in India? And is not the poorer one the will?

"I did not think so when I was young. I thought that human volition sought to make history. And where did history go? That stumbling old beggar woman.

"Some are all the same endowed with the faculty to cut time short at the pinnacle. I know it to be true, for I have seen examples with my own eyes.

"What power, poetry, bliss! To be able to cut it short, just as the white radiance of the pinnacle comes into view. There comes a foreknowledge in the delicate excitement offered by the slopes, in the changing distribution of the alpine flora, in the approach of the watershed.

"Just a little more and time will be at the peak, and

without pausing it will begin its descent. Most people beguile the downward course by taking in the harvest. And what is that? The trails and the waters are only plunging downward.

"Endless physical beauty. That is the special prerogative of those who cut time short. Just before the pinnacle when time must be cut short is the pinnacle of physical beauty.

"Clear, bright beauty, in the knowledge that the radiant white pinnacle lies just ahead. And unhappy purity. In that moment the beauty of a man and the beauty of a gazelle are in wonderful correspondence. Raising its horns proudly, raising the hoof of the white-spotted leg ever so slightly in the face of the denial. Replete with the pride of the farewell, crowned with the white mountain snows.

"It would not have become me to raise my hand in farewell to those who were below, where time still ran on. Had I raised my hand in sudden farewell at a street crossing, I would only have stopped a cab.

"Perhaps, unable to stop time, I had to be content with stopping a succession of cabs. For the purpose, and that only, with firm resolve, of being taken to yet another place where time does not stop. Without the poetry and the bliss.

"Without the poetry, without the bliss! That is the important thing. And I know that only in them lies hidden the reason for life.

"Even if time is stopped there is rebirth. That I know too.

"And I must deny Tōru the terrible poetry and bliss. That must be my policy."

Honda was by now quite awake. With dull pains here and there and with mucus in his throat to tell him that a new day had begun, he became captive of the need to bring together again things that had fallen apart while he slept. As if opening an old folding chair, he brought himself out of bed. The room was light. It was his practice to give notice of his having awakened through the interphone, but today he preferred not to. Instead he took a lacquered box from the shelf, and from it the report on Tōru he had had from the detective agency.

> Report on proposed adoption
> Number M-2582
> Client 1493: Mr. Shigekuni Honda
> August 20, 1970
> Dainichi Investigating Agency

Tōru Yasunaga, born March 20, 1954; aged sixteen

Permanent residence: 6–152 Yui, Ihara-gun, Shizuoka Prefecture

Present residence: Meiwasō, 2–10 Funabara-chō, Shimizu, Shizuoka Prefecture

Character and deportment:

The subject is highly intelligent, with the unusual I.Q. of 159. As against 47 percent of examinees with an I.Q. of a hundred, only .6 percent have an I.Q. of over 140. It seems regrettable that such a talented boy should have lost his parents early and, reared by an uncle in straitened circumstances, have been forced to stop his education at middle school. A knowledge of his own abilities, moreover, has not been allowed to go to his head. He has acquitted himself of his rather simple and routine duties with the utmost conscientiousness and diligence, and his modesty and good manners have won him the affection of his colleagues and superiors. Since he is only sixteen, it is too early for a great deal to be reported on his behavior, but it would seem that his ministrations to a demented girl named Kinué who is the sport of the neighborhood have nothing to do with sex but are evidence of a gentle, charitable humanism. She looks up to a youth younger than herself as a god.

Interests and hobbies:

He would seem to have no pronounced interests. On holidays he goes to the library or to a movie, or watches the ships in the harbor. Usually by himself in these pursuits, he would seem to have solitary inclinations. One may perhaps explain his addiction to tobacco despite the fact that he is still a minor as a result of the solitary and routine nature of his work. Smoking would seem to have had no effect on his health.

Marital status:

He is of course single.

Ideological tendencies and associations:

Perhaps because he is still so young, he has shown no interest in extreme political movements. He would on the contrary seem to have a distaste for politics and political movements. The company is without a union, and he has taken part in no movement toward unionization. He is a voracious reader despite his youth, and his interests would seem to be wide. He owns almost no books, but is a devoted user of libraries who relies on remarkable powers of memory to master what he has read. There is no evidence that he has been addicted to extremist writings of either the left or the right. The evidence is rather that he has sought knowledge of a general and varied kind. He sees comrades from his middle-school days occasionally but would seem to have no close friends.

Religious and other beliefs:

The family is Buddhist, but on the subject himself seems to have little interest in religion. He belongs to none of the newer religious sects. He has resisted strong pressure from their adherents.

Family:

Investigations to the third generation on both sides of the family have revealed no evidence of mental illness.

17

HONDA CHOSE a day late in October for Tōru's first lesson in foreign table manners. The small parlor was set for a banquet in the French style, complete with caterer and butler, and Tōru wore a new navy-blue suit. He was informed that he must sit well back in the chair and bring it close to the table, that he must not put his elbows on the table or lean too low over his soup, and that he must keep his arms close to his sides. There followed instructions in the disposition of the napkin and the taking of the soup, with the spoon tilted toward the mouth for purposes of avoiding noise. Tōru followed all the instructions carefully, repeating over and over again sequences that did not come easily.

"Foreign table manners may seem a trifle stupid," said Honda, "but when they come in an easy, natural way they give a person a sense of security. Evidence of good breeding gives a person status, and by good breeding in Japan we mean a familiarity with the Western way of doing things. We find the pure Japanese only in the slums and in the underworld, and may expect them to be more and more narrowly circumscribed as time goes by. The poison known as the pure Japanese is thinning, changing to a potion acceptable to everyone."

There can be little doubt that Honda was thinking of Isao as he spoke. Isao knew nothing of Western table manners. Such elegant accessories were no part of the grandeur of his world. And so Tōru, still sixteen, must be taught Western table manners.

Food was served from the left and drink from the right. Knives and forks were taken in order from the outside. Tōru looked at his hands like one engulfed in a torrent.

The instructions continued. "And you must make polite conversation while you eat. That puts your table companion at ease. You must be careful about timing your swallows, because there is a danger, when you talk with food in your mouth, of spitting something out. Now, then. Father"—Honda referred to himself as "Father"—"will say something to you, and you must answer. You must think of me not as your father but as a very important man who might be able to do a great deal for you if he likes you. We are acting out a play. All right, now. 'You are studying hard, I see, and you have your three tutors all speechless with admiration; but it seems a little odd that you should have no real friends.' "

"I don't feel any great need for them."

"That's no answer at all. If you give that sort of answer people will think you queer. Now, then. Give me a proper answer."

Tōru was silent.

"It won't do. Studying will do you no good if you don't use common sense. This is the sort of answer you should give, as pleasantly as can be: 'I'm studying so hard that I really don't have time at the moment for friends, but I'm sure I'll have some as soon as I start prep school.' "

"I'm studying so hard that I really don't have time at the moment for friends, but I'm sure I'll have some as soon as I start prep school."

"That's it, that's it. That's the style. And all of a sudden the conversation turns to art. 'Who is your favorite Italian artist?' "

There was no answer.

"Who is your favorite Italian artist?"

"Mantegna."

"No, no. You're far too young for Mantegna. Probably your table companion has never heard of Mantegna, and you'll make him uncomfortable, and give an unpleasant impression of precociousness. This is how you answer. 'I think the Renaissance is just wonderful.' "

"That's it, that's it. You give your table companion a feeling of superiority and you seem all cute and charming. And he has an opening for a long lecture on things he only half understands. You must listen all aglow with curiosity and admiration even though most of what he says is wrong and the rest is old hat. What the world asks of a young person is that he be a devoted listener, nothing more. You're the winner if you let him do the talking. You must not forget that for a moment.

"The world does not ask brilliance of a young person, and at the same time too firm a steadiness arouses suspicions. You should have a harmless little eccentricity or two, something to interest him. You must have little addictions, not too expensive and not related to politics. Very abstract, very average. Tinkering with machinery, or baseball or a trumpet. Once he knows what they are, he feels safe. He knows where your energies can go. You can even seem a little carried away by your hobbies if you want to.

"You should go in for sports but not let them inter-

117

fere with your studies, and they should be the sports that show off your good health. It has the advantage of making you look a bit stupid. There are no virtues more highly prized in Japan than indifference to politics and devotion to the team.

"You can graduate with the highest marks in your class, but you have to have a sort of vague stupidity that puts people at their ease. Like a kite full of wind.

"I'll tell you about money once you're in prep school. You're in the happy position for the moment of not having to worry about it."

As he lectured to the attentive Tōru, Honda had the feeling that these were really instructions for Kiyoaki and Isao and Ying Chan.

Yes, he should have spoken to them. He should have armed them with the foreknowledge that would keep them from flinging themselves after their destinies, take away their wings, keep them from soaring, make them march in step with the crowd. The world does not approve of flying. Wings are dangerous weapons. They invite self-destruction before they can be used. If he had brought Isao to terms with the fools, then he could have pretended that he knew nothing of wings.

He had only to say to people: "His wings are an accessory. You needn't trouble yourself about them. Just keep company with him for a while, and you'll see that he's an ordinary, reliable boy." Such tidings could have been remarkably effective.

Kiyoaki and Isao and Ying Chan had had to make do without them, and had been punished for their contempt and arrogance. They had been too proud even in their sufferings.

18

THE THREE TUTORS were all highly gifted students from Tokyo University. One taught sociology and literature, one mathematics and science, and one English. It was known that in 1971 the prep-school entrance examinations would have more essay questions and fewer short-answer questions, and that there would be more emphasis on English dictation and Japanese composition. Tōru was suddenly set to English newscasts. He took them on tape and repeated them over and over.

Here is a question on geography and the movements of the heavenly bodies:

In what position is Venus present longest for morning observation? Indicate on the chart. What is the shape of Venus when viewed in this position? Please indicate which of the following you believe to be the correct answer:
1. The east half is light.
2. The west half is light.
3. It is shining in a thin crescent, like the moon.
4. It is round.
What is the position of Mars when it is visible in the southern evening sky? Please indicate on the chart.

What is the position of Mars when it is visible in the southern midnight sky? Please indicate on the chart.

Tōru immediately circled "B" on the chart, and so answered the first question successfully. He chose the third possibility for the second question, circled "L" for the third question, and, finding spot "G" at which the sun, the earth, and Mars were in a line, circled it.

"Have you been asked this question before?"

"No."

"Then why were you so quick?"

"I see Venus and Mars every day."

Tōru answered quite as if he were a child describing the habits of his pets. As a matter of fact Venus and Mars were like the mice that occupied the signal station. He knew all about their feeding habits.

It was not, however, as if he felt nostalgic for nature or regretted the loss of his telescope. He did have a sense of that uncommonly simple work as his own, and the world beyond the horizon was a source of happiness for him; but he did not feel in the least deprived by the loss of them. It was his task, from now until he was twenty or so, to explore a cave with an old man.

Honda had taken pains to choose as tutors bright, companionable, talented young men of a sort Tōru might look to as models. He made a slight miscalculation in the case of Furusawa, Tōru's literature teacher. Much pleased with Tōru's disposition and intelligence, Furusawa would take him to nearby coffeehouses when they were tired of their lessons, and sometimes they would go on long walks together. Honda was grateful for these services and liked the cheerful Furusawa.

Furusawa did not at all mind saying unpleasant things about Honda. Tōru enjoyed them, though he was careful not to nod too quick an assent.

One day the two of them walked down Masago Rise past the ward office and turned left toward Suidōbashi. The street was torn up for a new subway line, and Kōrakuen Park was hidden behind construction towers. The twilight of late November came through the framework of a roller coaster as through an empty basket.

Passing trophy shops and sports shops and short-order resturants, they had came to the Kōrakuen gate. Two rows of lights over the red gate flashed from left to right: "We will no longer be open in the evening after November 23." So the shining nights would soon be over.

"How about it?" asked Furusawa. "How about a good shaking in a teacup?"

"Well." Tōru thought of himself in a dirty pink teacup, now rather lonely and short of customers among its blinking little lights. He thought of himself being so shaken and twisted by it that objects became streaks of light.

"Well, do you want to or don't you? You only have ninety-two days left till the examinations, but I'm sure you have nothing to worry about."

"I'd rather have a cup of coffee."

"Such dissipation."

Furusawa led the way down the steps of a coffee-house called the Renoir. It was across the street from the third-base side of the baseball stadium, which was like a huge trophy pouring forth darkness.

The Renoir was larger than Tōru would have expected from the outside. The tables were generously spaced around a fountain. The lights were soft and the carpet was beige. There were few other guests.

"I had no idea there was such a place so close to home."

"A cloistered maiden like you wouldn't."

Furusawa ordered two cups of coffee. He offered Tōru a cigarette, upon which Tōru leaped.

"It's not easy to keep it out of sight."

"Mr. Honda's much too strict. It's not as if you were an ordinary middle-school boy. You've been out in the world. He wants to make a child of you again.

But you just have to wait till you're twenty. You can spread your wings once you're in the university."

"Exactly my own idea. But I have to keep it to myself."

Furusawa frowned and laughed a pitying lough. It seemed to Tōru that he was trying to be older than twenty-one.

Furusawa wore glasses, but his good-natured face was very engaging when he smiled, and wrinkles formed around his nose. The horns were bent, and he was forever shoving the glasses back up on his nose, the gesture with his forefinger as if he were reprimanding himself. He had large hands and feet, and he was considerably taller than Tōru. He was the gifted son of a railway worker. Hidden in him was a spirit like a squirming red lobster.

Tōru had no urgent wish to destroy the image Furusawa had of him, as another son of the poor, holding onto the windfall that had come to him. Others, all of them, painted free pictures of him, but it was their freedom. What was most certainly his own was contempt.

"I don't really know what Mr. Honda is up to, but I should imagine he's making a guinea pig of you. But that's all right. He has a big fat estate, and you don't have to dirty your hands the way other people do clawing your way to the top of the garbage heap. But you do have to hang on to your self-respect. Even if it kills you."

"Yes," answered Tōru succinctly. He refrained from saying that he had a great deal of self-respect in reserve.

He was in the habit of tasting his answers. If they seemed sentimental he bit them back.

Honda was off at a dinner with some legal colleagues. Tōru would have something to eat with Furusawa before they went home. He was required, whatever else might happen, to have dinner with Honda at seven every evening when Honda was at home. Sometimes there were other guests. The evenings with Keiko were the greatest trial.

His eye was cool and clear when he had finished his coffee. But there was nothing to see. He looked at the half circle of coffee dregs. The bottom of the cup, round like the lens of a telescope, obstructed his view. The bottom of this world showed a clean white face of porcelain.

Turned half away, Furusawa suddenly spoke as if throwing the butt of his words into the ashtray. "Have you ever thought of suicide?"

"No." Tōru was startled.

"Don't look at me like that. I haven't thought of it all that seriously myself. I don't like the weak and the sick sort of people that commit suicide. But there is one variety I accept. People who commit suicide to establish themselves."

"What sort of suicide is that?"

"Are you interested?"

"A little, maybe."

"Then I'll tell you.

"Take a mouse that thinks it's a cat. I don't know how, but it does. It's gone through all the tests and concluded that it's a cat. Its view of other mice changes. They are its meat, that's all, but it tells itself it refrains from eating them just to hide the fact that it's a cat."

"A rather large mouse, I suppose."

"It doesn't matter. It's not a question of size but of confidence. It's sure that the concept 'cat' has taken on the guise 'mouse,' nothing more. It believes in the concept and not the flesh. The idea is enough, the body doesn't matter. The happiness from the contempt is all the greater.

"But then one day"——Furusawa shoved his glasses

up and drew a persuasive line beside his nose—"but then one day the mouse meets a real cat.

" 'I'm going to eat you,' says the cat.

" 'You can't,' replies the mouse.

" 'And why not?'

" 'Cats don't eat cats. It's impossible as a matter of instinct and as a matter of principle. I'm a cat myself, whatever else I may look like.'

"The cat rolls over laughing. It laughs so hard it's clawing the air and its white furry belly is heaving. Then it gets up and starts to eat the mouse. The mouse protests.

" 'What are you eating me for?'

" 'Because you're a mouse.'

" 'I'm a cat. Cats don't eat cats.'

" 'You're a mouse.'

" 'I'm a cat.'

" 'Prove it.'

"So the mouse jumps into the laundry tub, all white with suds, and drowns itself. The cat wets a forepaw and has a lick. The suds taste horrible. So it leaves the body floating there. We all know why the cat goes off without eating the mouse. Because it's not something for a cat to eat.

"That's what I'm talking about. The mouse commits suicide to establish itself. It doesn't of course make the cat recognize it as a cat, and it didn't think when it killed itself that it would. But it was brave and perceptive and filled with self-respect. It saw that there are two parts to mouseness. First is that it is a mouse in every physical detail. Second is that it is, for a cat, worth eating. Those two. It has long ago given up in the first matter, but in the second there is still hope. It dies in front of the cat without being eaten, and it establishes itself as something that cats don't eat. In those two respects it has proved it wasn't a mouse. That much. To prove besides that it was a cat is simple. If something that had the form of a mouse wasn't a mouse, then it can be anything else. And so the suicide is a success. The mouse has established itself. What do you think?"

Tōru was weighing the parable. He had no doubt that Furusawa had polished it by telling and retelling it to himself. He had long been aware of the disjuncture between Furusawa's genial appearance and his inner workings.

If only Furusawa himself was concerned, there was nothing to worry about; but if he had detected something in Tōru to make fun of, then Tōru must be careful. Tōru sent out a probing mental hand. It came upon nothing dangerous. Furusawa had sunk deeper and deeper into himself as he talked; he could not see out from so far below the surface.

"And did the mouse's death shock the world?" Furusawa was no longer paying attention to his audience. Tōru saw that he had only to listen as to a soliloquy. It was a voice of slow, moss-covered pain, such as he had not before heard from Furusawa. "Did the view the world had of the mouse change in any way? Did the true word spread that there existed something that had the form of a mouse but was not a mouse? Was there a crack in the confidence of the cats? Were the cats sufficiently concerned to obstruct the spread of the word?

"Do not be surprised. The cat did nothing at all. It had forgotten. It was washing its face and settling down for a nap. It was full of catness, and not even aware of that fact. And in the sluggishness of its nap it became with no effort at all what the mouse had so desperately wanted to become, something other than itself. It could become anything, through inaction, through self-satisfaction, through unconsciousness. The blue sky spread over the sleeping cat, beautiful clouds drifted by. The wind carried to the world the cat fragrance, the heavy snores were music."

"You're talking about authority now." Tōru felt compelled to put in a word of recognition.

Furusawa's face broke into a good-natured smile. "Yes. You're very quick."

Tōru was disappointed. It had ended up as the sad sort of political parable the young are so fond of.

"You'll understand some day yourself." Although there was no danger of being overheard, Furusawa lowered his voice and brought his face close to Tōru's. Tōru remembered the smell of his breath, forgotten for a time.

Why had he forgotten? He had smelled Furusawa's breath frequently enough in the course of their lessons. He had not been especially repelled by it; but now he was.

There had been no touch of malice in the story, and yet it had somehow angered Tōru. He did not choose to reprove Furusawa for it, however, and feared that to do so would be only to lower himself. He needed another reason, a quite adequate one, for disliking and even being angry at Furusawa. So the smell of his breath became unendurable.

Oblivious to what was happening, Furusawa went on: "You'll understand, one of these days. With deception as its starting point, authority can only sustain itself by spreading deception. It's like a germ culture. The more we resist, the greater are its powers of endurance and propagation. And before we know it we have the germs in ourselves."

They left the Renoir and had a bowl of noodles nearby. Tōru found it far more appetizing than a dinner with his father and all those dishes.

As he ate, eyes narrowed against the steam, Tōru was measuring the degree of danger in his relations with this student. He could not doubt that there was sympathy between them. But somehow the harmony was muted. It was possible that Furusawa had been hired by Honda to test Tōru. He knew that after one of these expeditions Furusawa presented a report on where they had been and a bill for his expenses. Honda had of course asked that he do so.

They passed the Kōrakuen again on their way back, and again Furusawa suggested a ride in the teacups. Tōru assented, knowing that Furusawa wanted a ride. The teacups were just inside the gate. No other customers appeared, and presently, with reluctance, the attendant turned on the switch for just the two of them.

Tōru got into a green cup, and Furusawa chose a pink cup a considerable distance off. They were decorated with a cheap flower design, reminiscent of teacups on special sale somewhere out in the suburbs, at the too brightly lighted front of a tableware shop.

The cup started moving. Furusawa was suddenly close, and then, shoving his glasses up on a smiling face, he darted off again. The cold Tōru had felt at the seat of his trousers became a cold blast. He turned up the speed. He liked to have it so fast that he could feel nothing and see nothing. The world became a gaseous Saturn.

When the cup had come to a stop, shaking gently from the inertia, like a floating buoy, Tōru stood up. Dizzy, he sat back down again.

"What's the trouble?" Furusawa came smiling toward him over a platform that still seemed to be moving.

Smiling back, Tōru remained seated. It displeased him to have the world, until now all a blur, importunately line up its sordid details, the peeling posters and the backs of Coca-Cola signs, like great red electric heaters.

19

"FURUSAWA TOOK ME to the Kōrakuen," said Tōru at breakfast the next morning. "We had a ride in the teacups, and then we had Chinese noodles for dinner."

"That's nice," said Honda, showing his false teeth. It should have been the bland, insubstantial old smile that went with false teeth; but Honda seemed to be genuinely pleased. Tōru was wounded.

Since he had come to Honda's, Tōru had known every morning the luxurious pleasure of scooping up the meat of an imported grapefruit, cut into sections by a thin curved knife. The rude abundance of juice, in the faintly bitter, glossy white meat of fruit ripe to bursting, sank into his lazy morning gums with its warmth.

"Furusawa has bad breath. I can hardly stand it when we're studying together." Tōru smiled an equivocal smile.

"I wonder why. Do you suppose he has stomach trouble? But you're too fussy. You can put up with that much. You're not likely to find a more able tutor."

"I suppose not." Retreating a step, Tōru finished his grapefruit. A carefully scrutinized piece of toast gave off in the November morning light a glow as of well-tanned leather. Tōru watched the butter melt into it, and then took a bite, careful to follow the instructions he had had from Honda.

"Yes, Furusawa is a good man," he said after the first bite. "But have you looked into his ideas?"

It pleased him to see confusion of the most vulgar sort come out on Honda's face.

"Has he said something to you?"

"Nothing specific. But I can't get over feeling that he either has been or still is involved in some political movement."

Honda was startled. He trusted Furusawa, and was sure that Tōru liked him. From Honda's point of view, Tōru's warning was based on confidence and understanding; but from Furusawa's it was clearly the report of a secret informant. It amused Tōru to observe how Honda would dispose of this delicate ethical problem.

Honda saw that he was not to pass the light judgment he usually passed upon good and evil. Judged against a broader humanity of which Honda was fond of thinking, Tōru's behavior was ugly; but judged against the image Honda had for Tōru himself, it passed muster. Honda was at the point of confessing that what he looked for in Tōru was ugliness.

To put Honda at his ease and offer occasion for mild reproof, Tōru tore off a childish mouthful of toast, spreading crumbs liberally on his knee. Honda took no notice.

It would not do to reprove Tōru for the element of meanness in this first mark of trust he had vouchsafed. On the other hand Honda's old sense of ethics demanded that he inform Tōru of the impropriety of turning informant, whatever the reason; and so something rather petty was by way of coming into this happy breakfast scene.

Their hands bumped awkwardly as they both reached for the sugar bowl.

A sugar bowl bright with betrayal in the morning sunlight. Feelings of guilt for having reached out simultaneously. It wounded Honda to think that this had been the first suggestion of a parental bond.

Tōru was pleased at more than this open confusion. He could see the hesitation as Honda found himself unable to preach the obvious lesson: that one must show more confidence in and respect for a person whom one has even tentatively called teacher. For the first time the controversy within Honda and the evil hidden in his educational policies became clear. Tōru felt like a liberated child spitting out a watermelon seed.

"Well, leave it to me. You just go on doing as you've always done. Don't worry yourself over anything but your studies. Leave everything else to me. The first thing is to get you through your examinations."

"How right you are." Tōru smiled a beautiful smile.

Honda deliberated for a day. The next day he asked an acquaintance in the Public Security Division of the Metropolitan Police to investigate. A report came some days later. Furusawa had been a member of an extremist student faction. Honda invented a trivial pretext for dismissing him.

20

Tōru occasionally wrote to Kinué, and got long answers. He had to be careful when he opened them, because each one contained a pressed flower for the season. Sometimes she would apologize for having sent a hothouse flower, there being no wildflowers in bloom.

Wrapped in paper, the flower would be like a dead

butterfly. There was pollen for wing dust, letting one imagine that when it lived it had flown. Dead wings and dead petals are the same. The remembrance of color that has flown through the sky, and the remembrance of color in stillness and resignation.

Only after reading the letter did he recognize one fragment, dry and brown like the skin of an Indian, strong red threads torn and jagged from having been pressed flat, as the petal of a red hothouse tulip.

The letters were the endless confession she had brought to the signal station. And she always offered in much detail a description of her loneliness for Tōru and her wish to come to Tokyo. He always replied that she must be patient, however many years passed. He would find an occasion to summon her.

Sometimes he almost thought, after having been away from her for so long, that she was beautiful. And immediately he would laugh. Yet he was coming to see what the mad girl had meant to him.

He needed lunacy to dim his own clarity. He had to have someone beside him who would see as something quite different all the things he saw with such clarity, clouds or ships or the gloomy old hallway of the Honda house, or the schedule of all his lessons until examination day posted on the wall of his room.

Tōru sometimes longed for liberation. The direction was clear. It must be the direction of uncertainty, the realm behind the clearly defined world, a realm whose phenomena were flowing over a waterfall.

Kinué unconsciously played the role of the gentle guest who brought freedom into the cage.

Nor was that all.

She brought balm for certain itches within him. He itched to do injury. His heart was a sharp drill protruding from a sack, itching to cut someone. Having cut down Furusawa, it was looking for someone else. Its cleanness, free of the least speck of rust, must sooner or later turn savage. Tōru saw that he could do something other than observe. The awareness brought tension, and Kinué's letters brought rest from it. Because of her madness she was beyond his harming.

The strongest bond between them was his certainty that he could not himself be wounded.

A successor to Furusawa was found, a student of the most ordinary common-sense sort. Tōru hoped that within the next two months he could get rid of the other tutors as well, for he did not want to seem in their debt when he had passed his examinations.

But caution held him back. Honda would begin to have certain suspicions were Tōru to waste his energies on such minor personages. He could come to discount Tōru's complaints, and, accepting the faults complained of, find fault in the complaints themselves. And the secret pleasure would disappear. Tōru concluded that he must be patient. He must wait until someone far more worth wounding appeared. Whoever it was would provide a way, albeit an indirect one, of wounding Honda himself. A way that left no room for resentment. A clean, unsullied way of Tōru's very own, leaving Honda with no one but himself to blame.

And who would come into his life, like a ship on the far horizon? As the ships had first taken firm shape in Tōru's mind, so would his victim appear one day, a shadow neither ship nor mirage, unsuspecting and vulnerable, following the dictates of the drill in his heart. Tōru came almost to have hopes.

21

Tōru ENTERED the preparatory school of his choice.

In his second year there came a proposal, through a suitable mediator. A certain person had a marriageable daughter he thought Tōru might be interested in. Tōru had reached the legal age of consent, but he was still only eighteen. Honda laughed the proposal off. The other person was persistent, however, and the proposal came through another mediator. Since the second man was an eminence in the legal world, Honda could not turn him away unconditionally.

Honda longed for something: a young bride who would be twisted with grief at the loss of her twenty-year-old husband. She would wear the pale, beautiful hues of tragedy; and so, at no expense, Honda would have another meeting with a pure crystallization of beauty.

The dream was rather out of accord with his educational policies. Yet if there had been no margin at all for the dream, and if there had been no sense of crisis, Honda would scarcely have bothered with policies calculated to give Tōru a long and beautyless life. What Honda feared was what Honda hoped for, what Honda hoped for was what Honda feared.

The proposal was repeated at appropriate intervals, like water dripping through a floor. It amused Honda to be visited by this eminence and to hear his desperate plea. He thought it too early to tell Tōru.

Honda was fascinated with the photograph the old

man brought. The girl was eighteen and a beauty, with a thin delicate face that had in it nothing of the bright and modern. There was beauty in the faint air of bewildered resentment with which she faced the photographer.

"Yes, she is very beautiful. And is she strong physically?" asked Honda, the intent of his question quite the opposite of what his friend must have supposed it to be.

"I can assure you that I know her very well. She is much stronger than this picture would lead you to believe. She has had no serious illnesses. Health is of course the most important thing. It was her father who chose the picture, and I think he chose a rather old-fashioned one."

"She is of a cheerful disposition, then?"

"Not, I fear, if that expression contains a suggestion of frivolity."

It was an equivocal response. Honda wanted to meet the girl.

•　　•　　•

It was clear that the proposal had taken Honda's wealth into account. Only that could explain the eagerness for an eighteen-year-old bridegroom, however talented he might be. The tempting object must be snatched up before someone else saw its possibilities.

Honda was perfectly aware of all this. And if he were to accept the proposal, the obvious reason would be to control the urges of a difficult eighteen-year-old. But Tōru here before him seemed quite under control already. So the interests of the two parties were more and more divergent, and Honda saw no reason at all to pursue the talks. He felt a certain curiosity about the contrast between the parents and the beautiful candidate herself. He wanted to see greedy self-respect give way. The family that made the proposal was of much prominence, but such considerations no longer troubled Honda.

A dinner party was proposed at which Tōru and the girl would be present. Honda declined. Instead he and the person who had brought the proposal had dinner with the girl's family.

For two or three weeks the seventy-eight-year-old Honda was in the grip of temptation. He had seen the girl at dinner, and they had exchanged brief remarks. He had received several more photographs. Hence the temptation.

He had not given a favorable answer, nor had he reached a decision; but his aging heart was the victim of impulses which his reason could not control. The willfulness of old age gave him the itch. He longed to show the pictures to Tōru and see his response.

Honda did not himself know what had possessed him, but happiness and pride were at work in the temptation. He knew that if in fact he were to inform Tōru of the proposal he would have passed the point of no return. But willfulness did not see reason.

He longed to see all the results of the match, of bumping the two of them together, a white billiard ball and a crimson. It would be good if Tōru was fond of the girl and it would be good if she was fond of him. She would mourn him when he died, he would be aroused by her greed and come to see humanity for what it was. Either would for Honda be a pleasing result. A sort of festival.

Honda was much too old to have solemn thoughts about the nature of human life. He was at an age when he could justify malicious games. Whatever the malice, death was near, to make amends. He was at an age when youth was a plaything, humanity a collection of clay dolls, an age when, putting ceremony to his own uses, he could turn honesty and sincerity into the play of the evening sky.

When others were as nothing, surrender to such temptations became a kind of destiny.

Late one evening Honda called Tōru into his study. Mildewed by the summer rains, it was the English-style study he had inherited from his father. Honda disliked air-conditioning, and there was a faint glow of sweat on Tōru's white chest. It seemed to Honda that a doomed white hydrangea was in bloom before him.

"It will soon be summer vacation."

"But exams come first." Tōru bit at the chocolate mint Honda had offered.

"You eat like a squirrel." Honda smiled.

"Oh?" Tōru too smiled, the smile of one whom it is not possible to injure.

Looking at the pale face, Honda thought that this summer the sun must burn it to a crisp. It was a face that did not seem in danger of pimples. With a studied casualness, he opened a drawer and laid a photograph on the table before Tōru.

Tōru was rather splendid. Honda missed no detail. Tōru first examined it with the solemn attention of a guard examining a pass. His questioning eyes looked up at Honda and back again at the picture. Then came boyish curiosity, and he flushed to the ears. Putting the photograph back on the table, he plunged a rough finger into an ear.

"She is very beautiful," he said, a touch of anger in his voice.

Very, very splendid, thought Honda. There was something poetic in the youthfulness of the response (and it had been in a moment of crisis). Honda forgot that Tōru had responded as he had wanted him to respond.

It was a complex amalgam, as if Honda's self-awareness had itself for an instant played a boyish role, hiding confusion with a touch of roughness.

"Would you like to meet her?" Honda asked quietly.

He coughed somewhat nervously, hoping that the next response would be as appropriate. Tōru sprang lightly to his feet and went over to beat on Honda's back.

"Yes."

The word was almost a growl. Taking advantage of the fact that his father could not see, his eyes were aglow as he said to himself: "The wait has been worth it. Here is someone worth injuring."

Yet farther on, beyond the window, it was raining. A sad, lonely rain, like a black liquid, giving the bark of the trees a steamy glow in the light from the window. At night the subway trains, here running on elevated tracks, shook the ground. The bright lights in the windows as the train plunged underground again brought a vision to Tōru, still beating on his father's back. There was no sign tonight of a ship.

22

SUPPOSE YOU keep company with her for a while. If you don't like her you just have to say so. There is no commitment."

Tōru went to dinner one night when summer vacation had begun. After dinner, upon a suggestion from her mother that it might be nice to show him her room, Momoko Hamanaka led him upstairs. It was a large

Western room, girlish from corner to corner, Tōru's
first experience of the utterly girlish. It was luxuriantly
pink. There was girlishness in every detail of the wall-
paper, the dolls, the accessories. They quite breathed a
beguiling young charm. Tōru took a seat in an arm-
chair. The thick multicolored cushion made sitting
difficult.

Momoko had a mature look, and yet there could be
no doubt that all these details were of her own choos-
ing. The cool pallor, somewhat blanched, was in
keeping with old-fashioned features not too deeply
carved. The solitary earnestness made her the only
object at odds with the beguiling charm. Her beauty
was too formally perfect; and as in the formal perfection of a paper crane it had in it something ominous.

Her mother brought tea and withdrew. The two had
met several times before, but for the first time they
were alone. That fact did not produce new tensions.
Momoko was safe in the knowledge of having obeyed
instructions. He must awaken her to danger, thought
Tōru.

He had been put off by all the solemn attentions
during dinner. But his annoyance was about to leave.
A match was being made. Delicate love was being
picked up in pincers, tinted. The bonbon had already
been put in the oven. To Tōru it made no difference
whether he had gone in of his own accord or been put
in. He had no reason to be dissatisfied with himself.

The first thing Momoko did when they were alone
was to choose an album from four or five numbered
ones and offer it to Tōru. Thus he was made aware
of her essential mediocrity. He opened it on his knees,
and he saw an infant in a bib, its legs spread wide.
Pants all swollen with diapers, like a Flemish knight's.
The dark pink of a mouth not yet filled out with teeth.
Tōru asked who the infant might be.

Momoko's consternation was rather wondrous. She

glanced at the album and put a hand over the picture and snatched the album from him. Clutching it to her breast, she turned to the wall. Her breathing was heavy.

"How perfectly dreadful. The numbers were wrong. I didn't mean for you to see this one. Whatever will I do?"

"Is it such a secret that you were once a baby?"

"Aren't you cool. Like a doctor."

Calm again herself, Momoko replaced the album. Tōru was sure, from his misstep, that in the next album he would see Momko at seventeen.

But the next album was most ordinary, pictures from a recent trip. Each picture showed how popular Momoko was. It was a record of tedious happiness. Far more than to pictures of a recent trip to Hawaii, Tōru was drawn to Momoko in the garden beside a bonfire, one evening the previous fall. The bonfire was a rich, sensuous vermilion. Crouched beside it, Momoko had the grandeur of a witch.

"Are you fond of fires?" he asked.

He caught hesitation in her eyes. He had a strange confidence that she had been menstruating as she sat looking into the fire. And now?

How pure abstract malice would have been if it had been free from sexual attraction! He saw that this new challenge would not be as easy as dismissing his tutor had been. But he had confidence in his coldness, however much he might be loved. It lay in the indigo realm within him.

23

RELUCTANT TO LEAVE Tōru by himself, Honda took
him to Hokkaido that sumer. Their schedule was an
easy one. They did not want to tax themselves. Keiko,
for whom it had become difficult to travel with Honda,
went off by herself to Geneva, the Japanese ambassador
to Switzerland being a relative. The Hamanakas wanted
to have two or three days with the Hondas, and so
the two families took rooms in Shimoda. Overwhelmed
by the summer heat, Honda rarely left his air-con-
ditioned room.

It was agreed that they would have dinner together
each night. The Hamanakas came for Honda. Where
was Momoko, they asked. She had come a little earlier,
said Honda, and was out in the garden with Tōru.
And so the Hamanakas sat down and waited for the
young couple to return.

Honda was standing by the window, a cane in his
hand.

It was all very stupid. He was not hungry, and the
menu was an impoverished one. He knew without
going to the dining room that vulgar family merriment
awaited him. And Hamanaka table conversation was
tedium itself.

The old had politics forced upon them. Even though
he ached in all his joints, a man of seventy-eight could
hide his want of interest only under a show of wit and
good humor. A want of interest was important all the
same. It was the only way to win out over the idiocy

of the world. The unconcern of a beach receiving each day the waves and the driftwood.

Honda had thought that, purse-lipped and surrounded by lackeys, he had yet a little life in him, a little sharpness with which to hinder the purse-lipped days and the lackeys; but it had deserted him. All he really had was an overwhelming sense of folly, and of a vulgarity that melted into a monotone. How myriad were the manifestations of the vulgar. The vulgarity of elegance, the vulgarity of ivory, the vulgarity of holiness, the vulgarity of the craze, erudite vulgarity, the vulgarity of the academic pretender, coquettish vulgarity, the vulgarity of the Persian cat, the vulgarity of monarchs and beggars, of lunatics, of butterflies, of blister beetles. Reincarnation was retribution for vulgarity. And the chief and indeed the only source of it all was the wish for life. Honda himself was without doubt a part of it. What distinguished him was his uncommonly keen sense of smell.

He glanced sideways at the aging couple before him. Why had the two of them come into his life? The superfluity of their presence ran against his sense of order. But there was no help for it now. There they were, smiling on his sofa, as if prepared to wait a decade or so.

Shigehisa Hamanaka, aged fifty-five, was the former chief of a feudal clan in the northeast. He sought to cover the now-empty pride of family in Bohemianism, and had even written a book of essays, *The Chief*, which had been a modest success. He was the president of a bank, the head office of which was in his old fief, and he had made a name in the pleasure quarters as an old-style man of taste. There was still a full, rich head of black hair over the gold-rimmed glasses and the almond-shaped face, but the stronger impression was of vapidity. A confident raconteur, he always allowed an appropriate pause before a witty conclusion.

A clever talker who made a great point of skipping the preliminaries, a person of gentle irony who never forgot his respect for the aged, he would not have dreamed he was a bore.

His wife Taeko too came from the military aristocracy. She was a fat, rough-featured person, and fortunately the daughter looked like the father. All Taeko could talk about was family. She had seen neither movies nor plays. She passed her life before a television set. They were very proud of the fact that their other three children were married and on their own, and only Momoko remained.

Old-fashioned elegance had thus become shallowness. It was more than Honda could bear to hear Shigehisa talk permissively of the sex revolution, and to hear Taeko's shocked responses. Shigehisa used his wife's old-fashioned responses as part of his act.

Honda wondered why he could not be more tolerant. He knew, as it became more and more of a burden to make new acquaintances, how difficult it was to muster a smile. Contempt was of course the emotion that came first, but even that was rather a lot of trouble these days. He thought how much easier it would be to respond with spittle than with words, even as the words came to his lips, but words were the task that remained. With them an old man could twist the world as he might squash a willow lattice.

"How young you look standing there," said Taeko. "Like a soldier."

"A very inappropriate simile, my dear. You must not liken a judge to a soldier. I have never forgotten an animal trainer I once saw in a circus in Germany. That is what Mr. Honda is like."

"A far more inappropriate simile, I should think, my dear." Taeko was dreadfully amused.

"I am not striking a pose, you must believe me. I

142

am standing here so that I can see the sunset and the young people in the garden."

"You can see them?"

Taeko came and stood beside Honda, and Shigehisa too, with dignity, left his chair.

The garden was spread below the third-floor window. It was circular, bordered by a walk that led down to the sea, and there were two or three benches among the shrubs. A few family groups were returning, towels over shoulders, from the pool a level below. They cast long evening shadows over the lawn.

Momoko and Tōru were walking hand in hand halfway along the circle. Their shadows stretched far out to the east. It was as if two great sharks were biting their feet.

Tōru's shirt was full in the evening breeze, and Momoko's hair was blowing. They were a most ordinary boy and girl; but to Honda they were as insubstantial as gossamer mosquito nets. The shadows were the substance. They had been eaten away by the shadows, by the deep melancholy of a concept. That was not life, thought Honda. It was something less easy to excuse. And the terrible fact was that Tōru probably knew.

If the shadow was the substance, then the all too transparent something clinging to it must be wings. Fly! Fly over the vulgarity! The limbs and the heads were a superfluity, too concrete. If the contempt in him was only a little stronger, Tōru could fly off, the girl's hand in his; but Honda had forbidden it. Honda longed with all the powers of his senile impotence to put his envy to work and give the two of them wings; but not even envy burned very hot in him any more. Only now did he see it for what it was, the most fundamental emotion he had felt toward Kiyoaki and Isao, the source of all lyricism in intellectual man, envy.

Very well, then. Suppose he were to think of Tōru

and Momoko as the basest, the least tempting morsels of youth. They would act, fall into each other's arms, like a pair of puppets. He only had to move a finger. He moved two or three of the fingers on his stick. The pair on the lawn walked toward the cliff path.

"Just look at them, would you. Here we are waiting, and it seems they mean to go farther away."

Taeko stood with her hand on her husband's elbow. There was a touch of excitement in her voice.

Facing the sea, the young couple went through the shrubbery and sat down on one of the rough wooden benches. Honda could see from the angle of the heads that they were looking at the sunset. A lump of black came out from under the bench. Honda could not make out whether it was a cat or a dog. Momoko stood up in surprise. Tōru, standing up beside her, took her in his arms.

"Well, now." The voices of her parents, watching through the window, floated up gently as dandelion floss.

Honda was not watching. The cognizant one was not watching through his peephole. There at the bright window, he was half enacting in his heart the movements his awareness had ordered, directing them with the strength of all his faculties.

"You are young, and you must give evidence of a far stupider vitality. Shall I put thunder into you? A sudden flash of lightning? Shall we have some queer sort of electric phenomenon: perhaps send flames darting from Momoko's hair?"

A tree stretched its branches spider-like toward the sea. They started to climb it. Honda could feel the tension in the pair beside him.

"I shouldn't have let her wear pants." Taeko seemed on the edge of tears. "The little hussy."

They entwined their legs around the branches and swung up and down. Leaves scattered toward the ground. One tree among the others seemed to have gone mad. The two were like a pair of great birds against the evening sky.

Momoko jumped from the tree first. But she did not jump boldly enough, and her hair was entangled in one of the lower branches. Tōru followed her and sought to disentangle it.

"They're in love," Taeko, in tears, nodded again and again.

But Tōru was taking too long. Honda knew immediately that he was deliberately entangling the hair more tightly. The delicately overdone efforts brought a twinge of fear. Secure in these ministrations, Momoko sought to pull away from the branch. The pain was sharp. Pretending to make matters unintentionally worse the more he tried, Tōru mounted the low branch like a jockey. Momoko pulled at the long rope of hair, her back to him. She was weeping, and her hands were at her face.

From the third-floor window, across the wide garden, it was like a scene in wax, a quiet little pantomime. The grandeur was in the evening light, an avalanche falling off to the sea, in the high glow of the light glancing off toward the sea from the clouds, relics of sun showers through the afternoon. Because of the light, the trees and the islands in the bay, closer and closer, spread color on hard, thin lines. The clarity was terrible.

"They're in love," said Taeko once more.

A bright rainbow arched over the sea, like an outcropping of the sunlight in Honda's heart at the idiocy of it all.

24

EXCERPTS from Tōru Honda's diary.

I cannot excuse the several mistakes I am making in
the matter of Momoko. That is because one must
proceed from clarity, and the smallest element of
miscalculation produces fantasy, and fantasy produces
beauty.

I have never been a sufficiently ardent devotee of
beauty to believe that beauty produces fantasy and
fantasy miscalculation. When I was still new at the
signal station, I sometimes misidentified a ship.
Especially at night, when it is difficult to calculate
the distance betwen mast lights, I would sometimes
take a puny little fishing boat for an international
freighter, and send out a signal asking it to identify
itself. Unaccustomed to such formal treatment, the
fishing boat would sometimes flash back the name of
a movie star. It was not however a thing of great
beauty.

Momoko's beauty of course meets all the ob-
jective standards. Her love is necessary for me, and
I must give her the blade with which to cut herself.
A paper knife will not suffice.

I know well enough that the more firmly insistent
demands come not from reason or will but from
sexual desire. The detailed demands of sex are sometimes mistakenly thought logical. I think that, lest
I confuse the two, I must have another woman for

sex. That is because the most subtle and delicate wishes of evil are not for a physical wound but for a spiritual. I know well enough the nature of evil within me. It is in the insistent demands of awareness itself, awareness transformed into desire. Or to put the matter differently, it has been clarity in its most perfect form acting out its part in the darkest depths.

I sometimes think it would be better if I were dead. For my plans can be realized on the far side of death. For there I can find true perspective. To do it while still alive is more difficult than the difficult. Especially when you are only eighteen!

I find it very hard to understand the Hamanakas. There can be no doubt that they want us to be engaged for five or six years, and that they will presently exercise their option and bring the two of us together, fully recognized members of society, in high matrimony. But what guarantee have they? Should they have such confidence in their daughter's beauty? Or is it that they put high hopes on payments for breach of promise?

No, I doubt that they have made any real calculations at all. They take the crudest, most common-sense view of relations between man and woman. To judge from their gasps of admiration when they heard my I.Q., I should imagine that all their energies go into the study of talent, and especially talent with money.

Momoko telephoned from Karuizawa the day I got back from Hokkaido. She wanted to see me and so I must come to Karuizawa. I have no doubt that her parents were behind it. There was just a touch of artificiality in her voice, and so I made bold to be cruel. I replied that since I was deep in studies for my university entrance examinations I was unable to accept her kind invitation. And when I hung up I felt a quite unexpected twinge of sadness. Denial is itself a sort of concession, and it is natural that the concession should bring a shadow of sadness over one's self-respect. I am not afraid of it.

Summer is almost over. I am very much aware of its passage. As strongly as words can express. There were mackerel clouds and cumulus clouds in the sky today, and a faint touch of sharpness in the air.

Love should follow along, but my emotions must not follow anything.

The little present Momoko gave me in Shimoda is here on my desk. It is a framed bit of white coral. On the back, in two pierced hearts, it carries the inscription: "From Momoko to Tōru." I do not understand how she can go on being prey to these childish tastes. The case is filled with little bits of tinfoil that float up like the white sands of the sea when you shake it, and the glass is half frosted with indigo. The Suruga Bay I have known is compressed into a frame five inches square, it has become a lyrical miniature forced on me by a girl. But small though it is, the coral has its own grand, cold cruelty, my inviolable awareness at the heart of her lyric.

Whence come the difficulties in my being? Or to put it another way, the ominous smoothness and facileness of my being.

I sometimes think that the ease of it all comes from the fact that my being is a logical impossibility.

It is not that I am asking any difficult questions of my being. I live and move without motive power, but that is as much an impossibility as perpetual motion. Nor is it my destiny. How can the impossible be destiny?

From the moment I was born on this earth, it

would seem, my being knew that it flew in the face of reason. I was not born with any defect. I was born like an impossibly perfect human being, a perfect film negative. But this world is full of imperfect positives. It would be a terrible thing for them to develop me, change me into a positive. That is why they are so afraid of me.

The source of greatest amusement to me has been the solemn injunction that I be faithful to myself. It is an impossibility. Had I sought to follow it I would immediately have been dead. It could only have meant forcing the absurdity of my existence into unity.

There would have been ways if I had not had self-respect. It would have been easy, without self-respect, to make others and myself as well accept all manner of distorted images. But is it so very human to be hopelessly monstrous? Though of course the world feels secure when the monstrous is reality.

I am very cautious, but I am greatly wanting in the instinct for self-preservation. And I am so brightly wanting in it that the breeze through the gap sometimes makes me drunk. Since danger is the ordinary, there is no crisis. It is very well to have a sense of balance, since I cannot live without a miraculous sort of balance; but suddenly it becomes a hot dream of imbalance and collapse. The greater the discipline the greater the tendency toward violence, and I grow weary of pressing the control button. I must not believe in my own docility. No one can know what a sacrfice it is for me to be gentle and docile.

But my life has been only duty. I have been like an awkward novice sailor. Only in seasickness and nausea have I escaped from duty. The nausea corresponded to what the world calls love.

For some reason, Momoko is reluctant to come home

149

with me. We talk for an hour or so after school at the Renoir. Sometimes we have our innocent fun in the park, riding the roller coaster. The Hamanakas do not worry a great deal about having their daughter come home late if it is not after dark. Though I sometimes take her to a movie, of course, I must let them know in advance that we are going to be later. There is not much pleasure in these public dates, and so we also have our assignations, brief ones.

Momoko came to the Renoir again today. She may seem old-fashioned, but she is just like any other girl in the unpleasant things she has to say about her teachers, in gossip about her friends, in talk, all contemptuously masked with indifference, of the scandalous behavior of movie stars. I humor her a little, showing a manly tolerance.

I lack the courage to write further, for my reservations on the surface seem no different from the unconscious reservations of all other teen-agers. Whatever my perversity, Momoko does not feel it as such. So I let my feelings have their way. Unintentionally, I become sincere and honest. If I really were, then the ethical contradictions in my being should be exposed like mud banks at low tide; but the troublesome ones are the banks not yet exposed. As the waters recede they pass a point at which my frustrations are no different from the frustrations of any other young person, the sadness that furrows my brow draws a line no different from that on the brow of any other. It would not do for Momoko to catch me there.

I have been wrong in thinking that women are tormented by doubts as to whether they are loved. I have wished to plunge Momoko into doubt, but the swift little beast has eluded capture. It would do no good to tell her I do not love her. She would think I was lying. My only recourse is to bide my time and make her jealous.

I sometimes ask myself if I was not somehow changed by the dissipation of my sensibilities in welcoming all those ships. There had to be some effect on me. Ships were born of my consciousness and grew into giants and had names. Only so far were they my concern. Once in port, they were of a different world. I was too busy receiving other ships. I did not have the art to become alternately ship and harbor. That is what women demand. The concept of woman, become sensible reality, would in the end refuse to leave port.

I have known secret pride and pleasure in seeing the concept on the horizon gradually take shape. I have put my hand in from outside the world and created something, and I have not tasted the sensation of being brought into the world. I have not felt myself brought in like laundry brought in before a shower. No rain has fallen to give me existence within the world. On the verge of intellectual drowning, my clarity has been confident of proper sensual rescue. For the ship has always passed. It has never stopped. The sea winds have turned everything to spotted marble, the sun has turned the heart into crystal.

I have been self-reliant to the point of sadness. I wonder when I first fell into the habit of washing my hands after each brush with humanity, lest I be contaminated. People have diagnosed the habit as uncommon fastidiousness.

My misfortune has clearly had its origins in nonrecognition of nature. It is natural that I should not have recognized nature, for nature, containing all rules, should be an ally, and "my" nature has not been. I have accomplished the nonrecognition with gentleness. I have not been spoiled or pampered. Always feeling the shadow of persons clamorous to do me injury, I have been careful about expenditures of gentleness certain to do injury to others. One may see in the care a very human sort of solicitude. But mixed in with the very word "solicitude" are unpleasant shreds of weariness.

I have thought that, in comparison with the nature of my own being, the affairs of the world, delicate and complicated international problems and the like, have not been problems at all. Politics and art and ideology have been so many watermelon rinds. Only watermelon rinds left on the seashore, mostly white but tinged with the faint pink of sunrise. For though I have hated the vulgar, I have recognized in them the possibility of eternal life.

Incomprehension and error have seemed preferable to a relentless probing of my depths. This last means indescribable rudeness and discourtesy, not possible without the nastiest hostility. When did a ship ever understand me? It was enough for me to understand. Spiritlessly, punctiliously, it gave me its name and without another word slipped into harbor. It has been fortunate for the ships that not one of them was aware of the situation. Had any one of them shown the slightest misgivings, in that instant it would have been wiped out by my consciousness.

I have put together a delicate machine for feeling how it would be if I were to feel like a human being. The naturalized Englishman is more English than the native Englishman, they say; and I have become more of an expert on humanity than a human being. More, in any case, than an eighteen-year-old. Imagination and logic are my weapons, more precise than nature or instinct or experience, quite waterproof in awareness of and accommodation to probability. I have become a specialist in humanity, as an entomologist might become a specialist in South American beetles. With odorless flowers I have explored the ways in which human beings are captured by the odor of certain flowers, caught up in certain feelings.

So it is to see. I have seen from the signal station how an international freighter sets its sights from a certain distance out at sea, and makes toward shore at twelve and a half knots with the most urgent dreams of home. That was mere probing, my eye was really turned on an invisible realm far beyond the horizon. What is it to see the invisible? That is the ultimate vision, the denial at the end of all seeing, the eye's denial of itself.

But sometimes I fear that all these thoughts and all these plans of mine begin in me and end in me. It was so, in any event, at the signal station. All the images flung into that little room like fragments of glass cast their light upon the walls and ceiling and left no trace behind. Is it not the same with other worlds too?

I must be my own support and go on living. Because I am always floating in air, resisting gravity, on the borders of the impossible.

Yesterday in school one of our more ostentatiously erudite teachers taught us a fragment of a Grecian lyric:

> Those born with the bounty of the gods
> Have the duty to die beautiful,
> Not dissipating the bounty.

For me, for whom the whole of life is a duty, this particular duty does not exist. Because I have no knowledge of having received a bounty.

Smiling has become a heavy burden, and so I have taken it upon myself to be out of sorts with Momoko for a time. I leave room for the perfectly ordinary view, even while offering a glimpse of the monster, that I am a sulky, frustrated boy. And because it is an unrelieved piece of acting, because it is altogether too stupid, I too must have a measure of passion. I have looked for a reason. I have found the most plausible one. It is the love born in me.

I almost burst out laughing. For I had become aware of the significance of lovelessness as a self-evident premise. It is in the freedom to love indiscriminately at any time. Like a truck driver napping in the summer shade, certain that the moment he awakens he can drive off again. If freedom is not the essence of love but its enemy, then I have friend and enemy in hand at once.

My sulkiness seems to have been convincing. That is most natural, for it is the form taken by love that is free, asking while denying.

Momoko promptly lost her appetite. She looked at me with a worried face, as she might look at a pet bird. She had the vulgar notion that happiness is to be apportioned to all, like a big loaf of French bread. She did not understand the mathematical principle that happiness for one must be unhappiness for another.

"Has something happened?" It was an inappropriate question coming from those elegant lips, on that face shaded over with quiet tragedy.

I laughed vacantly and did not answer.

It was the only time she asked the question. She was soon lost in her own talk. It was the part of the faithful listener to be silent.

She noticed the middle finger of my right hand, which I had injured on the buck in gymnastics class that day. I saw the relief on her face the moment she saw the bandage. She thought she had found the cause of my ill temper.

Apologizing for not having noticed earlier, she said with a great show of concern that it must hurt a great deal. I answered brusquely that it hurt scarcely at all.

As a matter of fact it did not. I was unable to excuse her for finding such a simple explanation. And it displeased me that, despite the fact that I had been at pains to hide the bandage from her, she had taken so long in finding it.

I turned off her symapthies with stronger and stronger assurance that it did not hurt in the least. With an expression on her face as of having seen through all the pretense and all the feigned bravery, she was more and more insistently sympathetic, having convinced herself that she must extract an admission from me.

She insisted upon going off to a drugstore immediately for a fresh bandage. The old one was already a dirty gray, and dangerous. The stronger my denials the greater her awareness of my powers of abnegation. Finally we went off together and had the bandage changed by a lady who was obviously a former nurse. Momoko looked aside in terror, and so I was able to hide the fact that the wound was only a scratch.

How was it now, she asked earnestly.

"The bone is showing."

"No! How horrible!"

"You needn't be alarmed," I said sullenly.

She was terrified at a casual hint that the finger might have to be amputated. The extravagant horror showed all too clearly her sensual egotism, but it did not displease me.

We talked as we walked along. As usual, the chief burden of conversation was hers. She was happy in the warmth, the brightness and the propriety of her home. It irritated me that she felt not the slightest doubt about her parents.

"I should imagine that your mother has spent quiet

nights with another man or two. She's lived a long time."

"Absolutely not."

"How do you know? There were things that happened before you were born. Ask your brothers."

"It isn't true."

"And I imagine your father has a pretty woman off somwhere."

"No, no. Absolutely not."

"What's your proof?"

"You're dreadful. No one has ever said such dreadful things to me before."

We were on the point of a quarrel, but I do not like quarrels. Sullen silence was called for.

We were on the sidewalk below the Kōrakuen pool. As always, it was teeming with people in search of inexpensive pleasure. Few of the young people could have been described as well dressed. They were in the ready-made shirts and machine sweaters of the fashionable provincial set. A child suddenly squatted in the middle of the street and began picking up beer caps. It was scolded by its mother.

"Must you be so nasty?" Momoko seemed near tears.

I was not being nasty. It was kindness on my part not to tolerate smugness. I sometimes think I am a fearfully moral beast.

We had turned as our stroll took us, and were at the gate to the Kōrakuen garden of the Mito Tokugawa family. "The gentleman troubles himself on the world's behalf; only then does he take his pleasure"—hence the name Kōrakuen, "Garden of After-Pleasure." Near though it is, I had not before visited it. The sign informed us that the garden closed at four thirty and that tickets were not sold after four. It was ten minutes till four. I urged Momoko inside.

The sun was directly ahead as we west through the gate. The insects of early October were singing.

We passed a party of perhaps twenty people on their way out. Otherwise the paths were empty. Momoko wanted to hold my hand, but I showed her the bandage.

Why, with precarious emotions, were we walking in the late afternoon like lovers, down the quiet path of the old garden? I had of course a picture of our unhappiness in my heart. A scene of beauty threatens the heart, gives it fever and chills. Had she been of sufficient sensibility, I would have liked to hear her rambling on in a delirium. I would have liked to see her lips parched with the horror of having met the unfathomable.

Seeking complete solitude, I walked down past the Waterfall of Awakening. It was dry and the pool was cloudy. The network on its surface like a mesh of threads was from water striders. Seated on a rock we gazed down into the pond.

I could see that she at length found my silence threatening. I was confident that she did not know its source. I had introduced an emotion experimentally, and was fascinated to see it producing agnosticism in another. Without emotion we can link together in any number of ways.

The surface of the pond—rather the swamp— was screened off by leaves and branches, but here and there it caught the rays of the western sun. The inappropriate light set off the accumulation of leaves on the shallow bottom like an unpleasant dream.

"Look at it. If you were to turn a light on them, our hearts would be just as shallow and dirty."

"Not mine. Mine is deep and clean. I'd like to show it to you."

"How can you say you're an exception? Give me your proof."

— An exception myself, I was irritated at another's claim to be an exception. I did not see in any case how mediocrity could claim to be an exception.

"I just know it, that's all."

I could sense well enough the inferno into which she had fallen. She had not once felt the need to prove herself. Soaked in a bliss that dripped sadness, she had dissolved everything from the girlish gewgaws to love itself in the obscure liquid. She was up to the neck in the bathtub of herself. It was a dangerous position, but she was not prepared to ask for help, and indeed refused the helping hand. To wound her, it was necessary to drag her out of it. Otherwise the blade would fall short, deflected by the liquid.

There were autumn cicadas in the evening groves, and the roar of the subway came through the calls of the birds. A yellow leaf dangled from a spider web on a branch far out over the swamp, catching a divine light each time it revolved. It was as if a tiny revolving door were floating in the heavens.

We gazed at it in silence. I was asking what world would be opening beyond the dark gold each time it turned. Perhaps, as it revolved in the busy wind, it would give me a glimpse of the bustle in some miniature street beyond, shining through some tiny city in the air.

The rock was cold. We had to hurry. There was only a half hour till closing time.

It was a walk as irritating as a hangnail. The quiet beauty of the garden was caught up in the restlessness of sunset. The waterfowl on the pond were astir, the pink of the bush clover beside the wasted iris had faded.

THE DECAY OF THE ANGEL

The closing hour was our pretext for hurrying, but it was not our only reason. We were afraid of the mood of the autumn garden, sinking into our hearts; and we wanted the swiftness of our pace to turn up voices inside us more shrilly, like a record that is revolving too fast.

We stood on a bridge along the circular path. There was no one else in sight. Our shadows stretched out over the moving carp, with the shadow of the bridge. We turned our backs to the pond, out of distaste for the huge patent-medicine sign beyond. We were facing a little round artificial hillock tangled with dwarf bamboo, and the net flung by the setting sun upon the groves beyond. I felt like the last fish resisting the violent light and refusing to be caught in the net.

Perhaps I was dreaming of another world. I felt as if a moment containing death had brushed past the two of us, high-school students in pale sweaters on a bridge. The sexual fullness of love suicide crossed my heart. I am not one to call for help, but if help were to come, I thought, it would come only with the end of consciousness. There would be joy in the rotting of consciousness there in the evening light.

The little pond to the west was choked with lotuses.

Like jellyfish in the evening breeze, the lotus pads blocked off the water. Covered with a powder, the green leathery pads buried the valley below the hillock. They softened the light radically, catching the light of other pads, the delicate shadow of a maple branch. They wavered uncertainly, competing for the evening light. It was as if I could hear them in faint chorus.

I saw how complicated their movements were. The wind might come from one direction, but they did not bow obediently in the other. One spot was forever in motion, another obstinately still. One pad would show its underside, but the others would not imitate it. They bowed sluggishly, painfully, to the left and right. Winds that brushed the surfaces and winds that loitered along the stems produced immense disorder. I was beginning to find the evening breeze chilly.

Most of the pads were fresh at their centers but eaten by rust at the edges. The decay seemed to spread from the spots of rust. There had been no rain for two days, and there were brown water stains at the concave centers. Or dead maple leaves.

The sun was still bright, but from somewhere darkness pressed in. We exchanged brief remarks. Though our faces were near, it was as if we were calling out to each other from far off in an inferno.

"What is that?" As if in fright, Momoko pointed to a cluster at the foot of the hillock, a tangle of rich red threads.

It was a cluster of shining spider lilies, a powerful red.

"It's closing time," said the old attendant. "Hurry up, please."

Our afternoon at the Kōrakuen brought me to a decision.

It was a trivial decision. If I was to wound Momoko not in the flesh but in the spirit, then there was an urgent need for another woman.

To make Momoko taboo was at the same time a responsibility and a logical contradiction. And if my carnal interest in her was the hidden source of my rational interest, then my dignity was left with nothing to stand on. I must wound her with the shining scepter of "love that is free."

To have another woman did not seem difficult. I went to a go-go hall on my way home from school. All I had to do was dance as I had learned to at the houses of friends, whether skillfully or not did not matter. I had several friends who had a healthy routine. Each day after school they would spend an hour or so alone at a go-go house before settling down after dinner to studies for entrance examinations. I went with one of them, and persevered over Coca-Cola after the hour had passed. A countrified girl with thick makeup spoke to me, and I danced with her. She was not, however, what I was after.

I had heard from my friend that there were certain to be "chastity eaters" at such a place. One would imagine rather older women, but such is not always the case. Women are sometimes interested in education even when they are young. A surprising number of them are good-looking. Their pride dictates against submitting to a sexual virtuoso. They prefer to become tutors and leave a lasting impression on young hearts. The interest in young male purity derives from the pleasure of leading into temptation; and yet, because it is quite clear that the women themselves have no sense of guilt, the pleasure must derive from leaving the man with the guilt which has carefully been nurtured elsewhere. Some are bright and happy, others of a melancholy turn. There is no standard, but they are all like hens warming eggs of sin. They are less interested in hatching the eggs than in cracking the heads of young roosters.

In the course of the evening I made the acquaintance of one of them, a rather well-dressed girl of twenty-five or twenty-six. She said I must call her Nagisa, "Miss Brink," and did not tell me her real name.

Her eyes were almost uncomfortably large, and she had thin, malicious lips. Yet there was in her face a warm richness as of a rustic orange. Her bosom was a startling white and she had good legs.

"Really!" That was her favorite expression. She was not at all reluctant to ask questions herself, but she greeted every question in return with a "Really!"

Since I had told Father that I would be home at nine, there was only time for dinner. She drew a map and gave me a telephone number and said that since she lived alone there was no need for shyness.

I want to be as precise as possible about what happened when, some days later, I went calling. Because the event itself is so filled with sensual exaggeration and imaginings and disappointments and the events are so distorted, a person departs from the truth in the very effort to be cool and objective; and if he seeks to portray the intoxication, he falls into conceptualizing. I must take up all three, sexual pleasure and the trembling curiosity of a new experience and an oppressive disharmony that could be either sensual or rational. I must cleanly separate them, allowing none to encroach upon the others, and I must transplant them, perfect and undamaged. The task will not be an easy one.

She seemed at first to have overestimated my shyness. She reassured herself repeatedly of the fact that I was "new to the experience." I did not want to appear under false colors, nor, on the other hand, did I want to be one of those young men who seek to attract a certain sort of woman with their inexperience—not after all a very attractive trait. And so I assumed a delicate arrogance, which was nothing but shyness cloaking itself in vanity.

The woman seemed torn between a desire to put me at my ease and a desire to excite me; but she was really thinking of herself. She knew from experience that over-ardent instruction can make the young person stumble. That was the reason for her sweet reserve. It was the perfume with which she had carefully touched herself. I could see a little gauge wavering in her eyes.

Since it was quite obvious that she was using my eagerness and curiosity to arouse herself, I was reluctant to have her look at me. It was not that I was feeling particularly shy; but I made the gestures as I brushed her eyes shut seem like a demand of shyness. I suppose that thus rolling in the dark a woman feels only the wheel that runs over her.

It goes without saying that my feelings of pleasure were over as soon as they began. I was much relieved. Only with the third try did I feel anything like real pleasure.

And so I saw: pleasure has an intellectual element in it from the start.

Which is to say: a certain distance is established, a play of pleasure and awareness is established, calculation and reckoning are established, and so, until one is able to look clearly down upon one's pleasure from without, as a woman looks down at her breasts, there is no pleasure. To be sure, my pleasure took a rather thorny shape.

But the knowledge that the shape of something attained after considerable practice lies concealed in the initial brief and insubstantial satisfaction was not good for my pride. That very first something was not at all the essence of impulse, it was the essence of concept, long in the making. And the intellectual operations of pleasure thereafter? Do they perhaps make the slow (or precipitous) collapse of concept a small dam, and use the electric power to enrich impulse bit by bit? If so, the intellectual road to the beast is very long.

"You're great," said the woman afterward. "You have real possibilities."

How many ships has she seen out of harbor with that same bouquet?

I am avalanching.

Yet I have nothing at all to do with the collapse and ruin of self. This avalanche, willfully destroying family, house, doing injury, bringing shrieks from an inferno, is something that the winter sky has caused to fall gently upon me, and it has nothing to do with my own basic nature. But in the instant of the avalanche, the softness of the snow and the hardness of the cliff change places. The agent of the disaster is the snow and not the self. It is the softness and not the hardness.

For a very long time, indeed since the beginning of natural history, my sort of heart, a heart of irresponsible hardness, has been ready. Most commonly, in the form of a stone. In the purest form of all, a diamond.

But the too-bright sun of winter penetrates even into the transparency of my heart. It is at such times that I see myself with wings that have no obstacles, and I see too that I shall do nothing at all with my life.

I shall probably achieve freedom, but freedom akin to death. None of the things I have dreamed of will come to me in this world.

Like the winter view from the signal station on Suruga Bay, when I could see even the reflections from the automobiles on the Izu Peninsula, I can see with these eyes every detail of the future.

I will no doubt have friends. The clever ones will betray me, and only the stupid ones will remain. It is strange that betrayal should come to a person like me. I suppose that everyone, faced with my clarity, feels the urge to betray. There can be no greater victory for betrayal than to betray such clarity. Probably all the people who are not loved by me are confident that they are so loved. The ones who are loved by me will probably guard a beautiful silence.

The whole world will wish my death; and, each trying to outdo the others, seek to prevent it.

My purity will presently wander beyond the horizon to that invisible realm. Probably at the end of unbearable pain I shall seek to become a god. The pain! I will know all of it, the pain of absolute silence, of a world of nothing at all. I will crouch trembling in a corner, like a sick dog. And the happy ones will sing songs around me.

There is no medicine for it. No hospital. It will be written in tiny gold letters, somewhere in the history of the race: that I was evil.

I vow it: that when I am twenty I will cast Father into hell. I must start making plans.

It would have presented no difficulty at all to go walking arm-in-arm with Nagisa where I had promised to meet Momoko. But I did not wish so hasty a solution, nor did I wish to see Nagisa stupidly intoxicated with victory.

She had given me a little silver chain and medal inscribed with her monogram, "N." It would not do for school or home wear, but I wore it around my neck when I met Momoko. I knew from the bandage incident that it was not easy to attract Momoko's attention. Despite the cold, I wore an open shirt and a V-neck sweater, and made sure that my shoe was badly tied. The medal was sure to fall out and catch the sun when I retied it.

It was a considerable disappointment that though I tied my shoe three times Momoko did not notice the medal. The inattentiveness came from complete confidence in her own well-being. I could not, for my own part, make too obvious a show.

In desperation I took Momoko swimming at the heated pool of a large Nakano sports center. She was delighted at this little reminder of our happy summer days in Shimoda.

"You're a man, aren't you?"

"I believe so."

This classical exchange between man and woman was taking place here and there beside the pool, where one of those Harunobu scenes, men and women indistinguishable, was being posed in the nude. There were long-haired men indistinguishable from women. I have the confidence to fly symbolically over the head of sex, but I have never felt the urge to melt into the other sex. I have no wish to be a woman. The very structure of woman is the foe of clarity.

I had had a swim and was sitting on the edge of the pool. Momoko was leaning toward me. The medal was no more than three or four inches away.

Finally it caught her eye.

She took it in her hand.

"What does 'N' stand for?" Finally she asked the question.

"Guess."

"Your initials are T.H. What might it be, I wonder."

"Think about it for a moment."

"I know. It stands for Nippon."

I felt rather let down. I began putting myself at a disadvantage by asking questions in return.

"It was a present. Who from, do you think?"

" 'N.' I have relations named Noda and Naka-mura."

"And why would I be getting presents from your relatives?"

"I know. It's for 'north.' It did occur to me that

the design around the edge was like a compass. You got it from a shipping company or something. At a launching. North, for a whaler. Right? Am I right? A whaler, and it was sent to your signal station. No doubt about it."

I cannot be sure whether Momoko really thought so, or whether she was trying to put herself at ease, or whether she sought to conceal her uneasiness in a play of innocence. I had lost the urge, in any case, to tell her she was wrong.

And so my operations turned to Nagisa. She was a phlegmatic sort, and I could appeal to her bland, harmless curiosity. If she had time to spare, I said, she might like to see my young fiancée from a distance. She accepted immediately. She asked me over and over again whether I had slept with Momoko. She seemed very interested in the practical application her pupil had made of her lessons. I told her when I was to meet Momoko at the Renoir and made her promise to act like a stranger. I knew that she was not one to keep a promise.

I was aware that shortly after our arrival Nagisa had arrived and taken a seat behind us, on the other side of the fountain. Silently and lazily, like a cat, she seemed to be glancing at us from time to time. Since Momoko was the innocent one, the understanding between Nagisa and myself was suddenly closer, and it was as if most of my remarks were being directed at her. The silly expression "physical bond" took meaning.

I was sure that she could hear us through the murmur of the fountain. In the awareness of being overheard, my words took on a certain appearance of sincerity. Momoko was delighted that I was in such good spirits. She was congratulating herself,

I could see, that we got on so nicely, though she did not know why.

Tired of conversation, I took the medal from my collar and bit at it. Far from reproving me, Momoko laughed happily. I caught a taste of silver, and against my tongue it felt like an indissoluble pill. The chain brushed my lip and chin. It was pleasant all the same. I felt like a bored dog.

Through the corner of my eye I saw that Nagisa had stood up. I knew from Momoko's wide eyes that she was standing beside us.

Suddenly a red-nailed hand was tugging at the medal.

"You're not to eat my medal."

I stood up and introduced the two.

"I'm sorry to have interrupted you." Nagisa walked off. "I'll see you later."

Momoko was blanched and trembling.

It was snowing. I spent a tedious Saturday afternoon at home. There is a window at the landing of the Western staircase. Only from it do you get a good view of the street. My chin on the sill, I knelt looking out at the snow. It was a quiet street even on ordinary days, and today the automobile tracks were blotted out.

There was a dim light from the snow. Though the sky was dark, the light of the snow signaled a strange time of its own, different from the time of day. Behind the house across the street it settled into hollows between the blocks of a concrete fence.

An old man, umbrella-less, in a brown coat and black beret, came up from the right. There was a pronounced swelling toward the bottom of his coat. He was embracing it. It would seem that he had a parcel of some sort which he wanted to keep dry.

I could see a gaunt, hollow face under the beret, quite out of keeping with the stout figure.

He stopped at our gate. There was a low gate beside the main one. I thought he would be some unusually impoverished caller with a request to make of my father. He looked around him, however, not bothering to brush the snow from his now white coat and making no motion toward coming in.

The swelling disappeared. A parcel fell to the ground, as if he had laid a great egg. I gazed at it. At first I could not make out what it might be. A spherical object of many colors glowed darkly from the snow. I saw that it was scraps of fruits and vegetables in a plastic kerchief. The kerchief bulged with bits of red apple, orange carrot, pale green cabbage. If he had gone out to throw them away, then he must be a strict vegetarian who lived alone. In such quantities, they gave the snow a strange, fresh spectrum. Even the bits of green cabbage seemed to breathe with a strangled breathing.

Riveted on the bundle, my eyes fell behind the old man as he walked off. He took tiny steps through the snow. I saw him from behind. Even taking into consideration the hunched shoulders, the coat was shapeless and unnatural. It was still swollen, though not so much as before.

He walked off. He was probably unaware of it himself, but five or six yards from the gate something fell from his coat like a great ink spot.

It was a dead bird, a crow, apparently. Or perhaps a turkey. I even thought I could hear the sound of the wings as it struck the snow; but the old man walked on.

The bird was a puzzle. It was a considerable distance away, blocked by the trees in the garden and further obscured by the snow, and there was a limit to my powers of vision. I thought of going for binoculars or going out to look, but an over-powering inertia held me back.

What sort of bird was it? As I looked at it, for almost too long a time, it came to seem not a bird but a woman's hair.

Momoko's sufferings had begun, like a conflagration from a cigarette. The perfectly ordinary girl and the great philosopher are alike: for both, the smallest triviality can become the vision that wipes out the world.

As planned, I became the petitioner. I sought to cajole her, and I followed her lead in saying the most dreadful things about Nagisa. She wept as she told me I must put an end to the affair. I said I would like nothing more, but needed her help. With some exaggeration, I said I would need her help if I was to break off with that devil of a woman.

She agreed to help me, but on one condition. I must throw away the necklace, and she must be witness to the act. Since it was nothing to me, I agreed. The two of us went to the bridge in front of Suidōbashi Station. I took it off and handed it to her, and told her to throw it with her own hand into the filthy canal. She flung it from her, arching it high into the sunlight of the winter evening. It hit the stinking water over which a barge was just then passing. She fell on me, her breathing as heavy as if she had just committed murder. Passers-by looked at us curiously.

It was time for my special night classes. I left her, with a promise to meet on Saturday afternoon.

I had Momoko write to Nagisa a letter of my dictating.

I wonder how many times I used the word "love" that Saturday afternoon. I said that if I loved

Momoko and Momoko loved me, then we must plan together to avert disaster, we must write a fraudulent letter.

We met at a bowling alley by the Meiji Gardens. After several strings, we went out hand in hand through the warm winter afternoon, through the shadows of the bare gingko trees, and into a new coffeehouse on Aoyama Avenue. I had brought paper and stamp and envelope.

Applying the anesthetic, I whispered of love as we walked along. In the course of time I had turned her into a person no different from the mad Kinué. She breathed easily only under the most obvious misconception, that our love was unchanging.

The two of them are alike in their denial of reality, Kinué in her belief that she is beautiful, Momoko in her belief that she is loved. Momoko needs help with her delusion, however, while Kinué needs no word from outside. If only I could raise Momoko to the same level! Since there was in the wish a pedagogical urge—love, so to speak—my protestations of love were not wholly without substance. But was there not a methodological contradiction in having an affirmer of reality like Momoko become a denier? It would not be easy to have her, like Kinué, do battle with the whole world.

But while reading the sacred formula "I love you" over and over, endlessly, a change comes to the heart of the reader. I could almost feel that I was in love, that some corner of my heart was drunk in the sudden and abandoned liberation of the banished word. How similar the tempter is to the flying instructor who must go flying with a beginner!

Momoko's other requirement, altogether appropriate for a somewhat old-fashioned girl, was no more than a purely "spiritual" affirmation, and all that was needed to satisfy it was a word or two. Words,

casting a clear shadow on the earth in their passage
—might they not have been the essential I? I had
been born to use words thus. If so (these sentimental
locutions greatly annoy me, of course), then perhaps
the basic mother tongue I have kept hidden is after
all the language of love.

While the patient himself is ignorant of the truth,
his family goes on telling him that he is certain to
recover. So, with the most intense earnestness, I
whispered over and over to Momoko of love, there
in the beautiful network of shadows from the winter
trees.

Once we were at our ease in the coffeehouse, I
told her of Nagisa's nature, as if I were asking her
advice and following it. I described in outline certain stratagems likely to be effective. I of course
created my Nagisa with complete license.

Since Momoko was my fiancée and loved me,
Nagisa was not the sort of woman likely to be
moved by a plea that she give me up. Such a plea
would only arouse her contempt and lead her on to
greater unpleasantness. She was a woman who did
battle with the word "love" and sought to bring
it down by assault from the rear. She had resolved
to leave her brand on boys who would one day
be good husbands and fathers, and so to jeer from
the shadows at marriage itself. Yet she had her
amiable defects. She gave no ground in her hatred
of love, but she had a certain strange sympathy for
a woman who was struggling to make her way. I
had heard her describe several representatives of the
species. The argument most likely to move her was
that she was obstructing not love but money and
security.

So what should we do?

"Make me a girl who does not love you but needs
you for your money."

"Precisely."

The thought greatly excited Momoko. What fun, she said dreamily.

The excitement that had replaced her gloom was altogether too bright and open. It put me out of sorts.

She continued. "And of course there is a grain of truth in it. Mother and Father make a great secret of it, and I have never said anything myself; but we're not all that well off. There was trouble in the bank and Father took responsibility and all the land at home is mortgaged. Father is such a good-natured man. He was the victim."

She was as entranced with the effort to make herself into a mean, crass woman (certain that she could never be one) as a young girl with her part in the school play. This is the letter which, to that end, I devised for her there in the coffeehouse.

Dear Nagisa,

Because I am about to make a request of you, please read my letter through to the end. The truth is that I want you to stop seeing Tōru.

I will tell you the reasons as honestly as I can. Tōru and I would seem to be tentatively engaged, but we do not love each other. I do think of us as good friends, but my feelings go no deeper. What I really want is affluence and freedom, married to an intelligent husband who has no difficult family problems. In this I am following my father's wishes. Tōru's father has not much longer to live, and when he dies Tōru will inherit the whole of his estate. My father has his own interests in the matter. There have been difficulties at the bank, of which we do not speak, and we are somewhat pressed financially, and need the help of Tōru's father and of Tōru himself once his father is dead.

I do love my mother and father, and if Tōru's affections were to turn elsewhere it would mean the end of all my plans and hopes. And so, to put the matter quite bluntly, the marriage is of very great importance for financial reasons. I have come to think that there is nothing more important in this world than money. I do not see anything dirty in it, and I think expressions like "love" and "affection," leaving it out of consideration, are misplaced. What may for you be a moment's dalliance is a matter of the greatest importance for my whole family. I am not saying that because I love Tōru you must give him up. I am speaking as a more mature and calculating girl than you may think.

This being the case, you are mistaken if you tell yourself that it will be all right for you to go on seeing Tōru in secret. The secret is certain to leak out, and it will not do to have Tōru think me a woman willing to close her eyes to everything for the sake of money. It is precisely for the sake of money that I must watch over him and preserve my pride.

You must not show this letter to Tōru. It has taken all my resolution to write it. If you are an evil woman, then show it to him and make it your weapon for getting him away from me; but you will have to live the rest of your life with the knowledge of having taken from another woman not love but her very living. We must dispose of the matter with cool heads, since the emotions of neither of us are involved. I feel quite capable of killing you if you show this letter to him; and I doubt that it will be an ordinary sort of murder.

Most sincerely,
Momoko

"The ending is good." Momoko was still excited.

"If I were to see it anything could happen." I smiled.

"I'm not worried." She leaned toward me.

I had her address the envelope and put a special delivery stamp on it, and we went off hand in hand to mail it.

Today I went to Nagisa's apartment and saw the letter. Trembling with anger, I snatched it from her and ran out. At home later that night, I went into Father's study and, heartbroken, showed it to him.

25

TŌRU BEGAN preparatory school at seventeen, two years later than most boys, and he would enter the university at twenty, in 1974, when he reached legal maturity. During his third year in preparatory school he had no recess from studies for the university examinations. Honda cautioned him against overwork.

One autumn day in that third year Honda dragged a protesting Tōru out for a weekend of nature. Tōru did not want to go far from home, and so they followed his wishes and drove to Yokohama for a look at the ships, his first in a very long time. The plan was that they would have dinner in the Chinese quarter of Yokohama.

Unfortunately the sky of early October was clouded over. The sky is high and wide over Yokohama. They got out at South Pier. The sky was an expanse of rough mackerel clouds, with only here and there a spot of white. Like the aftertone of a bell, there was a touch of blue beyond Central Pier. It seemed on the verge of disappearing.

"If we had our own car I could drive you. A driver is a useless expense."

"Not yet. I'll buy you one, I promise, when you get into the university. It will only be a little longer."

Sending Tōru off to get tickets for the terminal building, Honda leaned on his stick and looked wearily up at the stairs he must climb. He knew that Tōru would be willing enough to help him, but did not want to ask.

Tōru was happy from the time they reached the harbor. He had known that he would be. Not only Shimizu but every harbor was like a crystalline medicine that worked an immediate cure on him.

It was two in the afternoon. The register for nine in the morning had been posted: the *Chung Lien II*, Panamanian, 2,167 tons; a Soviet ship; the *Hai-i*, Chinese, 2,767 tons; the *Mindanao*, Philippine, 3,357 tons. The *Khabarovsk*, a Soviet ship bringing numbers of Japanese passengers from Nahodka, was due at two thirty. The view of the ships was good from the second floor of the terminal building, slightly higher than their decks.

They looked out over the prow of the *Chung Lien*, and the stir in the harbor beyond.

It was not unusual for the two of them, as the seasons passed, to stand thus side by side in confrontation with grandeur. Perhaps indeed it was the position best for the Hondas, father and son. If the "relationship" between them consisted in using nature as a mediator between their separate awarenesses, knowing that evil results from a direct meeting, then they were using nature as a giant filter to turn brine into potable water.

Below the prow of the *Chung Lien* was the lighter anchorage, like an accumulation of bobbing driftwood. Marks and signs on the concrete pier forbidding automobiles suggested the aftermath of a game of hopscotch. A dirty smoke drifted in from somewhere, and there was an incessant chugging of engines.

The paint had flaked from the dark hull of the *Chung Lien*. The bright red of the rust-preventive painted a pattern around the prow like an aerial map of harbor installations. The rusty stockless anchor clung to the hawse pipe like a great crab.

"What is the cargo, all done up in neat, long bundles? Like spindles." Honda was already scrutinizing the stevedores at work on the *Chung Lien*.

"Boxes of some sort, I'd imagine."

Satisfied that his son knew no more than he, Honda turned his attention to the shouts of the stevedores and labor such as he had not known in his life.

The astonishing thing was that the flesh, the muscles, the organs (the brain aside) given to a human being should through the whole of a long life of indolence have been blessed with health and a superfluity of money. Nor had Honda wielded great powers of creativity or imagination. Only cool analysis and solid judgment had been his. He had made money enough through them. He felt no pangs of conscience at the sweating stevedores he saw in action or in pictures, but he did feel a nameless irritation. The scenes and the objects and the movements before him were not the reality of something he had touched and taken profit from. They were a barrier, an opaque wall forever laughing derisively at both sides, daubed all over with smelly paint, between him and some unseen unreality and the unseen people taking profit from it. And the figures so vivid on the wall were themselves in the tightest bondage, controlled by someone else. Honda had never wanted to be thus in opaque bondage, but he had no doubt that they were the ones who had their anchors like ships, deep in life and being. Society paid recompense only for sacrifice. Intelligence was paid in measure proportionate to the sacrifice of life and being.

But there was no point in worrying at this late date. All he had to do was enjoy the movements before him. He thought of the ships that would come into the harbor after he was dead, and sail off for sunny lands. The world overflowed with hopes of which he was not part. If he were a harbor himself, however hopeless a harbor, he would have to give anchorage to a number of hopes. But as it was, he might as well declare to the world and to the sea that he was a complete superfluity.

And if he were a harbor?

He glanced at the single little boat in Honda Harbor, Tōru here beside him, engrossed in the unloading operations. A boat that was exactly the same as the harbor, rotting with the harbor, refusing forever to leave. Honda, at least, knew it. The ship was cemented to the pier. They were a model father and son.

The great dark holds of the *Chung Lien* were agape. The cargo overflowed the mouths of the holds. The figures of stevedores in brown sweaters and green bellybands of gold-threaded wool were half visible on the mountains of cargo, their yellow helmets bobbing as they shouted up at the cranes. The myriad iron lines of the derrick shook with their own shouts, and as the cargo wavered precariously in the air it blotted out and then revealed again the gold-lettered name of the passenger ship tied up at Central Pier.

An officer in a white cap was supervising the operations. He was smiling. It would seem that he had shouted a loud joke to encourage the stevedores.

Tired of the unloading operations, the father and

son walked to a point from which they could compare the stern of the *Chung Lien* with the prow of the Soviet ship.

The prow was astir with life, the low stern was deserted. Ochre vents pointed in several directions. Rough piles of garbage. Ancient casks with rusty iron hoops. Life jackets on white railings. Ships' fittings. Coils of ropes. The delicate white folds of lifeboats under ochre covers. An antique lantern still burned under the Panamanian flag.

The stillness was like that of a Dutch still life, tinged over with the sadness of the sea. It was as if napping with its private parts exposed to the forbidden gaze of landsmen, all the long hours of tedium aboard ship.

The black prow of the Soviet ship with its thirteen silver cranes pressed down from above. The rust of the anchor clinging to the hawse pipe had streaked the hull with red spider webs.

The ropes tying them to land marked off great vistas, three crossed ropes each, trailing beards of Manila hemp. Between the immovable iron screens moved the unresting bustle of the harbor. Each time a little tug with old black tires hanging at its sides or a white streamlined pilot boat moved past, it would leave a smooth track in its wake, and the dark irritability would for a time be soothed.

Tōru thought of Shimizu as he had studied it alone on holidays. Something was wrested from his heart each time, he would feel something like a sigh from the great lungs of the harbor, and as he covered his ears against the shouting and roaring and grating, he would taste simultaneously of oppression and liberation, and be filled with a sweet emptiness. It was the same today, though his father had an inhibiting effect.

"I think it was a good thing," said Honda, "that we broke off with the Hamanaka girl early in the spring.

179

I can talk to you now that you have gotten over it and seem so lost in your studies."

"It doesn't matter." Annoyed, Tōru put a touch of boyish melancholy and gallantry into his words. They were not enough to stop Honda. Honda's real purpose lay not in apology but in the question he had long been wanting to ask.

"But that letter. Doesn't it strike you as altogether too stupid? Wasn't it really too much to have a young girl speak openly of what we had been perfectly aware of and closed our eyes to? Her parents made all sorts of excuses, and the man who first came with the proposal had nothing to say at all when he saw the letter."

It displeased Tōru that Honda, who had until now not touched upon the matter, should be speaking so plainly, almost too plainly. He sensed that Honda had taken as much pleasure in breaking the engagement as in making it.

"But don't you suppose all the proposals that come to us are the same?" Elbows on the railing, Tōru did not look up. "Momoko was honest, and so we were able to take early measures."

"I quite agree. But we mustn't give up. We'll find a good girl yet. But that letter—"

"Why should you be so worried about it now?"

Honda gave Tōru a gentle nudge with his elbow. Tōru felt as if he had been jabbed by a bone. "You had her write it?"

Tōru had been expecting the question. "Suppose I did. What would you do?"

"Nothing at all. The only point is that you have found a way of getting through life. We must describe it as a dark way, with no sweetness in it."

Tōru's self-respect had been affronted. "I would not want to be thought sweet."

"But you were very sweet while it was all in process."

"I was doing as you wanted me to do, I should imagine."

"Yes."

Tōru shuddered as the old man bared his teeth to the sea wind. They had reached a point of agreement, and it brought Tōru to thoughts of murder. He could easily enough let them have their way by pushing Honda over; but he feared that Honda was aware of even that impulse. It left him. To have to live was blacker than the most cheerless black. To have to see every day a man who sought to understand, and did understand, the deepest thing inside him.

They had little more to say. After a round of the terminal building, they stood for a time looking at the Philippine ship on the far side.

Directly in front of them was an open door to the crew's cabins. They could see the scarred linoleum, glowing dully, and, around a corner, the iron rail of a stairway leading downward. The short, empty corridor of the quotidian, of frozen human life, never for a moment away from human beings, on whatever remote seas. In the great white transient ship, that one spot was representative of a dark, dull afternoon corridor in every house. In a vast, unpeopled house as well, where lived only an old man and a boy.

Honda ducked. Tōru had just made a violent motion. Honda caught a glimpse of the word "Notebook" on the rolled-up tablet Tōru had take from his briefcase. He flung it past the stern of the Philippine ship.

"What are you doing?"

"Notes I don't need. Scribblings."

"You'll be fined if they catch you."

But there was no one on the pier, and on the ship only a Philippine sailor who looked down at the sea in surprise. The rubber-bound tablet floated for an instant and sank.

A white Soviet ship with a red star on its prow and

the name "Khabarovsk" in gold letters was being brought against the pier by a tugboat with masts the color of a thorny broiled lobster. There was a cluster of welcomers at the rail, their hair blowing in the wind. Some were on tiptoes. Children on the shoulders of adults were already shouting and waving.

26

THE VERY QUESTION was indignant when Keiko asked Honda how Tōru meant to spend the Christmas of 1974. Since the September incident, the eighty-year-old Honda had been afraid of everything. His incisiveness had quite left him. He seemed to cower and tremble perpetually, to be a victim of unrelieved disquiet.

This state of affairs was to be explained not only by the September incident. They were now in the fourth year since Honda had adopted Tōru. Through most of those years Tōru had seemed quiet and docile, and there had been little change in him; but this spring he had reached maturity and entered Tokyo University, and everything was changed. He had suddenly come to treat his father as an adversary. He was prompt in putting down every sign of resistance. After Tōru had hit him on the forehead with a fire poker, Honda went to a clinic for a few days to have the wound treated—he told the doctors that he'd had a bad fall. Thereafter he was most attentive in reading and deferring to Tōru's wishes. Tōru was studiously rude to Keiko, whom he recognized as Honda's ally.

From long years of avoiding relatives who might be after his money, Honda had no allies prepared to sympathize with him. Those who had opposed the adoption were pleased. Everything had turned out as expected. They set no stock whatsoever by Honda's complaints. He was only trying to arouse sympathy. Their sympathies were rather with Tōru. Such beautiful eyes, such impeccable deportment, such a devoted sense of filial duty—they could only conclude that a suspicious old man was maligning him. And indeed Tōru's manners were above reproach.

"There seem to be troublemakers around. Who can have told you such a silly story? Mrs. Hisamatsu, I'm sure. She's a nice person, but she believes everything Father tells her. I'm afraid he's pretty far gone. He has delusions. I imagine that's what happens when you spend so many years worrying about money; but he treats even me, right here under the same roof, like a thief. After all, I am young, and when I talk back he starts telling people I'm not good to him. The time he fell in the garden and hit his head against the root of the plum tree—remember?—he told Mrs. Hisamatsu I'd hit him with a poker. She actually believed it, every last word of it, and that doesn't give me much room to fight back."

He had that summer brought the mad Kinué from Shimizu and installed her in the garden cottage.

"Her? Oh, she's a very sad case. In my Shimizu days she helped me this way and that. She wanted to come to Tokyo because at home everybody made fun of her and the children were always chasing after her and shouting at her. So I persuaded her parents to let me have her. They'd kill her if they put her in an asylum. Yes, she's crazy, no doubt about it, but she's harmless."

Casual acquaintances among the elders of the family were much taken by Tōru, but they were courteously

and skillfully turned away when they sought to enter
his life. They were inclined to lament that a man once
so keen and intelligent as Honda should have fallen
so hopelessly into senile delusions. They had long
memories, remembering that windfall of more than
twenty years before. Envy was at work.

A day in Tōru's life.

There was no longer a need to look at the sea and
await ships.

There was no need to attend classes either, but
Tōru did so to inspire confidence. He went by automobile, despite the fact that the university was a ten-
minute walk away.

The habit of rising early had not left him. Judging
from the light through the curtains that a quiet summer rain was falling, he would go over the ordering of
the world he controlled. Were the evil and the arrogance going like clockwork? Was no one yet aware of
the fact that the world was wholly under the control
of evil? Was order being preserved, everything pro-
ceeding after the laws, with not the smallest spot of
love to be detected anywhere? Were people happy
under his hegemony? Had transparent evil, in form a
poem, been spread over their heads? Had "the human"
been carefully wiped away? Had careful arrangements
been made for every sign of warmth to be ridiculed?
Was spirit quite dead?

Tōru was confident that if he but laid a beautiful
white hand upon it, the world would succumb to a
beautiful illness. And it was natural too that he should
expect windfall to follow unanticipated windfall. For
reasons that he did not know, an impoverished signalman had been chosen as the foster son of a rich old
man, and an old man with one foot in the grave. One
of these days a king would come from some country
or other and ask to adopt him.

Even in the winter he would run to the shower room he had had installed next to his bedroom and have a cold shower. It was the best thing for waking a person up.

The cold water would liven his pulse, lash at his chest with its transparent whip, thousands of silver needles would stab at his skin. He would take it against his back for a time and turn to face it again. His heart had still not quite made friends with it. It was as if a sheet of iron were pushing at his chest, as if his naked flesh were encased in a tight suit of armor. He twisted and turned, like a corpse dangling from a rope of water. Finally his skin had awakened. Young skin stood there regally, turning off the drops of water. At that moment Tōru raised his left arm and looked down at the three moles like three shining black pebbles in a cascade. They were the sign of the elite, visible to no one, hidden under a folded wing.

He dried himself. He breathed deeply. His body was flushed.

It was the duty of the maid Tsuné to bring his breakfast the moment he called for it. Tsuné was a girl he had picked up in a Kanda coffeehouse. She obeyed all his orders.

It was only two years since he had first known a woman, but he had quickly learned the rules for making a woman serve a man who did not love her. And he know how to spot instantly a woman who would do what he told her. He had dismissed all the maids likely to follow Honda's wishes and hired women who he had discovered and slept with, and given them the title "maid," using the English word. Tsuné was the stupidest one among them, and the one with the largest breasts.

When breakfast was on the table, he poked at a breast by way of good morning.

"Nice and firm."

"Yes, in very good shape." Tsuné answered respectfully if expressionlessly. The heavy, dark flesh itself was respectful. Particularly deferential was the navel, deep as a well. The beautiful legs were somehow incompatible with the rest of Tsuné. She was aware of that fact. Tōru had seen how, as she brought coffee past on the uneven floor of the coffeehouse, she had brushed her calf against the lower branches of the starving rubber plant, like a cat rubbing against a bush.

Tōru thought of something. Going over to the window, he looked down into the garden, the chest of his bathrobe open to the morning breeze. Even now Honda scrupulously respected the hour for his morning walk, just after he was out of bed.

Tottering along on his stick in the stripes of November sunlight, Honda smiled and managed a good morning Tōru could barely hear.

Tōru smiled and waved. "I'll be damned. The old man's still alive." That was his good morning.

Still smiling, Honda skirted a dangerous steppingstone. He did not know what would come flying down upon him if he were so incautious as to say more. He had only to endure this moment of humiliation. Tōru would be out of the house at least until evening.

"Old people smell bad. Go away." Honda's offense had been to come too near.

Honda's cheek twitched with anger, but he had no recourse. If Tōru had shouted at him, he could and would have shouted back. But Tōru had spoken softly and coolly, gazing at Honda with his clean, beautiful eyes, a smile on his pale face.

Tōru's dislike seemed to have grown through the four years they had been together. He disliked everything, the ugly, impotent flesh, the useless chatter that covered the impotence, the tiresome repetitiveness, five and six times over, the automatism that became fretful at the repetitiveness itself, the self-importance and the cowardice, the miserliness and the self-indulgence, the pusillanimity in the constant fear of death, the complete permissiveness, the wrinkled hands, the gait like a measuring worm, the mixture of arrogance and obsequiousness on the face. And Japan was teeming with old people.

Back at the breakfast table he kept Tsuné on duty to pour his coffee. He had her put in sugar. He complained about the toast.

It was a sort of superstition that the success of a day depended upon a smooth beginning. The morning must be an unflawed crystal. He had been able to endure the boredom of life at the signal station because observation did not damage self-respect.

Once Tsuné said: "The manager of the coffee shop used to call me Asparagus. Because I am long and white, he said."

Tōru replied by pressing his lighted cigarette against the back of her hand. Stupid though she was, Tsuné thereafter minded her words. Especially when she served him at breakfast. The four "maids" took turns on duty. Three of them looked after Tōru, Honda, and Kinué, and the fourth was off duty. The one who served Tōru his breakfast was the one he received in his bed at night. When he had finished with her she was dismissed. No one was permitted to spend the night with him. They thus enjoyed his favors once every four days, and were allowed to leave the house once a week. Honda secretly admired the tightness of the control and the want of dissension. The maids followed Tōru's orders as if to do so were in the nature of things.

He had taught them all to call Honda "the old master," and otherwise trained them impeccably. Occasional callers would say that nowhere else these days did they see such beautiful and well-trained maids.

Tōru left Honda wanting for nothing even while humiliating him.

Having made himself ready for school. Tōru always looked in at the garden cottage. Carefully made up, wearing a negligee, Kinué always received him from the chaise longue on the veranda. Her newest coquetry was illness.

Tōru would sit on the veranda and face the ugly woman with the warmest, most sincere gentleness.

"Good morning. And how are you feeling this morning?"

"Not too bad, thank you. I doubt if there is anything more beautiful in this world than the moment when a beautiful woman with only the strength to make herself up, all weak on her couch, receives a caller and manages a feeble 'Not too bad, thank you.' The beauty of it all waves like a heavy flower, and it is there on her eyelids as she closes her eyes. Isn't it? I think of it as the one thing I can do for all your kindness. But I'm very grateful. You're the one kind man in the world who gives me everything and asks nothing in return. And now that I'm here I can see you every day and don't have to go out. If only your father weren't here."

"Don't worry about him. He'll give up and die one of these days. The September business has been taken care of and everything is going fine. I think next year maybe I can buy you a diamond ring."

"How nice! That's what will keep me alive, the thought of it. But today I'll have to make do with flowers. The white chrysanthemum in the garden is my flower for today. Will you pick it for me? How nice. No, not that one. The one in the pot. That's it. The big white one with the petals all drooping like threads."

Heedlessly, Tōru broke off the white chrysanthemum so carefully tended by Honda. Like an ailing beauty, Kinué turned it languorously in her fingers.

Then, with an all-too-fleeting smile on her lips, she put it in her hair.

"Be off with you. You'll be late for school. Think of me between classes." And she waved him good-bye.

Tōru went to the garage.. He started up the Mustang sports car he had had Honda buy him that spring upon his entry into the university. If the absent, romantic engine of a ship could cut through waves so cleanly, kick up such wake, then why could not the six delicately alert cylinders of the Mustang scatter the stupid crowds, cut through the masses of flesh, scatter splashes of red as the other scattered splashes of white?

But it was held in quiet control. It was coaxed and wheedled into a gentle pretense of docility. People admired it as they admire a sharp, shining blade. It forced a smile from its beautiful hood, paint all ashine, to assure them that it was not dangerous.

Capable of a hundred and twenty-five miles per hour, it debased itself by keeping to the twenty-five-mile speed limit as it made its way through the Hongō morning crowds.

The September third incident.

It began with a little spat Tōru and Honda had in the morning.

Through the summer Tōru had been happily rid of Honda, who had taken refuge from the heat at Hakoné. Reluctant to rebuild after his Gotemba villa burned down, Honda had left the land as it was and, always sensitive to he heat, spent his summers at a Hakoné inn. Tōru preferred to stay in Tokyo and drive here and there, to the mountains and the sea, with friends. Honda returned to Tokyo on the evening of September second. He saw Tōru for the first time in some weeks. There was clear anger in the eyes that greeted him from the sun-blackened face. Honda was frightened.

Where was the crape myrtle, he asked in surprise as he went out into the garden on the morning of the third. The old crape myrtle by the garden cottage had been cut at the roots.

Kinué, who had been in the main house, had moved to the cottage early in July. It had been from fear of Tōru after the poker incident that Honda had first taken her in.

Tōru came out. He had the poker in his left hand. His room was a remodeled parlor. It had the only fireplace in the house. Even in summer there was a poker on the nail beside it.

Tōru of course knew that the mere sight of it would make Honda cower like a whipped dog.

"What are you doing with that thing? This time I'll call the police. Last time I kept quiet because I didn't want publicity, but it won't be so easy for you this time." Honda's shoulders were quivering, and it had taken all his courage to speak.

"You have a stick, don't you? Defend yourself with that."

Honda had been looking forward to the crape myrtle in bloom, its blossoms shining against a trunk smooth like the white skin of a leper. But there was none. The garden had been made over, he knew, in the Ālaya, the Storehouse, into a different garden. Gardens too must change. But in the instant that he so felt, uncontrollable anger came from another source. He cried out, and even as he cried out he was afraid.

The summer rains had ended and the heat had come after Kinué had moved to the cottage. The crape myrtle was in bloom. She disliked it, she said. It gave her a headache. She started saying that Honda had planted it there to drive her mad; and so Tōru cut it down after Honda's departure for Hakoné. It was as simple as that.

Kinué herself was out of sight, far back in the dusky recesses of the cottage. Tōru offered Honda no explanation. There would be no advantage in it.

"I suppose you cut it down?" said Honda, more softly.

"That I did." Tōru's answer was cheerful.

"Why?"

"It was old and useless." Tōru smiled a beautiful smile.

At such times Tōru would lower a thick glass door before his eyes. Glass that came down from the sky. Glass made from exactly the same material as the limpid morning sky. Honda knew that no shout, no word would reach Tōru's ears. Tōru would only see false molars. Honda already had inorganic teeth. He was already beginning to die.

"I see. It makes no difference."

All through the day Honda sat still in his room. He barely touched the food that the "maid" brought. He knew what she would report to Tōru.

"The old man's being awful sulky."

Perhaps the suffering of the old man did in fact come to nothing more than sulkiness. Honda could see in them foolishness beyond defending. It had all been his own doing and not Tōru's. There was no need for surprise at the change in Tōru. Honda had seen at the first glance the "evil" in the boy.

But at the moment he wanted to measure depth of the wound inflicted on his self-respect by what he had asked for.

Honda disliked air-conditioning and was at an age when he feared stairs. He had a large twelve-mat room on the ground floor, looking out over the garden to the cottage. Built in the medieval *shoin* style, it was the oldest and gloomiest room in the house. Honda ranged four linen cushions in a row. He lay down and then sat up on his heels. With all the sliding doors pulled shut, he let the heat accumulate. Sometimes he would crawl to the table for a drink of water. It was as warm as in full sunlight.

Time went past along the indefinable line between waking and sleeping, like a nap at the ultimate end of anger and sadness. Even the pain in his hips would have been a distraction, but today there was none. He was only exhausted.

An unfathomable disaster seemed to be coming down on him, only made worse by the fact that it had precise, delicate gradations, and, like a subtly compounded potion, was having the predicted effect. Honda's old age should have been free of vanity, ambition, honor, prestige, reason, and above all emotion. But it wanted cheer. Although he should have forgotten all feeling long ago, black irritation and anger continued to smolder like a bed of embers. Stirred, they sent off a reeking smoke.

There was autumn in the sunlight on the paper doors, but isolation contained no signs of movement, of change into something else, like the change of the seasons. All was stagnation. He could see them clearly in himself, anger and sadness that should not have been there, like puddles after a rain. The feeling born this morning was like a bed of leaves ten years old, and new each instant. All the unpleasant memories poured in upon him, but he could not, like a youth, say that his life was unhappy.

When the light at the window told him that evening was near, sexual desire stirred in the crouching Honda. It was not a sudden onset of desire, but rather something tepid that had gestated through hours of sadness and anger and coiled round his brain like a red worm.

The driver he had used over the years had retired, and his successor had been guilty of certain indiscretions. And so Honda had sold his automobile and now used rented cars. At ten he called a maid on the interphone and asked her to order a car. He took out a black summer suit and a gray sports shirt.

Tōru was out. The maids looked with curiosity upon the nocturnal departure of the eighty-year-old Honda.

When the car turned into the Meiji Gardens, Honda's desire had become something like a faint attack of nausea. Here he was again, after twenty years.

But it was not sexual desire that had burned in him all through the ride.

His hands on his stick, more erect than usual, he had been muttering to himself: "I only have to endure it six months more. Just six months more. If he's the real thing."

That "if" made him tremble. If Tōru were to die in the six months before his twenty-first birthday, everything could be forgiven. Only the awareness of that birthday had made it possible for Honda to endure the arrogance. And if Tōru was counterfeit?

The thought of Tōru's death had been a great comfort. In his humiliation he had concentrated upon Tōru's death, in his heart already killed him. His heart was quiet, happiness welled up, his nose twitched with tolerance and pity when he saw death, like the sun through isinglass, beyond the violence and cruelty. He could be drunk on the open cruelty of what is called charity. Perhaps that was what he had found in the light upon the vast, empty Indian plain.

He had not yet detected in himself symptoms of a fatal illness. There was nothing to be alarmed about in his blood pressure or his heart. He was confident that if he lasted another half year he would outlive Tōru, perhaps by only a few days. What quiet, secure tears he would be able to shed! Before the foolish world, he would play the part of the tragic father deprived of the son he had come upon so late in life. He could not deny that there was pleasure in looking forward to Tōru's death, in looking ahead to it with the quiet love, oozing sweet poison, of one who knows everything. Tōru's violence, beguiling and lovable, seen through the time ahead as through a Mayfly's wing. People do not love pets that will outlive them. A short life is a condition for love.

And perhaps Tōru was fretting at a prospect like a strange, unheard-of ship suddenly appearing on a horizon which he had been scanning for days. Perhaps a foretaste of death was moving him, irritating him. The possibility brought unbounded gentleness over Honda. He felt that he could love not only Tōru but the whole human race. He knew the nature of human love.

But if Tōru was counterfeit? If he was to live on and on, and Honda, unable to keep up with him, to waste away?

The roots of the strangling desire within him were in the uncertainty. If he was to die first, then he could not refuse the basest of desires. He might all along have been destined to die in humiliation and miscalculation. The miscalculation about Tōru may itself have been the trap laid by Honda's destiny. If a person like Honda had a destiny.

The fact that Tōru's awareness was too much like his own had long been a seed of disquiet. Perhaps Tōru had read everything. Perhaps Tōru knew that he would live a long life, and, reading the determined malice in the practical education given him by an old man confident of his early death, had plotted his revenge.

Perhaps the eighty-year-old and the twenty-year-old were even now engaged in close combat over life and death.

Night in the Meiji Gardens, for the first time in

twenty years. The car had turned left from the Gondawara entrance and was on the circular drive.

"Keep going, keep going." Each time Honda gave the order he added a cough, like a bothersome accessory.

Egg-colored shirts appeared and disappeared among the night trees. For the first time in a very long while, Honda felt that very special throb in his chest. Old desire still lay piled under the trees like last year's leaves.

"Go on, go on."

The car turned right behind the art gallery, where the groves were thickest. There were two or three couples. The lighting was as inadequate as ever. Suddenly there was a glaring cluster of lights to the left. In the middle of the park the entrance to the expressway gaped with a multitude of lights, like a deserted amusement park.

To the right would be the grove on the left side of the art gallery. The night trees cut off the dome, and branches poured out over the sidewalk, a tangle of firs, plantains, pines. Even from the moving car he could hear the insects in the clump of agaves. As if it had been yesterday, he remembered the ferocity of the mosquitoes in the thickets and the sound of slapping against naked skin.

He dismissed the car at the parking lot by the art gallery. The driver glanced at him from under a narrow forehead. It was the sort of glance that can sometimes work collapse. You may go, Honda said again, more strongly. Pushing his stick out on the sidewalk ahead of him, he climbed from the car.

The parking lot was closed at night. A sign said that access was forbidden. A barricade blocked off the entrance. There was no light in the attendant's shelter, and no sign of life.

Looking after the car, Honda walked down the sidewalk past the agaves. They flung out harsh leaves, a pale green in the darkness, quiet, like a clump of malice. There were few passers-by, only a man and woman on the sidewalk opposite.

Having come as far as the façade of the art gallery, Honda stopped and looked at the great empty scheme in which he found himself. The dome and the two wings rose powerfully into the moonless night. The rectangular pond and the white gravel of the terrace, long streaks of light from the lamps cutting off the dim white of the gravel like the line of the tide. To the left loomed the round wall of the Olympic Stadium, its now-dark floodlights high against the sky. Far below, lamps, like a mist, touched the outermost branches of the trees.

In the symmetrical plaza, which contained no shadow of desire, Honda felt as if he were at the center of the Womb Mandala.

The Womb Mandala, one of the two elemental worlds, is paired with the Diamond Mandala. Its symbol is the lotus, and its Buddhas manifest the virtue of charity.

The womb has also the meaning of inclusiveness. Just as the womb of the beggar woman held the embryo of the Lord of Light, so the muddied heart of the ordinary man holds the wisdom and mercy of all Buddhas.

The perfect symmetry of the shining mandala holds at its center the Court of the Eight-Petaled Lotus, abode of the Lord of Great Light. Twelve courts stretch out in the four directions, and the abodes of the several Buddhas are fixed with delicate and detailed symmetry.

If the dome of the art gallery, high in the moonless night, was taken for the central court, then the avenue where Honda stood, separated from it by the pond, was perhaps the abode of the Peacock Lord, to the west of the Court of Emptiness.

With the Buddhas disposed geometrically on the golden mandala transferred to the dark groves of the symmetrical plaza, the expanse of gravel and the emptiness of the sidewalk were suddenly filled, merciful faces were everywhere, dizzying in the full light of day. The more than two hundred holy faces, and more than two hundred of the Diamond Mandala as well, were shining in the groves, and the ground was ablaze with light.

The vision faded as he walked off. The night was filled with the singing of insects, cicada voices stitched the shadows like needles.

The familiar path was still there through the groves, to the right of the art gallery. He remembered with longing that the smell of the grass and of the night trees had been an indispensable part of desire.

He felt the return of a sharp sense of pleasure, as if he were crossing a tideland, at his feet the workings of fish and shellfish and starfish and crustaceans and seahorses, as at night on a coral reef, the water lapping warm against the soles of his feet, in danger of being cut at each step by the pointed rocks. Pleasure dashed ahead, the body was unable to follow. Signs, indications, were everywhere. As his eyes grew accustomed to the dark he saw white shirts scattered through the groves, like the aftermath of a slaughter.

There was a previous caller in the shadows where Honda hid himself. Honda could tell from the dark shirt if from nothing else that it was a veteran peeper. The man was so short, coming only to Honda's shoulders, that Honda at first took him for a boy. When he made out the grizzled head, the moist breathing so near at hand seemed heavy and stupid.

Presently the man's eyes left their object and were trained on Honda's profile. Honda looked studiously away, but he had felt that the short gray hair bristling from the temples was somehow related to a disconcerting memory. He struggled to bring it out. The usual cough rose to his throat though he fought to keep it back.

A certain confidence came into the man's breathing. Raising himself to his full height, he whispered in Honda's ear.

"So we meet again. You still come, do you? You haven't forgotten?"

Honda turned and looked into the rodent eyes. A memory came back from twenty-two years before. It was the man who had stopped him in front of the Ginza P.X.

And he remembered with fear how coldly he had treated the man, asserting mistaken identity.

"You needn't worry. Here is here and there is there. Let's let bygones be bygones." This way of forestalling Honda's thoughts added to the uneasiness. "But you'll have to stop that coughing." He turned to look busily off beyond the tree trunks.

Breathing more easily as the man moved some distance away, Honda looked into the grasses beyond the tree. The throbbing had departed, however. It had been replaced by uneasiness and, again, anger and sadness. Self-forgetfulness withdrew as he pursued it. Though the spot was well suited for viewing the man and woman on the grass, there was a false quality about them, as if they knew they were being watched and were acting parts. There was none of the joy in seeing, there was neither the sweet pressure from the recesses of scrutiny nor drunkenness of clarity itself.

Though they were only a yard or two away, the light was too dim for him to make out details or the expressions on the faces. There seemed to be no screen between him and them, and he could approach no nearer. He hoped that if he went on looking the old throb would return. One hand against the trunk of the tree, one hand on his stick, he looked down at the couple.

Although the little man showed no disposition to interfere with his sport, Honda went on remembering things he should not have remembered. Since his own stick was uncurved, he could not hope to imitate the virtuosity of the old man who used his stick to lift skirts. The man had been old then, and no doubt he was dead by now. No doubt rather large numbers of the old men in the "audience" had died in the course of these twenty years. And not a few among the young "performers" too would have married and gone away, or died in traffic accidents or from juvenile cancer or high blood pressure or heart and kidney ailments. Because movements and transfers are far brisker among the performers than in the audience, some of them would be in apartment clusters in bedroom towns an hour or so by private railway from Tokyo, ignoring wives and children and abandoning themselves to the joys of television. And the day was at hand when some of them would join the audience.

Something soft brushed his right hand. A large snail was making its way down the tree.

He pulled his hand gently away. The flesh and the shell in succession, like the celluloid of the soap dish after the sticky suds, left revulsion. From just such a tactile impression the world could melt away, like a corpse in a tank of sulfuric acid.

Honda looked down again at the man and woman. There was almost a pleading in his eyes. Make me drunk, the earliest moment possible. Young people of the world, in ignorance and silence, let me get drunk to my heart's content on the forms of your passion, which have no room for the old.

Sprawled out in the singing of insects, the woman raised herself and put her arms around the man's neck.

The man, who was wearing a black beret, had his hand deep under her skirt. Her fingertips moved energetically over the wrinkles of his shirt. She was twisted against his chest, like a spiral stairway. Panting, she raised her head and kissed him, as if she were gulping down medicine.

As Honda gazed, so intently that his eyes ached, he felt a surge of desire, like the first rays of the morning sun, from depths until then empty.

The man reached into his hip pocket. The thought that in the very middle of desire he feared being robbed brought a sudden chilling of Honda's own desire. The next instant he was doubting his eyes.

The object the man took from his pocket was a spring knife. His forefinger touched it and there was a sound as of a rasping snake's tongue. The blade gleamed in the dark. Honda could not be sure where the woman had been stabbed, but there was a scream. The man sprang up and looked around. The beret had slipped back. For the first time Honda saw the hair and face. The hair was a pure white, and the emaciated face was that of a sixty-year-old, wrinkled to every corner.

The man brushed past Honda, now in a state of shock, and ran off with a speed that belied his years.

"Let's get out of here," muttered the rat-like little man in Honda's ear. "There's going to be hell to pay."

"I couldn't run if I wanted to," said Honda weakly.

"Too bad. They'll suspect you if you don't get away." The man bit at his fingernail. "Maybe you should stay and be a witness."

There was a whistle, a rush of footsteps, and a stir of people getting to their feet. The beam of a flashlight came from surprisingly near in the shrubbery. Policemen were standing around the woman, discussing the problem in loud voices.

"Where'd he get her?"

"In the thigh."

"It's not much of a cut."

"What sort of man was he? Tell us what sort of man he was."

The policeman who had been crouching beside the woman with his flashlight in her face stood up.

"An old man, she says. He won't have gone very far."

Trembling, Honda pressed his face against the tree. His eyes were closed. The bark was damp. It was as if a snail were crawling over his face.

He opened his eyes narrowly. He could feel the beam from the flashlight. Someone shoved at him, from so low that it had to be the little man. Honda stumbled from the shelter of the big tree. His face almost fell against one of the policemen. The policeman grabbed his wrist.

A reporter for a weekly magazine specializing in scandal happened to be at the police station. He was delighted at news of the stabbing in the Meiji Gardens.

The woman, her leg heavily bandaged, was asked to identify Honda. It took three hours for Honda's innocence to be established.

"I'm absolutely sure it wasn't this old gentleman," said the woman. "I met the other one a couple of hours ago on a streetcar. He was an old man, but he dressed very young, and he was a good talker, a good mixer, you might say. I'd never have dreamed he could do such a thing. That's right. I don't know the first thing about him, his name or where he lives or what he does or anything."

Before the woman confronted him, Honda was firmly tied up and his identity was established and he was forced to reveal the circumstances that had brought a person of his standing to the park at such an hour. It was a nightmare, that precisely the foolish story he had heard upward of twenty years ago from his old legal friend should now be his own experience. They all seemed to have the lucidity of a nightmare, quite divorced from reality; the shabby police station, the dirty walls of the interrogation room, the strangely bright light, the bald head of the detective.

He was allowed to go home at three in the morning. A maid got up and suspiciously opened the gate. He went to his room. He was troubled by bad dreams.

He came down with a cold the next day and was a week getting over it.

The morning he began to feel a little better, Tōru paid an unexpected visit. Smiling, he put a weekly magazine by Honda's pillow.

It carried this headline: "Troubles of His Excellency Mr. Judge-Voyeur, Falsely Accused of Stabbing."

Honda took up his glasses. There was an unpleasant throbbing in his chest. The article was astonishingly accurate, even carrying Honda's real name. This was the climatic sentence: "The appearance of an eighty-year-old voyeur would seem to indicate that the control of Japan by the aged extends even to the world of deviates."

The statement that his proclivities were not new but that for some twenty years he had had numbers of acquaintances among the voyeurs made Honda sure who the informant had been. The police themselves must have introduced the reporter to the little man. A suit for libel would only add to the embarrassment.

It was a vulgar incident that deserved to be laughed away; but Honda, who would have hoped that he no longer had prestige and honor to lose, saw in the loss of them that they were in fact still present.

It seemed certain that for rather a long time people would associate his name not with his spiritual and intellectual endowments but with the scandal. People were not quick to forget scandals. It was not moral indignation that made them remember. For encapsulating a person a scandal was the simplest and most efficient container.

The stubbornness of the cold told him that he was crumbling physically. To have been a suspect was an experience which, in the complete absence of intellectual dignity, seemed to bring a collapse of flesh and bones. Knowledge, learning, thought, could do nothing for it. What good would it have done to confront the detective with the fine details of the concepts he had acquired in India?

Henceforth Honda would take out his calling card:

"Shigekuni Honda"
"Attorney-at-Law"

People would insert a line in the cramped space between the other two:

Shigekuni Honda
Eighty-Year-Old Voyeur
Attorney-at-Law

And so Honda's career would be compressed into a single line.

"Former judge, eighty-year-old voyeur."

And so the invisible edifice which Honda's awareness had built through his long life had collapsed in an instant, and a single line was inscribed on the foundation. It was as concise as a white-hot blade. And it was true.

After the September incident Tōru moved coolly to have things his way.

He took as his lawyer an old lawyer with whom Honda had feuded, and consulted with him upon the possibility of having Honda declared incompetent. An examination would be required to establish mental debility, but the lawyer seemed confident of the results.

And as a matter of fact the change in Honda was clear. After the incident he stopped going out and he seemed afraid of everything. It should be easy enough to establish the symptoms of senile delusions. Tōru had only to appear before a court of domestic relations and have Honda declared incompetent, and the lawyer would be appointed his guardian.

The lawyer consulted a psychiatrist with whom he was on good terms. Behind Honda's much-publicized misconduct the psychiatrist drew a picture of senile unease. Two ailments emerged, "vicarious sexual desire," an obsession like a fire reflected in a mirror, not to be made light of, and incontinence resulting from senility. Everything else could be left to the legal system, said the lawyer. He added that it would be good if Honda were to begin spending his money unwisely, in such a way as to give rise to fears that the estate might be endangered, but unfortunately there were no such tendencies. Tōru was in any case worried less about money than about power.

27

LATE IN NOVEMBER a splendid engraved invitation, in English, came to Tōru from Keiko.

There was a letter with it.

Dear Tōru,
I have been very bad about keeping in touch.
Everyone seems to have made arrangements for

Christmas Eve, and so I am having a premature Christmas party on the twentieth. I have until now always invited your father, but I have had to conclude that because of his advanced years an invitation this year would be a disservice, and I am inviting you instead. I think we should keep the matter secret from him. That is why I have addressed the invitation to you.

I fear that to say so will be to reveal too much of myself, but the truth is that since the September affair I have found it difficult to invite your father, out of deference to the other guests. I know it will seem to you that I am a bad friend, but in our world it is the final stroke when the private becomes public. I must be very careful.

My real reason for inviting you is that through you I want to continue relations with the Honda family. I will be delighted therefore if you can accept this invitation.

And so do please honor me by coming alone. Among the other guests will be several ambassadors and their wives and daughters, the Foreign Minister and his wife, the president of the Federation of Economic Organizations and his wife, and numbers of other pretty ladies as well. You will see from the invitation that it is to be black tie. It would be a great help if you could let me know soon whether or not you will be able to attend.

Yours sincerely,
Keiko Hisamatsu

One could if one chose see the letter as a rude and haughty one, but Tōru smiled at the thought of Keiko's confusion after the September incident. He could read between the lines. Keiko, so proud of her immorality, retreated trembling behind bolted gates in the face of scandal.

But something in the letter aroused Tōru's delicate guard. That Keiko, so staunch an ally of his father, should be inviting him—might it not be to make sport of him? Might her intention in introducing him to all those pretentious guests as the son of Shigekuni Honda not be to excite them and so to embarrass not Honda but Tōru himself? That was it. There could be little doubt.

Tōru's combative instincts were aroused. He would go to the party as the son of the notorious Honda. No one of course would touch upon the matter. But he would shine as a son unapologetic for a notorious father.

The sensitive spirit would move silently among them, a faint, beautiful, somewhat sad smile on its lips, the skeletons of family scandal (such beastly little affairs), no doing of its own, ranged beside it. Tōru could see all the pale poetry. The contempt and interference of the old would push the girls irresistibly in Tōru's direction. Keiko's calculations would prove faulty.

Not owning a tuxedo, Tōru had to put in a quick order for one. He slipped into it when, on the nineteenth, it was delivered, and went over to show Kinué.

"You look very good in it. Lovely. I know how much you wanted to take me dancing in it. What a pity that I should always be so ill. What a real pity. And that's why you've come to show me. How very kind of you. That's why I like you."

It was obesity that had rendered Kinué immobile. She was in the best of health and she got no exercise, and in these six months she had fattened beyond recognition. The heaviness and immobility gave more immediacy to her illness. She was constantly taking liver pills, and she would gaze from the chaise longue through the trees at the blue sky, so soon to be lost. Her perpetual refrain was that she was not long for this world, and she was a great trial for the maids, whom Tōru had told that they were in no circumstances to laugh.

What Tōru admired was the cunning with which, offered a set of conditions, she would outflank them and raise defenses which would give her the advantage and reinforce her beauty and perhaps add a touch of the tragic to it. She had immediately sensed that he did not mean to take her out. So she had put her illness to the uses of the situation. Tōru thought he had things to learn from this so stubbornly guarded pride. She had become his teacher.

"Turn around. Oh, it's very nicely cut. The shoulder line is beautiful. Everything looks good on you. Just like me. Well, you must forget all about me tomorrow evening and enjoy yourself. But when you're enjoying yourself most, think for just a moment of the sick girl you've left at home. But just a moment. You need a flower in your lapel. If only I were strong enough I'd go and pick it for you myself. Maid, please. The winter rose, the red one, if you will."

She had the maid pick a little crimson rosebud just coming into bloom, and herself put it in his buttonhole.

"There." With the most languorous, evanescent of fingers, she pushed the stem through. She tapped the glossy silk of the lapel. "Go out into the garden and let me have another look at you."

The corpulent figure seemed to be breathing its last.

At the appointed time, seven in the evening, Tōru pulled up in his Mustang, as directed by the map, at a wide, white-graveled drive in Azabu. There were no other cars yet.

Tōru was astonished at how old-fashioned Keiko's mansion was. The lamps under the trees set off a circular Regency front. There was something rather ghostly about the place, the effect intensified by red ivy blackened by the night.

Tōru was ushered in by a white-gloved butler past the circular domed hallway to a parlor in the rich Momoyama style, and there seen to a Louis XV chair. He was rather ashamed to find himself the first guest. The house was brilliantly lighted but still. There was a large Christmas tree in one corner. It seemed out of place. Left by himself when the butler had taken his order for a drink, he leaned against the old-fashioned paned window and looked out through the trees at the lights of the city and a sky turned purplish by neon.

A door opened and Keiko came in.

The brilliant formal dress of the septuagenarian before him quite robbed him of speech. Sleeves trailing to the hem of the skirt, her evening dress was beaded over its whole surface. The shifting colors and patterns of the beads from the neck down over the skirt were such as to dazzle the eye. At the bosom, the wings of a peacock in green on a gold ground, waves of purple over the sleeves, a continuous wine-colored pattern down over the waist, purple waves and gold clouds on the skirt, the several boundaries marked in gold. The white of the organdy ground was set off by a threefold Western pattern in silver net. From the skirt emerged the toe of a purple satin slipper, and at the always proud neck was an emerald Georgette stole, draped down over the shoulders and reaching to the floor. Below her hair, cut shorter and closer than usual, hung gold earrings. Her face had the frozen look of one that had more than once been ministered to by plastic surgeons, but the parts that still remained under her control seemed to assert themselves all the more haughtily. The awesome eyes, the grand nose. The lips, like red-black bits of apple beginning to rot, tortured into a yet more shining red.

"I'm terribly sorry to have kept you waiting," she

said brightly. The face with its sculptured smile came toward him.

"My but you're looking grand."

"Thank you." Briefly and abstractedly, in the Western fashion, she showed him her well-shaped nostrils.

The aperitifs came.

"Perhaps we should turn down the lights."

The butler turned off the chandelier lights. In the flickering of the Christmas tree, Keiko's eyes flickered, as did the beads on her dress. Tōru was beginning to feel uneasy.

"The others are late. Or is it that I am too early?"

"The others? You're my only guest this evening."

"So you were lying about the others?"

"Oh, I'm sorry. I changed my plans. I thought I would have my Christmas alone with you."

"I think I'll ask to be excused, then."

"Why?" Seated quietly, Keiko made no motion toward stopping him.

"Some sort of plot. Or a trap. Something in any case you've talked over with Father. I'm tired of being made fun of." He had disliked this old woman from their first meeting.

Keiko was motionless. "If it were something I'd talked over with Mr. Honda, I wouldn't have gone to so much trouble. I invited you because I wanted to have a good talk with you, all by ourselves. It is true that I lied to you, because I knew you wouldn't come if you knew you were to be my only guest. But a Christmas dinner with only two people is still a Christmas dinner. Here we are both of us in party dress."

"I suppose you want to give me a good lecturing." Tōru was angry at himself for having let her make her excuses.

"Nothing of the sort. I just want to talk with you quietly about some things Mr. Honda would throttle me for if he were to find out. They are secrets that only Mr. Honda and I know. If you don't want to listen, well, that is that."

"Secrets?"

"Just sit down there quietly, if you will." An elegantly sardonic smile on her lips, she pointed to the somewhat worn Watteau garden party on the chair Tōru had just vacated.

The butler announced dinner. Opening doors Tōru had taken to be a wall, he ushered them into the next room, where the table was set with red candles. Keiko's dress jingled.

Not one to encourage conversation, Tōru ate in silence. The thought that the skill with which he managed his knife and fork was the result of Honda's assiduous tutelage enraged him all over again. Tutelage to make people think him a long-time adept of a cravenness he had not known until he met Honda and Keiko.

Keiko's fingers at knife and fork, beyond the heavy baroque candlesticks, absently quiet and diligent, like an old woman at her knitting, were a young girl's fingers brought into old age.

The chilled turkey was tasteless, like the dry skin of an old man. The chestnut stuffing and the cranberry jelly had for Tōru the sourly saccharine taste of hypocrisy.

"Do you know why you were so suddenly sought after to become heir to the house of Honda?"

"How should I?"

"Very easygoing of you. You haven't wanted to know?"

Tōru did not answer. Putting down her knife and fork, Keiko pointed through the candle smoke at his tuxedo front.

"It's all very simple. It's because you have three moles on your left chest."

Tōru was unable to hide his surprise. Keiko knew

of those three moles, the root of his pride, which through all his life should have attracted the attention of no one but himself. An instant later he had brought himself under control. The surprise had come from the fact that, by chance, the symbol of his own pride had coincided with a symbol of something for someone else. Though the moles may have set the something in motion, that need not mean that he had been found out. But Tōru had underestimated the intuitions of the aged.

The surprise so clear on his face seemed to give Keiko greater confidence. The words poured forth.

"See? You can't believe it. It was all too foolish, too nonsensical from the start. You have told yourself that you have managed everything coolly and realistically, but you swallowed the nonsensical premises whole. Who would be so foolish as to want to adopt a complete stranger on a single meeting just because he had taken a liking? What did you think when we first came with the proposal? We made all sorts of excuses to you and to your superiors, of course. But what did you really think? It puffed you up, I should imagine. People like to think they have their strong points. You thought that your childish dreams and our proposal matched admirably? That your strange childish confidence had been justified? That's what you thought?"

Tōru was for the first time afraid of Keiko. He felt not the slightest constraint because of class, but there are persons endowed with a special nose for scenting out worth. They are the angel-killers.

The conversation was interrupted by dessert. Tōru had let the moment for an answer pass. He knew that he had underestimated his adversary.

"Do you think that your hopes and those of someone else coincide, that your hopes can be smoothly realized for you by someone else? People live for themselves and think only of themselves. You who more than most think only of yourself have gone too far and let yourself be blinded.

"You thought that history has its exceptions. There are none. You thought that the race has its exceptions. There are none.

"There is no special right to happiness and none to unhappiness. There is no tragedy and there is no genius. Your confidence and your dreams are groundless. If there is on this earth something exceptional, special beauty or special evil, nature finds it out and uproots it. We should all by now have learned the hard lesson, that there are no 'elect.'

"You thought, didn't you, that you were a genius beyond compensation. You thought of yourself, didn't you, as a beautiful little cloud of evil floating over humanity.

"Mr. Honda saw it all the minute he saw your moles. He decided in that instant that he must have you with him, to save you from the danger. He thought that if he left you as you were, if he left you to your 'fate,' you would be killed by nature at twenty.

"He tried to save you by adopting you, by smashing to bits your 'godlike' pride, by drilling into you the world's rules for culture and happiness, by making you over into a perfectly ordinary young man. You did not recognize that you had the same starting point as the rest of us. The sign of your refusal to recognize was those three moles. It was affection that made him adopt you without telling you why he wanted to save you. The affection, of course, of a man who knew too much of the world."

Tōru was more and more uneasy. "Why do you say I will die at twenty?"

"I think probably the danger has passed. Let's talk about it in the other room."

A bright fire had been lighted in the fireplace. Below the mantel, a gold-clouded alcove in the Japanese style with a Kōtatsu hanging, two small golden doors opened to reveal the fireplace. Tōru and Keiko sat before the fire, a small table between them. Keiko repeated the long story of birth and rebirth she had had from Honda.

Tōru listened, gazing into the fire. He started at the faint sound of a collapsing log.

Clinging to a log with its smoke, the flame would twist and grow, and then show again in the darkness between log and log, its bed rich with a bright, still repose. Like a dwelling, the small floor dizzying in its reds and vermilions was deep in quiet, marked off by a rough frame of logs.

Sometimes the smoke bursting through the somber logs was like a grass fire far out on a night plain. There were great vistas in the fire, and the shadows moving in the depths of the fireplace were a miniature of the flames of political upheaval tracing shadows across the heavens.

As the flames died down on one log, an even expanse of quiet vermilion would show itself from under a delicate tortoiseshell bed of ashes, trembling like a heap of white feathers. The firm bind of logs would collapse at its foundations. Then, maintaining a precarious balance, it would burn up like a great rock in the air.

Everything was flowing, in motion. The quiet chain of smoke, so stable, was forever breaking up. The collapse of a log that had finished its work brought a sort of repose.

"Very interesting," said Tōru, rather tartly, when he had heard the story to the end. "But where's the proof?"

"Proof?" Keiko hesitated. "Is there proof for the truth?"

"When you say 'truth' it sounds false."

"If you demand proof, I should imagine Mr. Honda

has preserved Kiyoaki Matsugae's diary all these years. You might ask to see it. He wrote only of dreams, and Mr. Honda says all of them have come true. But maybe it doesn't matter. Maybe nothing I've said has anything to do with you. You were born on March twentieth and Ying Chan died in the spring, and you have those three marks, and so it would seem that you are her reincarnation. But we have not been able to find out exactly when she died. Her twin sister said only that it was in the spring, but she seems unable to remember the exact day. Mr. Honda has investigated in any number of ways, but without success. If she was bitten by a snake and died later than March twenty-first, you go scot free. The spirit wanders around for at least a week. So your birthday has to be a week after she died."

"Actually I don't know my own birthday. My father was at sea and there was no one to take care of the details, and the date of registration was put down as the birthday. But I was born before March twentieth."

"The earlier it was, the dimmer the possibility," Keiko said coldly. "But maybe it doesn't matter anyway."

"It doesn't matter?" Tōru showed signs of indignation.

Quite aside from whether or not he believed the terrible story he had heard, to be told that it did not matter seemed to him like a naked denial of his reasons for being. Keiko had the ability to make a person seem like an insect. It lay behind her unchanging gaiety.

In the light from the fire the multicolored evening dress was sending off deep, rich hues. It arched and coiled around her like a rainbow in the night.

"Maybe it doesn't matter. Maybe from the outset you were a fraud. In fact I myself am rather sure that you are a fraud."

He glanced at her profile. She had spoken into the fire as if presenting a petition. There was no describing the splendor of that profile, set aglow by the fire. The fire in the eyes enhanced the proud high bridge of the nose. It sent everyone else into childish fretfulness. It dominated relentlessly.

Thoughts of murder came to Tōru. How could he upset this woman, leave her pleading for her life? Were he to throttle her, to shove her head into the flames, he was sure she would look back at him with a proudly burning face, a grand mane of fire swirling around her. Tōru's self-respect was hurting, and he feared her next words, likely to bring blood. What he most feared was blood pouring from an open wound in his self-respect. Its hemophilia would not permit the flow to be stopped. And so he had until now used all emotions to draw a line between emotion and self-respect, and, avoiding the danger of love, armed himself with countless thorns.

Keiko seemed intent, quietly and ceremoniously, on saying what had to be said.

"We will know for certain that you were a fraud if you don't die in the next six months. We will know that you are not the regrowth of the beautiful seed Mr. Honda was after, and that you are what an entomologist would call a simulator. I doubt myself that we have to wait a year. It does not seem to me that you are doomed to die in six months. There is nothing inevitable about you, not a thing a person would hate to lose. There is in you not a thing to make a person imagining your death feel that a shadow had come over the world.

"You're a mean, cunning little country boy of the sort we see sprawled all over the place. You want to get your hands on your father's money, and so you arrange to have him declared incompetent. You're surprised, aren't you? I know everything. And when you have money and power, what do you propose to seek next? Success? Your thoughts don't go a step beyond those of any mediocre boy. The only way Mr. Honda's training has gone wrong is that it has done nothing more than bring out your essential nature.

"There is nothing in the least special about you. I guarantee you a long life. You have not been chosen by the gods, you will never be at one with your acts, you do not have in you the green light to flash like young lightning with the speed of the gods and destroy yourself. All you have is a certain premature senility. Your life will be suited for coupon-clipping. Nothing more.

"You cannot kill Mr. Honda or me. Your sort of evil is a legal sort of evil. All puffed up by illusions born of abstract concepts, you strut about as the master of a destiny even though you have none of the qualifications. You think you have seen to the ends of the earth. But you have not once had an invitation beyond the horizon. You have nothing to do with light or enlightenment, there is no real spirit in flesh or in heart. At least Ying Chan's spirit was in the shining beauty of her flesh. Nature has not had a glance for you, it has not had a glimmer of hostility toward you. The person Mr. Honda is looking for has to be one to inspire jealousy of nature at its own creation.

"You're a clever boy, no more. If someone pays your expenses you swim through the entrance examinations and a good job is waiting for you at the other end. A model student for the Education Fund. Propaganda material for the do-gooders who say that if material wants are taken care of, all sorts of hidden treasures will emerge. Mr. Honda was too good to you, and gave you too much confidence. He prescribed the wrong dose, that is all. Give you the right dose and you'll be back on the track. Make you the secretary to some vulgar politician and you'll wake up. I'll be happy to introduce you to one, at your convenience, any time.

"You will do well to remember what I have said. You have seen and think you have seen it all; but it is no more than the little circle in a thirty-power telescope. You would have been happier, I suppose, if we had let you go on thinking that was the whole world."

"It was you who dragged me out of it."

"And what made you come so happily was the thought that you were different.

"Kiyoaki Matsugae was caught by unpredictable love, Isao Iinuma by destiny, Ying Chan by the flesh. And you? By a baseless sense of being different, perhaps?

"If destiny is something that takes hold of a person from outside and drags him after, then the other three had destiny. And has anything caught you? Only we, Mr. Honda and I." Letting the green and gold peacock on her bosom take the fire as it would, Keiko laughed. "We are two bored, cold, cynical old people. Can your pride really permit you to call us destiny? A nasty old man and woman? An old voyeur and an old lesbian?

"You may think you have taken stock of the world. The ones who come summoning a boy like you are the ones who have taken stock of the world. The one who drags out the conceited purveyor of awareness is the veteran practitioner of the same trade. No one else would have come knocking on your door, you may be sure. You would have gone through life without the knock, and the results would have been the same. Because you have no destiny. The beautiful death was not for you. It was not for you to be like the other three. The drab, dreary heir, that is the role for you. I invited you tonight to let you learn all about it."

Tōru's hand was trembling, and his eyes were on the poker beside the fire. It would have been easy to reach for it, pretending to stir the fire. He would arouse no curiosity, and then he had only to swing it. He could feel the weight of it in his hand, he could see the blood spurting over gold chair and gold doors. But he did not reach out. He was fearfully thirsty, but he did not ask for water. The anger that enflamed his cheeks seemed to him like the first passion he had known. It remained shut up within him.

28

REMARKABLY, Tōru came to Honda with a request. He wanted to borrow Kiyoaki's diary.

Honda was reluctant to lend it, but even more reluctant not to.

He let Tōru have it for two or three days. They became a week. On the morning of the twenty-eighth, when he had resolved to have it back, he was startled by an outcry from the maids. Tōru, in his bedroom, had taken poison.

It being the end of the year, the family doctor was not available. Honda had to take the risk of publicity and call an ambulance. There was a wall of onlookers when the ambulance came shrieking up. They were eager for another scandal from a house that had already provided one.

Tōru remained in a coma and there were convulsions, but his life was not in danger. He felt severe pains in the eyes, however, when he regained consciousness. Impediments developed in both eyes, and he totally lost his sight. The poison had attacked the retina, which had deteriorated beyond hope of recovery.

The poison was industrial wood alcohol, stolen under cover of the year-end confusion from a factory that belonged to a relative of one of the maids. The maid, who followed Tōru unquestioningly, wept and insisted that she had not dreamed he would drink it.

The blind Tōru said almost nothing. After the turn of the year Honda asked him about the diary.

"I burned it just before I took the poison," he answered briefly.

His answer when asked for an explanation was much to the point.

"Because I never dream."

Honda asked for Keiko's help any number of times while all this was taking place. There was something strange about her. It was as if she alone knew the motive for the attempted suicide.

"He has twice the pride of most boys. I should imagine he did it to prove he's a genius."

When pressed, she admitted that she had revealed everything at her Christmas party. She said she had done it out of friendship, but Honda replied that he wished to see no more of her. He thus announced the end of a beautiful friendship that had lasted more than twenty years.

The declaration of incompetence was revoked, and now it was the blind Tōru who needed a guardian. Honda drew up a notarized will and named the most reliable guardian he could think of.

Tōru dropped out of the university, remained shut up in the house, and spoke to no one except Kinué. The maids were dismissed, and Honda hired a woman who had had experience as a nurse. Tōru spent most of the day in Kinué's cottage. All through the day

Kinué's soft voice could be heard through the doors. Tōru did not seem to weary of making reply.

His birthday passed on the twentieth of March. He showed no sign of dying. He learned to read Braille. When by himself he listened to records. He could recognize birds by their songs. One day, after a very long silence, he spoke to Honda. He asked that Honda let him marry Kinué. Though aware that her insanity was hereditary, Honda gave his permission immediately.

Decay advanced, the signs of the end appeared quietly. Like hairs tickling his neck when he came back from the barber shop, death, forgotten most of the time, would come tickling when remembered. It seemed strange to Honda that, though all of the preparations for receiving it had been made, death did not come.

Honda had been aware during the excitement of a certain heaviness in the region of his stomach, but he did not, as the old Honda might have been expected to, rush off to a doctor. He diagnosed the trouble as indigestion. He continued to have little appetite after the New Year came. It was not like him to pass it off as only a result of the troubles, nor was it like him to take emaciation as a result of mental anguish.

But it had come to seem that there was no distinguishing between pain of the spirit and pain of the flesh. What was the difference between humiliation and a swollen prostate? Between the pangs of sorrow and pneumonia? Senility was a proper ailment of both the spirit and the flesh, and the fact that senility was an incurable disease meant that existence was an incurable disease. It was a disease unrelated to existentialist theories, the flesh itself being the disease, latent death.

If the cause of decay was illness, then the fundamental cause of that, the flesh, was illness too. The essence of the flesh was decay. It had its spot in time to give evidence of destruction and decay.

Why did people first become aware of that fact only as old age came on? Why, when it buzzed faintly past the ear in the brief noontide of the flesh, did they note it only to forget it? Why did the healthy young athlete, in the shower after his exertions, watching the drops of water hit his shining flesh like hail, not see that the high tide of life itself was the cruelest of ills, a dark, amber-colored lump?

For Honda now, life was senescence, senescence was life. It was wrong that these two synonyms should forever be libeling each other. Only now, eighty-one years after he fell into this world, did Honda know the perverse essential at the heart of every pleasure.

Appearing now on this side and now on the other of human will, it sent up an opaque mist, the defense of the will against the cruel and terrible proposition that life and senescence are synonymous. History knew the truth. History was the most inhuman product of humanity. It scooped up the whole of human will and, like the goddess Kali in Calcutta, dripped blood from its mouth as it bit and crunched.

We are fodder to stuff some craw. In his shallow way, Imanishi, who died in the fire, had been aware of it. For the gods, for destiny, for history, the only human endeavor imitating the two, it was wise to leave man unaware of the fact until he had grown old.

What fodder Honda had been! What unnutritious, tasteless, dusty fodder! Instinctively refusing to become palatable, he now at the end of it all wanted to stab the mouth of his devourer with the tasteless bones of his awareness; but he was certain to fail.

Tōru went blind in an attempt at suicide. His twenty-first birthday came and went. Honda had no further wish to look into possible traces left behind by the person, unknown, dead at twenty, who was the true reincarnation. If there had been such a person, very well. Honda no longer had the energy to look into that person's life, nor would it have become him to make the effort. The movements of the heavenly bodies had left him aside. By a small miscalculation, they had led Honda and the reincarnation of Ying Chan into separate parts of the universe. Three reincarnations had occupied Honda's life and, after drawing their paths of light across it (that too had been a most improbable accident), gone off in another burst of light to an unknown corner of the heavens. Perhaps somewhere, some time, Honda would meet the hundredth, the ten thousandth, the hundred millionth reincarnation.

There was no hurry.

Why hurry? He did not know even where his own rut was taking him. So concluded Honda, a man who had not been in a hurry to die. What he had seen at Benares was human indestructibility as the fundamental essence of the universe. The other world did not lie quivering beyond time, nor did it lie shining beyond space. If to die meant to return to the four elements, to dissolve into the corporate entity, then there was no law holding that the place of birth and rebirth need be no other than here. It was an accident, an utterly senseless accident, that Kiyoaki and Isao and Ying Chan had all appeared beside Honda. If an element in Honda was of exactly the same quality as an element at the other end of the universe, there was no exchange procedure, once individuality had been lost, whereby they could purposely come together through space and time. The particle here and the particle there have precisely the same significance. There was nothing to keep the Honda of the next world from being at the farther side of the universe. When, after the string has been cut and the beads scattered on the table, they are strung in another order, the one indestructible rule, provided no beads have fallen under the table, is that their number must be as before.

Eternity does not come into being because I think I exist: Buddhist doctrine now seemed to Honda mathematically sound. The self was the order of beads determined by the self and therefore without validity.

These thoughts and the almost imperceptible decay of the flesh went together like the wheels of a cart. It was all right, even pleasant, to put the matter so.

In May or thereabouts he began to suffer from pains in the abdomen. They were very stubborn, and sometimes spread to the back. While he was still seeing Keiko, ailments inevitably came into the conversation. He would speak casually of some serious ailment, and with a great stir she would lay it out on the carving board. A stabbing sort of kindness competing with an amiable tendency to exaggerate, she would assign to it all the malignant medical terms she could think of, and he would be off to a hospital in a spirit of something like jest. Now that he was no longer seeing Keiko, he had to an astonishing degree lost this sort of enthusiastic disquiet. Pain such as he was able to endure he left to the ministrations of his masseause. Even the thought of a doctor was wearing.

Indeed general debilitation and rhythmical attacks of pain brought new powers to think. His aging brain had lost all ability to concentrate, but now it returned, and pain even worked aggressively upon it, to bring certain vital faculties other than the purely rational to bear. At the age of eighty-one Honda attained to a wondrous and mysterious realm that had before been denied him. He knew now that a more comprehensive view of the world was to be had from physical depression than from intelligence, from a dull pain in the entrails than from reason, a loss of appetite than analysis. The addition of a single vague pain in the back to a world that had been to the clear eye of reason a minutely detailed structure, and cracks began to appear in the pillars and vaults, what had seemed like hard rock proved to be soft cork, what had seemed to have solid form turned to inchoate jelly.

Honda had by himself reached that honing of the senses, achieved by few in this world, to live death from within. When he looked back upon life from its far side other than as a journey over a flat surface, hoping that what had declined would revive, seeking to believe that pain was transient, clinging greedily to happiness as a thing of the moment, thinking that good fortune must be followed by bad, seeing in all the ups and downs and rises and falls the ground for his own prospects—then everything was in place, pulled tight, and the march to the end was in order. The boundary between man and object disappeared. The portentous ten-floor building in the American style and the fragile human beings who walked beneath it had as a condition that they would outlast Honda, but as a condition of equal importance that they would fall, like the crape myrtle so rudely cut down. Honda no longer had cause to sympathize, and he had lost the imagination that gives rise to sympathy. The loss had been easy, for he had always been short on imagination.

Reason still worked, but it was frozen. Beauty had become a phantom.

And he lost that greatest ill of the spirit, to will and to plan. In a sense that was the great liberation provided by pain.

Honda heard the chatter that envelops the world like gold dust. Conditional talk, noisily claiming permanent residence.

"Let's go to a hot spring, Grandfather, when you're feeling better. Would you like Yumoto, or would Ikaho be better?"

"Let's have a drink when the contract is signed."

"Let's."

"Is it true that now is a good time to get into the stock market?"

"When I grow up can I eat a whole box of cream puffs all by myself?"

"Let's go to Europe next year."

"In three years I'll be able to buy a boat from my savings."

"I can't die till he grows up."

"I'll get my retirement pay and we'll build an apartment house and have a quiet old age."

"Day after tomorrow at three? I don't know whether I can make it or not. No, you have to believe me, I really don't. Suppose we say you'll be there if you feel like it."

"We'll have to get a new air-conditioner next year."

"It's a real problem. Can't we at least cut down on entertainment expenses next year?"

"They say you can have as much tobacco and liquor as you want when you're twenty."

"Thank you. It's very kind of you. Next Tuesday evening at six."

"That's just the point. That's the way he is. Just wait two or three days and he'll be around with a sheepish look on his face to apologize."

"Good-bye. See you tomorrow."

Foxes all, walking the path of foxes. The hunter had only to wait in the thicket.

It seemed to Honda that he was a fox with the eyes of a hunter, walking the path of the foxes even though he knew that he would be caught.

Summer and ripeness were approaching.

It was mid-July when Honda finally stirred himself to make an appointment at the Cancer Research Institute.

On the day before the appointment he had one of his rare looks at television. It was a sunny afternoon, the summer rains having just lifted. There was a shot of a swimming pool. In the unpleasantly artificial blue of the water, young people were splashing and jumping and swimming.

The faint, fleeting scent of beautiful flesh!

To deny the flesh, to see them as skeletons disporting themselves by a pool in the summer sun, was ordinary, dull. Anyone could do it. Anyone could deny life, see through to the bones beneath the youthful surface. The most mediocre of persons could do it.

What revenge could there be in that? Honda would end his life without having known the feelings of the owner of beautiful flesh. If for a single month he could live in it! He should have had a try. What must it be like, to wear such a beautiful covering? To see people fall down before it. When admiration passed the gentle and docile and became lunatic worship, it would become torment for the possesor. In the delirium and the torment were true holiness. What Honda had missed had been the dark, narrow path through the flesh to holiness. To travel it was of course the privilege of few.

Tomorrow he would have a thorough examination. He did not know what the results would be. He should at least be clean. He had the bath drawn before dinner.

The middle-aged housekeeper, formerly a nurse, whom he had employed without consulting Tōru, was an unfortunate woman, twice widowed, but she was a model of kindness and devotion. Honda had been thinking that he must provide for her in his will. She even saw him to the bathtub lest he fall, and left behind the frays of her concern like cobwebs in the dressing room. Honda did not like being seen naked by a woman. He took off his bathrobe before the steaming mirror. He looked at himself. His ribs were in sharp relief, his stomach sagged, and in its shadow hung a shriveled white bean; and so down to whitish shins from which the flesh seemed to have been stripped away. The knees were like swellings. How many years of self-deception would it take to find rejuvenation in this ugliness? But he was able to console himself with a long smile of commiseration at the thought of how much worse it would be if he had been beautiful in the first place.

The examination took a week. He went to the hospital for the results.

"You must come in immediately. The sooner you come in the better." So it had happened. "We didn't catch a trace of it all those other times, and it seems unfair to have it jump out all of a sudden without warning. A person can't be too careful." The doctor smiled a beatific smile, as if reproving Honda for some dereliction. "But there seems to be no more than a benign growth on the pancreas. All we have to do is cut it away."

"It wasn't the stomach?"

"The pancreas. If the gastroscope pictures turn out I'll show them to you."

The diagnosis had coincided with his own personal one. He asked a week's reprieve.

He wrote a long letter and had it sent special delivery. It was to inform the Gesshū Temple that he would be visiting on July twenty-second. Since the letter would arrive on the twentieth, the day after posting, or the twenty-first, he hoped that the Abbess might be persuaded to receive him. He described his career over the past sixty years and apologized for not having awaited an invitation. The matter, he explained, was rather urgent.

On the twenty-first, the morning of his departure, he went out to the cottage.

The housekeeper had pleaded that he take her with him to Nara, but he had said that he must make the journey alone. She gave him elaborate instructions. She packed his suitcases with warm clothes to protect him from air-conditioning. It was almost more than an old man could lift.

She also gave elaborate instructions for his visit to the cottage. It seemed to Honda that she might be apologizing for what she considered oversights on her part.

"I must tell you that Mr. Tōru wears that one white kimono like a bird its feathers. Miss Kinué is terribly fond of it, and when I tried to take it off and wash it she bit my finger, and so there it is still on him. Mr. Tōru is, as you know, a very undemanding person, and it doesn't seem to bother him at all to wear that one kimono day and night. You must be prepared for it. And then, I don't know quite how to say it, the maid who takes care of the cottage says Miss Kinué vomits a great deal and has strange eating habits. She seems delighted that she should really be sick. I wonder. Anyway, you must be prepared."

She probably did not see how Honda's eyes shone at this oracle telling him his line would be cut off from the eye of reason.

Pushing at his cane, Honda sat down on the veranda. The door was open. He had been able to see into the cottage from the garden.

"Well, Father," said Kinué. "Good morning."

"Good morning. I'm off to Kyoto and Nara for a few days and I wanted to ask you to look after the house."

"A trip? How nice." Uninterested, she returned to her work.

"What are you doing?"

"Getting ready for the wedding. Do you like it? Not just for me, for Tōru too. People say they've never seen a more beautiful couple."

Tōru, in dark glasses, sat silently between the two.

Honda knew nothing of Tōru's inner life since he had lost his sight, and he kept his always limited powers of imagination under control. Tōru lived on. But nothing was more capable of conveying heaviness to Honda than this lump of silence no longer a threat.

The cheeks below the dark glasses were paler and the lips redder. Tōru had always sweated heavily. There were beads of sweat at the open neck of the kimono. He sat with legs crossed and left everything to Kinué, but the effort of putting Honda aside was evident in the nervousness with which he scratched his leg and wiped at his chest. There was no strength in the motions. It was as if he were moved by strings from the ceiling.

Though his hearing was apparently keen, he gave no sign that he was taking the outside world in through his ears. No doubt other people, save only Kinué, would have had the same impression, but however confidently the visitor approached, he was for Tōru a discarded scrap of the outside world, a rusty can overgrown by the summer grasses.

Tōru had no contempt, no resistance. He sat in silence.

Though known to be fraudulent, the beautiful eyes and smile had brought him the tentative recognition of the world. Now the smile had left him. There might be some comfort if even regret or sorrow were visible, but he showed emotion to no one except Kinué, and she did not speak of what she saw.

The cicadas had been noisy since morning. Through the branches of the neglected garden, the sky shone like a string of blue beads. The cottage seemed even darker than usual.

The tea garden was reproduced in the circles of dark glasses that would in any case have turned away the outer world. There were no flowering trees now

that the crape myrtle was gone from beside the stone
basin. The shrubs among stones that did not quite add
up to a landscape and the light through the trees were
caught in the glasses.

Tōru's eyes no longer took in the outside world.
The scene outside, no longer related to vision and
awareness, filled the black lenses in intricate detail.
It seemed strange to Honda that all he saw was himself and the little garden behind him. If the sea and
the ships Tōru had seen all through the day and their
strong funnel marks were an intimate part of his
awareness, then behind the glasses and the eyes moving whitely from time to time, the images must be
locked in forever. If for Honda and for everyone
Tōru's inner workings had become forever a mystery,
then it need not surprise them that sea and ships and
funnel marks too were shut up within.

But if they belonged to a world outside of and ir-
relevant to Tōru, they should be sketched in detail
on the lenses. Had Tōru perhaps completely merged
the outer world and the inner? A white butterfly flew
across the dark glass picture.

Tōru's heels looked up from the skirt of his kimono.
They were white and wrinkled as those of a drowned
corpse, and patches of dirt were scattered like bits of
foil over them. The kimono had gone quite limp. Sweat
drew clusters of yellow clouds at the neckline.

Honda had for some time been aware of a strange
odor. He saw that the dirt and oil on the kimono had
mixed with the sweat into the smell as of a dank canal
that young men put out in the summer. Tōru had lost
his fastidiousness.

And there was no smell of flowers. The room was
strewn with flowers, but they gave off no odor. There
were red and white hollyhocks everywhere, no doubt
ordered from a florist, but they were several days old,
and dry and wilted.

Kinué's hair was garlanded with white hollyhocks, not inserted into the hair but leaning this way and that, held unevenly in place by rubber bands. As her head bobbed they sent forth a dry rustling.

She would stand up and sit down again, decorating Tōru's still rich hair with red hollyhocks. There was a band around his head. She would poke three and four dry red hollyhocks into it and then, like a student of flower arranging, stand back and survey the results. Flowers falling over his ears and cheeks should have been an annoyance, but Tōru had abdicated control of the regions above his neck.

After a time Honda went to dress for the journey.

29

HAVING LEARNED that the road to Nara was now excellent, Honda took a room in Kyoto. He stayed at the Miyako Hotel and hired a car for noon on the twenty-second. The clouds were out of keeping with the heat. Showers seemed likely up in the hills.

So he was here, thought Honda, content. Sensations came as through screens to his weary body and heart, beneath old-fashioned unbleached linen. He had brought a blanket as defense against the air-conditioning. The shrilling of the cicadas in the Keagé district near the hotel sank through the windows.

He made a firm resolution as the car started off. "Today I am not going to see skeletons beneath flesh. They are only a concept. I will see and remember things as they are. It will be my last pleasure, my last effort. My last good look. I must look. I must take in everything, with an unoccupied heart."

The car passed the Sambōin Temple at Daigo. From the bridge at the Kajūji Temple it turned onto the National Nara Highway, and from Nara Park the Tenri Highway. In an hour it was at Obitoké.

Honda had noticed numbers of Kyoto women with parasols, not often seen in Tokyo. Some of the faces beneath were shining, some—because of the designs on the parasols, perhaps—were dark. Some were beautiful shining, some were beautiful dark.

As they turned from the northern outskirts of Yamashina they were in suburban wastes, a region of small factories burning in the summer sun. Waiting with several women and children at a bus stop was a pregnant woman, warm in a bold Western print. The faces wore a certain stagnation, as of tea leaves floating on the torrents of life. Beyond was a dusty tomato patch.

The Daigo district was a clutter of all the dreary details of new construction, to be seen throughout Japan: raw building materials and blue-tiled roofs, television towers and power lines, Coca-Cola advertisements and drive-in snack bars. Among heaps of rubble below cliffs where wild daisies stabbed at the sky were automobile dumps, blue and yellow and black, piled precariously one on the other, the gaudy colors molten in the sun. At this sad accumulation, kept hidden at most times by the automobile, Honda thought of an adventure story he had read as a child, and of the heaps of ivory in the swamp where elephants go to die. Perhaps, sensing the approach of death, automobiles too gather at their own graveyards. In any event, the brightness, the openness, the want of shame seemed to him quite automobilish.

From Uji the hills were for the first time green.

A billboard proclaimed "Delicious Chilled Sweets." Bamboo leaves arched over the road.

They crossed Moon Bridge in Uji and were on the old Nara Highway. They passed Fushimi and Yamashiro. A sign informed them that Nara was twenty miles distant. Times went by. At each marker Honda thought of the expression "milestones on the way to the grave." It seemed to him inconceivable that he would return over the same road. Sign followed sign, marking clearly the road he must travel. Nineteen miles to Nara. A mile nearer the grave. He opened a window, stealing an inch from air-conditioning, and the cicadas were ringing in his ears, as if the whole world were sounding in solitude under the summer sun.

Another filling station. More Coca-Cola.

The beautiful green embankment of the River Kizu stretched far away to the right. It was deserted, roily clouds defining its handsome groves. Blue patches glowed in the sky.

And what, thought Honda vacantly, might it be? The green platform was like a doll stand. The turbulent clouds made it seem that dolls had been lined up and then lost. Or perhaps transparent rows of dolls were still there. Would they be mortuary images? Perhaps images of darkness shattered by a tempest of light still left traces against the sky; and that was why the embankment was so grand, so solemnly respectful. It raised into the sky the light left behind by rows of dolls. Or perhaps the light which he seemed to see was the negative of a bottomless darkness.

He was aware of eyes once again seeking to go behind objects. They were what he had banned as he left the hotel. If he let them have their way the concrete world would once again collapse like a dike from the hole pierced by his glance. He must persevere yet a little more. He must hold it yet a little longer, the work of glass so delicate and ready to break.

The Kizu lay to their right for a time, its many shoals below them. A power line sagged down over it, as if melted and bent by the heat.

Presently the road turned to cross the Kizu on a steel bridge, and a sign told them that Nara was only five miles away. They crossed numbers of white country lanes bordered by grasses that had not yet sent forth plumes. The bamboo thickets were dense. The young bamboo leaves filled with sunlight as with warm water wore a soft, golden sheen, like the pelts of fox cubs, against the silent black of the evergreens.

Nara came into view.

As they descended through the pines along the hills, the great, soaring, protecting roof of the Tōdaiji and the golden kite tails at its gables were Nara.

The car moved through quiet streets, past plain, awning-shaded old shops with white gloves and other wares hung out for sale. They came to Nara Park. The sun was stronger, the cicada calls that hammered at the back of Honda's head were intenser. White spots on summer deer floated up through dappled sunlight.

Turning onto the Tenri Highway, they passed through shining fields. To the right from a casual little bridge a road led to Obitoké and Obitoké Station; to the left, another to the hills at the base of which lay the Gesshūji. Fringing the paddies, it was now paved, and the drive to the lower gate was an easy one.

30

THEY COULD perfectly well drive to the mountain gate, a considerable distance up the hill, altogether too far for an old man to walk, said the driver, looking up at the yet fiercer sun in the cloudless sky; but Honda refused, and told him to wait at the lower gate. He had to know for himself Kiyoaki's sufferings of sixty years before.

Leaning on his stick, he looked down from the gate, his back to the shade that invited from within.

Songs of cicadas and crickets filled the air. Into such quietness was woven the roar of automobiles on the Tenri Highway, beyond the fields. There were no automobiles on the road before him. White gravel delicately lined the shoulders of the road.

The serenity of the Yamato Plain was as it had always been. It lay flat as the world of man. Obitoké shone in the distance, its roofs like little shellfish. A trace of smoke hung over it. Perhaps it now had small factories. The inn where Kiyoaki had lain ill was at the foot of a flagstone slope such as was probably to be found in the village even now; but he thought it would be useless to look for the inn itself.

An endlessly blue sky arched over village and plain. Clouds trailed tatters of white satin like mirages from the misted hills beyond. The upper lines cut into the sky with a clear, statue-like beauty.

Honda squatted down, overcome by heat and fatigue. He felt as if the malign light from the sharp blades of summer grass were stabbing at his eyes. He felt that decay had been smelled out by a fly that brushed past his nose.

With his eyes he reprimanded the driver, who had climbed from the car, and, worried, was coming toward him.

He was beginning to doubt that in fact he could reach the mountain gate. His back and his stomach were aching. He waved off the driver and went inside the gate, determined to be healthy for as long as the man was watching. Gasping for breath, helped by the curves, he made his way up the uneven gravel road, catching through the corner of his left eye the bright yellow of moss, like a sickness, on the trunk of a persimmon tree, and, on his right, the lavender heads of bellflowers from which most of the petals had fallen.

The shadows that blocked off the road ahead had a sort of mystic quiet. The uneven road, which would be a river bottom in a rain, shone where the sun struck it like mineral outcroppings, and whispered with the coolness of its shadows. There was a reason for the shadows, but Honda doubted that it was in the trees themselves.

He asked himself and his stick at which shadow he might rest. The fourth shadow, already invisible from the automobile, quietly invited him. Coming to it, he sat, almost collapsed, on a chestnut root.

"In the beginning," thought Honda, as if of undisputed reality, "it was decided that I would rest on this day at this moment in the shade of this tree."

Sweat and insect songs, forgotten while he was walking, surged forward as he sat down. He pressed his forehead against his stick. The pressure of the silver head drowned out the pain throbbing in his stomach and back.

The doctor had told him he had tumor of the pancreas. Smiling, he had said that it was benign. *Smiling, benign.* To stretch out hopes on such words was to trample on the pride of a man who had lived through eighty-one years. Honda considered refusing surgery when he returned to Tokyo. If he did, however, the doctor was certain to bring pressure upon "near relatives." He had already fallen into the trap. He had fallen into one trap when he had been born into this world, and there ought not to be another trap waiting at the end of the way. He must laugh at it all, thought Honda. He must pretend to hope. The sacrificial kid in India had gone on struggling for so long after its head had fallen.

The eye of the troublesome supervisor no longer upon him, Honda leaned on his stick and reeled extravagantly as he made his way up the slope. He began to feel as if he were being funny. The pain left him and his step was brisker.

The smell of summer grasses filled the air. Pines were thick along the road. Leaning on his stick, he looked up at the sky. In the strong sunlight the cones among the thick branches were etched scale by scale. He came to an abandoned tea patch on the left, matted with spider webs and creepers.

There were strips of shadow ahead. The nearer ones were like the slate of a damaged blind, the farther ones were richly black, gathered in threes and fours, like sashes for mourning weeds.

A large pine cone lay fallen on the road. On the pretext of picking it up, he sat down on a giant pine root. His stomach was heavily, painfully hot. The fatigue, unable to find an outlet, bent like a rusty wire. As he toyed with the cone, fully opened and dried, the tea-colored scales put up a powerful resistance to his fingers. Dew-flowers dotted the way, their blossoms wilting in the sun, delicate traces of greenish lavender among leaves like young swallows' wings. The great pine tree against which he leaned, the

237

celadon of the sky above, the clouds like leavings from a broom—everything was ominously, threateningly dry.

Honda could not identify the insect songs that filled it all. A sound like the drone bass of all insects, a sound like a gnashing of teeth in a nightmare, a sound like an aimless echoing against the ribs.

He stood up again, and again he wondered whether he would reach the mountain gate. As he walked on, he could only count the number of shadows ahead. How many more shadows could he make his way past in the intensity of the heat, the torment of the slope? But he had already passed three since he had begun counting. A shadow stretched halfway across the road. Should he count it as a full shadow or only half a shadow?

Where the road curved gently to the left there were bamboo thickets. They were like settlements in the world of man. The delicate young leaves crowded thickly one against another, some light as asparagus, some black with a powerful malice and perversity.

As he sat down and wiped at the sweat once more, he saw a butterfly, the first. It was an outline in the distance, and cobalt freshly adorned the russet of the wings as it came nearer.

He came to a marsh. He rested under the strong green of a chestnut on the bank. There was not a breath of air. A dead pine tree lay like a bridge across a corner of the yellow-green marsh, the surface of which was disturbed only by the tracks of water striders. Around it shimmered tiny ripples, disturbing the dull blue reflection of the sky. The dead tree was a reddish brown to the tips of its needles. Propped up, it appeared, by branches in the marsh bottom, the trunk was above water, rusty red in a sea of green, its original shape still intact. It continued without a doubt to be a pine tree.

He started off again, as if following the hairtail butterfly that darted out happily from among the still plumeless grasses and foxtails. The tarnished green of the cypress grove across the marsh spread to the near side. Little by little the shadows were thicker.

He could feel the sweat coming through his shirt and soaking the back of his suit coat. He could not be sure whether it was a healthy sweat from the heat or a cold, oily sweat. In any event he had not sweated so profusely since he had reached old age.

Where the cypress grove gave way to a grove of cryptomeria, there stood a lone *nemu* tree. The soft clusters of leaves in among the hard needles of the cryptomerias were like wraiths, like afternoon slumber. They made him think of Thailand. A white butterfly from the *nemu* led him on his way.

The road was steeper. The mountain gate would be near. The cryptomerias were thicker, and a cool breeze came from among them. Walking was now easy. The bands across the road had until now been the shadows of trees. Now they were strips of sunlight.

The butterfly cut an uncertain path through the darkness of the crytomeria grove. It drew a low line across ferns shining liquidly in sunlight to the black gate within. For some reason, thought Honda, all the butterflies hereabouts flew low near the ground.

He passed the black gate. The mountain gate lay ahead. So finally he was at the Gesshūji. He had lived these sixty years only to come again.

Gazing at the prow-shaped pine that served as a carriage stop, Honda found it hard to believe that he was here. He felt strangely refreshed, even reluctant to reach his destination. He stood at a pillar of the mountain gate, which was flanked by two much smaller and lower gates. Sixteen-petal chrysanthemums were stamped on the ridge tiles. On the left pillar was a neat, lady-like sign identifying the temple as the Gesshūji, under the protection of the Imperial House. On the right pillar was a dim inscription in relief: "Peace on Earth. Within is Housed the Imperial Recitation Text of the *Prajñāparamitā-sūtra*. A Fortress of the Law of His Benign Majesty."

There were five stripes on the egg-colored earthen wall to indicate the high rank of the temple. Across yellowish gravel, steppingstones led to the doorway in a checkered pattern. Honda counted them with his stick, and when he had come to ninety he was at the closed doors. In the recessed grip his hand touched a chrysanthemum and clouds cut from white paper.

The farthest corner of the interior came back to him. He stood motionless, forgetting to announce himself. Sixty years ago the young Honda had stood on this same doorstep before this same door. The paper would have been changed a hundred times in those years, but a clean white expanse blocked the way now as it had that cold spring day. Though the grain of the wood was perhaps a little more prominent, it showed little sign of the wear of the winds and the snows. Only an instant had passed.

Ill at the Obitoké inn, Kiyoaki had staked everything on this trip to the Gesshūji. Feverish, he would still be waiting for Honda's return; and what would he think when he saw that in that instant Honda had become a bent, immobile old man?

A steward probably in his sixties, dressed in an open-necked shirt, came to receive him. He needed help in negotiating the last high step. Leading him to a suite of rooms, eight mats and six, in the main hall, the man said politely that they had received his letter and perused its contents, and motioned him to a cushion laid out with geometric precision on a mat with a figured border, white on black. He did not remember the rooms from six decades before.

On the scroll in the alcove, in the style of Sesshū, a dragon twisted and writhed among storm clouds. Below it was a crisp, tidy little arrangement of wild carnations. An old nun in a white kimono of cotton crepe and a white obi brought red and white sweets and cold tea on a rimmed tray. Through open doors green floated in from the garden. There was a thick growth of maples and arbovitae, and beyond it a white gallery; and nothing more.

The steward talked of this and that, and the moments passed. Honda sat quietly in the breeze. The sweat and the aching had left him. He felt that rescue had come.

He was in a room of the Gesshūji, which he had thought it would be impossible to visit. The approach of death had made the visit easy, had unloosed the weight that held him in the depths of being. It was even a comfort to think, from the light repose the struggle up the hill had brought him, that Kiyoaki, struggling against illness up that same road, had been given wings to soar with by the denial that awaited him.

The shrilling of cicadas remained in his ears, but here in the dusk it was cool, like the dying echo of a bell. The old man talked on, making no further reference to the letter. Honda could not bring himself to ask whether he would see the Abbess.

He began to fear that the empty passage of the moments was a circumspect way of informing him that the Abbess would not receive him. Perhaps the old steward had seen the article in the weekly magazine. Perhaps he had advised her to plead an indisposition.

Honda did not feel timid about seeing her, guilt-ridden though he was. Without the crime and the guilt and the mortality he would not have had the courage for that climb. He now saw that the scandal had given him his first dark prompting. Tōru's attempted suicide, his blindness, Honda's illness, Kinué's pregnancy, had all pointed to the same spot. It was true: they had frozen into a cluster and forced him up that burning road. Without them he could only have looked up at the radiance of the Gesshūji upon a distant summit.

If, after so much, the Abbess were to refuse him because of the incident, he could call it fate. He would not see her in this life. He was sure all the same he would see her one day, even if he was denied a meeting on this last spot in this last hour in this world.

Cool repose replaced fretfulness, resignation sorrow, to make the passage of time bearable.

The old nun appeared again, and whispered something in the steward's ear.

"Her Reverence has informed us that she is ready to see you," he said, in the accents of this West Country. "Come with me, if you will, please."

Honda wanted to believe his ears.

The green light from the northern garden was too strong, and for a moment he did not recognize it; but it was here, sixty years before, that the Abbess's predecessor had received him.

He remembered the bright review of the seasons on that earlier screen. It had been replaced by a plain screen of wattled reeds. Beyond the veranda burned the green of a small tea garden, alive with cicadas. Beyond a profusion of maples, plums, and tea bushes were the red buds of an oleander. The summer light fell sharply upon the white spears of dwarf bamboo among the steppingstones, repeating the white light from the sky above the wooded hills.

A beating of wings seemed almost to strike the wall. A sparrow flew in from the gallery and on again, its shadow wavering against the white wall.

The door to the inner apartments slid open. Before Honda, who had brought his knees together in stiff formality, the old Abbess appeared, led by a white-clad novice. The pale figure in a white kimono and a cloak of deep purple would be Satoko, now eighty-three.

Honda felt tears come to his eyes. He was powerless to look up at her.

She faced him across the table. The nose was the finely carved nose of those years before, and the eyes were the same beautiful eyes. Satoko had changed utterly, and yet he knew at a glance that it was Satoko. The bloom of youth had in a jump of sixty years become the extreme of age, Satoko had escaped the journey through the gloomy world. A person who crosses a garden bridge from shadow into sunlight may seem to change faces. If the beautiful young face was the face in the shadow, such, no more, was the change to the beautiful old face now in the sunlight. He remembered how, as he left the hotel, Kyoto faces had seemed bright and dark under parasols and how one could predict the quality of beauty from the brightness and darkness.

For Honda it had been sixty years. For Satoko had it been the time it takes to cross a garden bridge from shadow into sunlight?

Age had sped in the direction not of decay but of purification. The skin seemed to glow with a still light; the beauty of the eyes was clearer, shining through something like a patina. Age had crystallized into a perfect jewel. It was cold though diaphanous, roundly soft though hard, and the lips were still moist. There were wrinkles, deep and innumerable, but they were bright as if washed clean one by one. There was something brightly forceful about the tiny, somewhat bent figure.

Hiding his tears, Honda looked up.

"It was good of you to come," said the Abbess pleasantly.

"It was rude of me to introduce myself without

warning, and it is very kind of you to see me all the same." Wanting above all to avoid familiarity, Honda found himself using the stiffest of greetings. He was ashamed of the phlegm-choked old voice. He forced himself on. "I addressed myself to your steward. I wonder if he was kind enough to show you my letter."

"Yes, I saw it."

There was a pause. The novice took advantage of it to withdraw.

"How the memories come back. As you can see, I am so old that I cannot be sure of lasting the night." He took courage from the fact that she had read his letter. The words came more easily.

The Abbess laughed and seemed to sway gently. "Your interesting letter seemed almost too earnest." Like the steward, she spoke the West Country dialect. "I thought there must be some holy bond between us."

The last drops of youth leaped up within Honda. He had returned to that day sixty years before, when he had pleaded youthful ardor to the Abbess's predecessor. He discarded his reserve.

"Your revered predecessor would not let me see you when I came with Kiyoaki's last request. It had to be so, but I was angry. Kiyoaki Matsugae was after all my dearest friend."

"Kiyoaki Matsugae. Who might he have been?"

Honda looked at her in astonishment.

She might be hard of hearing, but she could not have failed to hear him. Yet her words were so wide of the mark that he could only believe he had been misunderstood.

"I beg your pardon?" He wanted her to say it again.

There was no trace of dissimulation as she repeated the words. There was instead a sort of girlish curiosity in her eyes, and below them a quiet smile. "Who might he have been?"

Honda saw that she wanted him to tell her of

Kiyoaki. Scrupulously polite, he recounted his memories of Kiyoaki's love and its sad conclusion.

The Abbess sat motionless through the long story, a smile always on her lips. Occasionally she would nod. She listened with care even as she gracefully took the cold refreshments the old nun had brought in.

Calmly, without a touch of emotion, she said: "It has been a most interesting story, but unfortunately I did not know Mr. Matsugae. I fear you have confused me with someone else."

"But I believe that your name is Satoko Ayakura?" He coughed in the urgency of his words.

"That was my lay name."

"Then you must have known Kiyoaki." He was angry.

It had to be not forgetfulness but unabashed prevarication. He knew that the Abbess had reasons enough to pretend ignorance; but that a woman far from the vulgar world, of her venerable state, should lie thus openly gave grounds for doubting the depth of her convictions. If she still carried with her all the hypocrisy of that other world, then there must be doubts about the validity of her conversion when she entered this one. The dreams of sixty years seemed betrayed in that instant.

His persistence passed a reasonable limit, but she did not seem to resent it. For all the heat, her purple cloak was cool. Her eyes and her always beautiful voice were serene.

"No, Mr. Honda, I have forgotten none of the blessings that were mine in the other world. But I fear I have never heard the name Kiyoaki Matsugae. Don't you suppose, Mr. Honda, that there never was such a person? You seem convinced that there was; but don't you suppose that there was no such person from the beginning, anywhere? I couldn't help thinking so as I listened to you."

"Why then do we know each other? And the Ayakuras and the Matsugaes must still have family registers."

"Yes, such documents might solve problems in the other world. But did you really know a person called Kiyoaki? And can you say definitely that the two of us have met before?"

"I came here sixty years ago."

"Memory is like a phantom mirror. It sometimes shows things too distant to be seen, and sometimes it shows them as if they were here."

"But if there was no Kiyoaki from the beginning—" Honda was groping through a fog. His meeting here with the Abbess seemed half a dream. He spoke loudly, as if to retrieve the self that receded like traces of breath vanishing from a lacquer tray. "If there was no Kiyoaki, then there was no Isao. There was no Ying Chan, and who knows, perhaps there has been no I."

For the first time there was strength in her eyes.

"That too is as it is in each heart."

A long silence ensued. The Abbess clapped gently. The novice appeared and knelt in the doorway.

"Mr. Honda has been kind enough to come all this way. I think he should see the south garden. I will take him there."

The novice led her by the hand. Honda stood up as if pulled by strings, and followed them through the dark rooms.

The novice slid open a door and led him to the veranda. The wide south garden was before him.

The lawn, with the hills behind it, blazed in the summer sun.

"We have had cuckoos since morning," said the novice.

The grove beyond the lawn was dominated by maples. A wattled gate led to the hills. Some of the maples were red even now in the summer, flames among the green. Stepping-stones were scattered easily over the lawn, and wild carnations bloomed shyly among them. In a corner to the left were a well and a well wheel. A celadon stool on the lawn seemed so hot in the sun that it would surely burn anyone who tried to sit on it. Summer clouds ranged their dizzying shoulders over the green hills.

It was a bright, quiet garden, without striking features. Like a rosary rubbed between the hands, the shrilling of cicadas held sway.

There was no other sound. The garden was empty. He had come, thought Honda, to a place that had no memories, nothing.

The noontide sun of summer flowed over the still garden.

THE END

November 25, 1970   The Sea of Fertility

About the Author

ON NOVEMBER 25, 1970, Yukio Mishima committed *seppuku* (ritual suicide). Forty-five years old and at the peak of a brilliant literary career, he had that morning written the last word of the final lines of his tetralogy, *The Sea of Fertility*. "The tetralogy is his masterpiece, as he knew," Donald Keene has said.

Mishima had written much about suicide and early death, and often told his friends he wished to die young. After he conceived the idea of *The Sea of Fertility* in 1964, he frequently said he would die when it was completed. In fact the second of the four novels, *Runaway Horses*, is a remarkable literary rehearsal of his *seppuku*. Just before his suicide, he wrote his closest friends that he felt empty, having put into the tetralogy everything he thought and felt about life and this world. "The title, *The Sea of Fertility*," he told Keene, "is intended to suggest the arid sea of the moon that belies its name. Or I might say that it superimposes the image of cosmic nihilism on that of the fertile sea."

Mishima's works have been compared to the works of Proust, Gide, and Sartre, and his obsession with courage and the manly virtues has been likened to Hemingway's. Arthur Miller said, "I felt Mishima had an admirable style. He was surrealistic. He was very erotic. He had an economy of means to create enormous myths—his novels are compressed visions." A British magazine called him "one of the outstanding modern writers of fiction, possessing a complex, subtle and frightening imaginative power."

He was often wrongly called a rightist because of his private "army" of a hundred unarmed young men, but it was not on the blacklist of the careful Japanese police because it had never been involved in violence and differed from conventional rightist organizations. It was a theatrical fantasy conceived by a poet, as was his death, about which Selig Harrison of the Washington *Post* wrote, "He forced the Japanese to consider where they are going more dramatically than anyone else since World War II, and he has done so with a distinctively Japanese symbolism."

Mishima was born into a samurai family and imbued with the code that apotheosized complete control over mind and body, and loyalty to the Emperor—the same code that produced the austerity and self-sacrifice of Zen. Much of the tetralogy shows that he viewed the self-seeking arrogance and corruption of the militarists of the thirties (and their contemporary successors) as inimical to the samurai code.

His first novel was published in his school magazine when he was thirteen. A perceptive teacher encouraged him and persuaded a magazine to publish a story, *The Forest in Full Bloom*, in 1941, when Mishima (a pen name the teacher suggested) was sixteen. Three years later, when he entered Tokyo Imperial University, his first collection of stories was published under the same title and pen name. The first printing sold out in a week. In 1946 he brought two essays in manuscript to Kawabata, later the Nobel Prize winner, whose protégé he became. Altogether, 257 works by him, including 15 novels, have been published in Japan, and 77 translations here and in Europe.

Mishima reverenced and mastered the martial arts of Japan, creating a beautiful body he hoped age would never make ugly. He began to practice body-building in 1955, and *kendo* (dueling with bamboo staves) in 1959.

In 1966 he took up *karate* as well. By 1968 he had become a *kendo* master of the fifth rank.

He traveled widely and often, and two travel books and many collections of articles are among his works. He also wrote countless short stories and thirty-three plays, in some of which he acted. Some ten films have been made from his novels; *The Sound of Waves* (1954, American edition 1956) was filmed twice, and one of the director Ichikawa's masterpieces, *Enjō*, was based on *The Temple of the Golden Pavilion* (1956, American edition 1959). Also available in English are *Five Modern Nō Plays* (1957) and the novels *After the Banquet* (1960, American edition 1963), *The Sailor Who Fell from Grace with the Sea* (1963, American edition 1965), *Forbidden Colors* (1951, American edition 1968), and *Thirst for Love* (1950, American edition 1969). The first novel of the tetralogy, *Spring Snow*, was published in its American edition in 1972, the second, *Runaway Horses*, and the third, *The Temple of Dawn*, in 1973.

About the Translator

EDWARD GEORGE SEIDENSTICKER was born in Castle Rock, Colorado, in 1921. He received his B.A. from the University of Colorado, his M.A. from Columbia University, and has done graduate work at Harvard University and Tokyo University. He is currently professor of Japanese at the University of Michigan.

Among the important contemporary Japanese novels Mr. Siedensticker has translated are *The Makioka Sisters* by Junichiro Tanizaki and *Snow Country, Thousand Cranes,* and *The Sound of the Mountain* by Yasunari Kawabata. For his translation of *The Sound of the Mountain* Mr. Seidensticker received the National Book Award.